MURDER

MURDER

Sarah Pinborough

Jo Fletcher

New York • London

JF

Jo Fletcher Books
An imprint of Quercus
New York • London

ISBN 978-1-62365-866-3

Library of Congress Control Number: 2014954166

Distributed in the United States and Canada by
Hachette Book Group
1290 Avenue of the Americas
New York, NY 10104

Manufactured in the United States

10 9 8 7 6 5 4 3 2 1

www.quercus.com

*For my mom, who taught me how to read
and gave me her love of a good story.*

PART ONE

PROLOGUE

Extract from letter from James Harrington
to Edward Kane, dated 1887

*. . . and I have just returned from their funerals. I suppose it is a blessing
that they are to lie at rest together and neither one must continue
living without the other (as I truly believe, as I told you in Venice, that
my parents did love each other), but my heart is heavy with grief, and
although I am almost recovered from the poisoning that took them from
me, I continue to feel plagued by the black cloud that has hung over me
since my return from Poland.*

*I wish you were here. I have never made friends very easily, and
the few friends I have made tend to be of a serious sort—there is not a
fellow among them I feel I could bare my soul to without judgment. Your
lively spirit and positive attitude would be a tonic to me in my present
predicament.*

*In my previous letter I mentioned that I had been ill in Poland, but
there was much that I omitted—perhaps because I wished to forget
most of the experience myself; I blamed the fevers I had suffered for
addling my brain somewhat. However, since my return to London,
I have begun to believe—and God help me in this—that there m*
be some truth in the madness. Or perhaps it is I who am craz

tried several times to write down what really occurred, about what the villagers and my poor dead guide, Josep, believed had infected me, but each time I have thrown the paper onto the fire. It is enough that I am plagued with doubts without driving you away with tales of monsters and legends that have no place in this modern world.

And yet I am still gripped by terror.

The night my mother and father fell fatally ill, we had eaten a jar of mushroom preserves that I had brought back with me from my travels. I heard myself tell the doctor as much as soon as I was well enough to speak, and there was an empty jar and the remnants of food to evidence this. And yet now that I am recovered, I cannot remember ever buying the mushrooms, or eating the dinner, although I must have done both. This is not because of the effects of the poisonous mushrooms. I have been suffering periods where my memories are vague, as if sometimes I am living in a fugue state, in which my desires and emotions are not entirely my own. I fought with my father that night—I have a memory of the anger, but not of why we argued. One day I found myself walking through a slum part of London, with no recollection of getting there other than vague dream-like memories that felt at once to be mine and not mine.

I had a similar experience in Paris, but that time, when I regained my senses, I had blood on my clothes. These moments are at their worst when the recurring fever is with me.

I fear, reading this back, that it must appear nonsensical. You probably think that my grief has left me "touched"—and believe me when I say most earnestly that I hope this is indeed the case. The madness I could live with, but I fear the dreams I can't help but think are real. And there is something almost worse: a constant weight on my back, as if there is something just behind me I cannot quite see.

I can picture your smile of disbelief from here, and in many ways that image is a comfort. Of course I am simply a victim of illness. There can be no more to it than that. I shall throw myself into running my father's business, as I need a distraction from these dark thoughts, and that will certainly provide a worthy one.

I must hope that you received my first letter as I have had no reply from you—you may well, of course, still be on your travels or you may be *at the Palazzo Barbaro in Venice, where I last saw you, but as I doubt that your family business commitments would have allowed you to stay in Europe for so long, I must presume my letter was lost rather than that you have forgotten our friendship. I shall continue to write, and I hope that one day you can visit me in London, and that by then these miseries that plague me will be long forgotten.*

Your dear friend,
James Harrington

1

The *Singleton Argus*
Saturday, June 27, 1896

JACK THE RIPPER

Carl Feigenbaum, who was executed in the electric chair at New York, has left a confession with his lawyer, from which it seems possible that he may be no other than Jack the Ripper. The account of the lawyer, which has been given to the Press, reads: "1 have a statement to make which may throw some light on this case [the murder for which the man was executed]. Now that Feigenbaum is dead and nothing more can be done for him in this world, I want to say as his counsel that I am absolutely certain of his guilt in this case, and I feel morally certain that he is the man who committed many, if not all, of the Whitechapel murders. Here are my reasons; and on this statement I pledge my honor: When Feigenbaum was in the Tombs awaiting his trial, I saw him several times. The evidence in his case seemed so clear that I cast about for a theory of insanity. Certain actions denoted a decided mental weakness somewhere. When I asked him point blank, 'Did you kill Mrs. Hoffman?' he made this reply: 'I have for years suffered from a singular disease, which induces an all-absorbing passion. This passion manifests itself in a desire to kill and mutilate the woman who falls in my way. At such times I am unable to control myself.' On my next visit to the Tombs I asked him whether he had not been in London at various times during the whole period covered by the Whitechapel murders. 'Yes, I was,' he answered. I asked him whether he could not explain some of these cases on the theory which he had suggested to me, and he simply looked tome in reply." The statement, which is a long one, proves conclusively that Feigenbaum was more or less insane, but the evidence of his identity with the notorious Whitechapel criminal is not satisfactory.

October 14, 1896

Dear Boss,
You will be surprised to find
that this comes from yours
as of old Jack the Ripper. Ha Ha
If my old friend Mr. Warren is dead
you can read it. you might
remember me if you try and
think a little Ha Ha. The last job
was a bad one and no mistake nearly
buckled, and meant it to
be best of the lot & what curse it,
Ha Ha Im alive yet and you'll
soon find it out. I mean to go
on again when I get the chance
wont it be nice dear old Boss to
have the good old times once
again. you never caught me
and you never will. Ha Ha
You police are a smart lot, the lot
of you could nt catch one man
Where have I been Dear Boss
you d like to know. abroad, if
you would like to know, and
just come back, ready to go on
with my work and stop when
you catch me. Well good bye
Boss wish me luck. Winters coming
"The Jewes are people that are
blamed for nothing" Ha Ha
have you heard this before

Yours truly
Jack the Ripper

Chief Inspector Henry Moore's report to
Chief Constable Melville Macnaghten

October 18, 1896

I beg to report having carefully perused all the old "Jack the Ripper" letters and fail to find any similarity of handwriting in any of them, with the exception of the two well-remembered communications which were sent to the "Central News" office: one a letter, dated September 25, 1888, and the other a postcard, bearing the postmark 1stOctober, 1888. . . .

On comparing the handwriting of the present letter with handwriting of that document, I find many similarities in the formation of letters. For instance the y's, t's and w's are very much the same. Then there are several words which appear in both documents—viz, Dear Boss"; ha ha (although in the present letter the capital H is used instead of the small one); and in speaking of the murders he describes them as his "work" or the last "job"; and if I get a (or the) chance; then there are the words "yours truly" and the Ripper (the latter on postcard) that are very much alike. Besides there are the finger smears.

Considering the lapse of time, it would be interesting to know how the present writer was able to use the words "The Jewes are people that are blamed for nothing"; as it will be remembered that they are practically the same words that were written in chalk, undoubtedly by the murderer, on the wall at Goulston Str, Whitechapel, on the night of September 30th, 1888, after the murders of Mrs. Stride and Mrs. Eddows [Eddowes]; and the word Jews was spelled on that occasion precisely as it is now.

Although these similarities strangely exist between the documents, I am of the opinion that the present writer is not the original correspondent who prepared the letters to the Central News; as if it had been, I should have thought he would have again addressed it to the same Press Agency; and not to Commercial Street Police Station.

In conclusion I beg to observe that I do not attach any importance to this communication.

2

LONDON. NOVEMBER, 1896
DR. BOND

By the time the brandy arrived, I was feeling pleasantly full. The warmth of the restaurant was a far cry from the bitter cold outside, and as Andrews passed the cigars around, the room had quieted. It was late in the evening, and many of the tables that had been full on our arrival were now being cleared away by brisk waiters.

"And so the letter was nothing?" I said. It was not unusual for Andrews and me to dine out together, but tonight Henry Moore had brought the three of us together, and I knew it was not just for the pleasure of our company.

"Just another to add to the hundreds of others," he said behind a small haze of smoke. "They're all worthless. Whoever our man was, he's either dead or he has fled."

He looked well. Unlike Andrews, who had retired from the police force a year or so after that bloody summer, Henry Moore had gone from strength to strength, being promoted to the rank of chief inspector after taking over the "Ripper" case from Inspector Abberline. He had retained his sense of earthy hardiness, and although he must surely feel the same frustration that plagued Andrews that their man had never been caught, he was a pragmatist. He would be disappointed, but he would not suffer as Andrews did.

"These are fine cigars." The smoke was sweet and strong. "Are we celebrating something?"

"Celebration might be too strong a word," Moore said, "but it's certainly the end of an era. We are no longer actively investigating the Ripper case. We've done all we can. We're not going to catch the bastard now. It's time to move on."

His words came as no real surprise to me, and in my heart I was glad for the news. It was the final door closing on a chapter of history I had done my best to make peace with and forget. Perhaps now that the decision was made, Andrews too would be able to let it go. He had become a close friend since his retirement from the police force. He was thinner than I, and although nearly ten years younger, he looked far older than a man yet in his forties should. He still mused on Jack's handiwork over our games of chess or backgammon, as if hoping one day to remember some small snippet of information that would lead to an arrest.

"Perhaps it is," Andrews said before sniffing his brandy. "But I wish to God we had got him."

"It's a wide world," I said. "It's possible that some policeman somewhere caught him."

"Then I shall imagine it's so. For my own peace."

We sat in comfortable silence for a moment as we sipped our drinks and smoked our cigars and reflected on those deeds that seemed at once a while ago and yesterday, as memories often did.

"It's not as if there isn't enough crime in London to keep me busy," Moore said after a moment, his eyes twinkling. "There are days I envy you, Walter, in your decision to change professions. Look at you now: the gentleman investigator, Sherlock Holmes himself."

We all laughed at that. Andrews had indeed moved into private investigations since leaving the force, but the reality of the job was a far more mundane affair than that presented in fiction, and it involved very little working alongside the police.

"Who knows?" Moore continued, smiling. "Perhaps it will soon be time for me to move on too. I'm starting to feel like the old dog trying to herd eager pups."

"Retirement?" Andrews said. "I'm certainly contemplating it—but you don't strike me as the sort."

"You see me dying on the job? Driven to an early grave by paperwork, maybe." He let out a gruff laugh. "I'll see a few more years on the force, I'm sure, but then—who knows? I imagine—and in many ways I hope, because I'm too tired to chase another damn lunatic like that one—I've already worked on the case I shall be defined by. We all have."

It was unlike Moore to be so reflective, but he had a point. London hadn't seen six weeks like Jack's before, and it was unlikely to again. We had played our parts in that, even if the man himself had never been brought to justice.

"Jack, and the torso man," Andrews said. "I hope we were wrong and they were one and the same—that way we failed to catch only one man."

My grip tightened on my brandy glass. We rarely talked of the Torso murders. For Andrews they had always been secondary to Jack's, and I was glad of that. For the first few years after those terrible events, my sleep had suffered. I kept the memories locked away in my soul, and I weaned myself from the laudanum, but often my days were wrecked with tiredness. I had not seen either the priest or Aaron Kosminski since that fateful night in Harrington's warehouse. I had slowly managed to convince myself that the drugs had induced a kind of madness in us, but still I felt an awful sense of dread when walking the streets of London.

But for the past eighteen months or so, that too had lifted, and the whole affair had begun to feel like a terrible dream. I had no doubt that Harrington was the killer, and so I felt no overwhelming guilt over his death, but neither did I like any reminder of those events for fear that once again my anxieties and insomnia would return.

"It's possible," Moore agreed, but I sensed more for Andrews's benefit than because he truly thought so.

"We should dwell less on the past," I said. "If the case is no longer active, then perhaps we too should let it rest. And ourselves as well."

"I'll drink to that," Moore said, and he signaled the waiter for more brandy.

It was late when I returned home to Westminster, but I had the pleasant buzz of having spent an evening with friends, and before going to bed, I went to my study to write a few more notes on my paper on the nature and treatment of hunting injuries. I wanted to push any dregs of thoughts of Jack and the torso killer to one side with practical work, and I found it was not too difficult in the comfort of my own home. The sense of being haunted had truly left me, and although I had moments of fear that it would return, with every day that passed, I relaxed a little more and allowed myself to feel content in my life. There would be no more opium. There would be no more madness. The priest and Kosminski were merely figures from a dream. They were not tangible, and as such, they could no longer affect me. Justice was done—even if it had been a crude version that I could never share with Andrews and Moore—and I refused to feel guilt for my part in it. It was far kinder for Juliana than any trial would have been, and I had no doubt whatsoever that the outcome would have been the same.

Finally, I turned out the lamps and climbed the stairs to the bed I no longer dreaded. *Yes,* I thought as I slipped into an easy sleep, *life was good at last.*

3

COLNEY HATCH LUNATIC ASYLUM.
MARCH, 1891
AARON KOSMINSKI

Medical report on admission

He goes about the streets and picks up bits of bread from the gutter and eats them. He drinks water from a standpipe and refuses food at the hands of others, he is very dirty and will not be washed.

Patient believes he is guided and controlled by an instinct that informs his mind.

4

LONDON. CHRISTMAS, 1896
DR. BOND

I stayed at Juliana's on Christmas Eve, and after little James had been put to bed, I helped her with the last of the present wrapping. Then we filled the stocking that hung from the edge of the mantelpiece before sipping sherry and allowing the enjoyment of the festive season to seep into us.

"The calm before the storm." She smiled, raising her glass to me. "Merry Christmas, Thomas."

"And a Merry Christmas to you too, Juliana."

We sat back, enjoying the silence in that particular way that two people who had grown used to each other's company could do. I was glad to see her looking healthier and more content. Her happiness made me happy, and even with the secret that I kept buried, I still dared to hope that one day she might consider me more than just a friend. Although I was now a man in my fifties and she had not quite reached thirty, still I wanted to look after her. Even without my impossible feelings of love for her, I knew I owed her that.

She had stopped wearing widow's weeds—reluctantly, but with a pragmatism that I was beginning to see was a part of her core—a few years earlier, but her grief still clung to her, almost as corporeal as the monster my madness had convinced me was attached to

Harrington's back. Nothing in that time had been easy for her: her husband's bloated body had been dragged from the river a few days after his death, and she, insisting on seeing him even though both her father and I strongly advised against it, had been heartbroken at the sight. Her pregnancy continued to make her sick, and her labor had been long and difficult—for a while, though we never told her, there were times when we feared we would lose both her and the child. And after that, she never regained the full bloom of health: though her red hair was still beautiful, it had lost its luster, and her face had thinned. Much as I tried to encourage her back out into the fresh air, even suggesting she join me at the hunt as she had been used to, she always declined. For the first year or so of little James's life, she was little more than a ghost of her former self. Once she left her sickbed, she moved and talked and walked, but her heart had gone in the river with her dead husband, and I rather felt that if her sickly child were to die too, it would be only a matter of days before she threw herself into the water as well.

But little James did not die, and Juliana slowly came back to us—perhaps not with the joie de vivre that had been so much a part of her before, but she was still a young woman and I hoped that Time, Mother Nature's healer, would rectify that. The young were resilient, and Juliana was an exceptional woman. I knew I was right in my decision: that it would be better if she had to bear only the grief of a husband robbed and murdered than the truth of what James Harrington had become: a brutal murderer of women and the killer of his own unborn child.

Juliana remained in the Chelsea house only until both she and the boy had recovered enough from the trauma of his birth. Then her parents and I encouraged her to sell the property and move, though I confess it was not difficult—she needed no persuasion from us, for that house held few happy memories for her. Selfishly, I too was happy that I would no longer have to visit that street, for not only had Harrington's parents died so horribly there but the ghost of Elizabeth Jackson lingered there too, and her death came back to me every time my gaze fell on the nearby house where she had been employed.

When Juliana moved into the new house in Barnes, the dark clouds I had carried with me everywhere began to lift. And as Juliana recovered, so did I.

Now, as the fire died down, her pale face was beautiful, lit by the glowing embers. When she had married James Harrington, she had been a girl, but now she had grown into a woman, and her face bore the marks of her suffering. I found that made her more perfect, if that were even possible.

"I think I shall go to bed," she said at last, rising. "Thank you for coming tonight, Thomas. It's been good to have some time alone before our guests arrive tomorrow." She leaned over my chair and kissed me softly on my cheek. "You are always so very kind to me. Sometimes I wonder what I would do without you."

"You will never have to do without me," I answered. "That I can promise you."

She smiled again, a wistful expression that made me hope one day to see her eyes twinkle with good humor as they had before. And although I dared not think it too often, perhaps she would one day start to love me as I loved her . . .

"I think I might read for a while," I said. "Sleep well. And Merry Christmas."

As I watched her leave the room, her skirts swishing as she walked, I thought I had never known such a woman, and never would again. I didn't read but instead, lost myself in the remains of the fire until it had burned down to a pale glow. As the air turned chilly, I too retired to my bedroom, seeking a good night's sleep before the Christmas festivities. Thankfully, that was no longer an idle wish.

The mood in the morning was as fine as in any house in London, and once Charles Hebbert, Juliana's father, had arrived, we left the cook preparing our feast and went to church before strolling back along the riverside to Juliana's house on The Terrace. It had been a mild month, and for all the slight crispness to the air, it could as easily have been a March day as a December one. Juliana relaxed her normal overprotectiveness a little, and she let James run ahead of us slightly, although she watched carefully as he peered over the bank to the river a few feet below us.

"He's starting to look just like his father," Charles said, adding with a smile, "and he seems well."

From under his hat, blond curls sprang around the child's face, and for once his pale cheeks were glowing from both excitement and the fresh air.

"He's got Mother's eyes," Juliana said, and she squeezed her father's arm. Mary Hebbert had been taken from them two summers before, the victim of a sudden fever. It was a swift death as her heart gave out, and although they had both grieved deeply, that grief had gradually transformed into fond remembrances rather than bouts of anguish. "And he is gentle, like her."

"And clever like his own mother," Charles added, his eyes twinkling. "A fine combination."

I did not join in with their talk of the boy, for whatever I said would sound stilted and awkward. Instead, I hung back a few paces and let them continue. I had never been able to bond with little James. The similarities with his father and the memories he engendered in Juliana comforted her, but for me they were darker triggers. James had his father's weak chest, and he had nearly killed Juliana arriving into this world. Even throughout her pregnancy he had made her terribly ill, and I could not help but wonder if some of his father's wickedness had passed into his unborn son. More than anything I loathed the child's fascination with the river. Juliana refused to let him on the water, despite their waterfront property—I wondered how she could bear to look out at the Thames, knowing that her husband had been pulled out of it, but I supposed in some way it allowed her to feel closer to him. For my own part I still could not look upon the river without a mild sense of dread.

"He's nearly six. He should be in school," I heard Charles say, "and mixing with boys his own age. It would be good for his chest to spend more time playing sports, and good for him to be around others."

"I prefer to school him myself," Juliana said, her tone abrupt, "until I know he is completely well."

Charles, to his credit, did not push her. It was Christmas Day and not the time to broach her controlling parenting.

"Look, Mother! Look!" The boy was pointing to a flurry of gulls wheeling and diving into the water.

"Don't lean over too far!" Juliana hurried forward, and Charles and I followed.

"But look!"

As their beaks nipped eagerly, the volume of gulls made the water foam and churn, but at their center I could just make out a dark hunk of something being tugged this way and that.

"It's a dead thing!" James squealed excitedly. "They're eating a dead thing!"

We turned away from the water after that.

Walter Andrews arrived in time for Christmas dinner, laden with parcels and a bottle of fine port, and by the time we had all eaten our fill and little James was playing with his new toys, we were truly a festive gathering. Crackers had been pulled, and nuts had been cracked, and then Juliana played the piano, and we sang carols. Outside, as if in a fine salute to the day, the temperature dropped, and the first snowflakes of the winter began to fall. I could not have wished for a more perfect Christmas.

"Say good night to Uncle Thomas and Inspector Andrews," Juliana said, ushering the sleepy child toward us. "And thank them for their presents."

"Just Mr. Andrews these days," Walter said, ruffling the boy's angelic curls. "Good night, young Master James."

"Thank you for the cricket bat," the boy murmured.

"We shall have you at the crease come summer." Andrews winked at him.

Little James turned to me and came in closer to where I sat so he could wrap his thin arms around me in a hug.

"Merry Christmas, Uncle Thomas," he said. I returned the embrace, but I felt stiff and awkward. I tried to like the boy, I truly did. It was not that he was an unpleasant child—that was not the case. He was quieter than most boys of his age, and he was somewhat reserved and clingy with his mother, but he was neither spiteful nor mean. It was merely that he was the child of a monster, conceived at the height of his father's murdering madness, and I could not help but wonder whether the sins of his father somehow lurked in his soul. And when those wide blue eyes were fixed on me, studious and somber, I found I could not help but believe it.

"Thank you for my books. And my train." He kept his arms round my neck and kissed my cheek, and knowing that Juliana was watching with fondness, I patted his back and forced a smile, though I could not bring myself to return the kiss.

"You're very welcome, young man," I said instead. He pulled back and stared at me for a moment, then returned to his mother's side.

"I shall come read you one of those new stories with your mother," Charles said as he got up from his seat. "How would you like that?"

"Thank you, Grandfather," he said politely as Charles swept him up in his arms and groaned as if the slight boy was far too much weight. He pretended to stagger slightly under the load, and little James laughed, a gentle giggle, and I felt a moment of sadness at my inability to like him.

"Good night, Uncle Thomas," he said again.

"We'll be down shortly," Juliana said, and she smiled at me. "Now come along, both of you."

When we were alone, Andrews poured me another glass of port and then added some coal to the fire before we went to the window and looked out at the snow and the gaslights flickering in the houses along the curved street. I thought of all the families who had decorated their trees and opened their presents, and I hoped they had enjoyed as happy a day as we had.

"The boy is very fond of you," Andrews said. "I think he wanted you to read his story to him rather than Charles."

"Oh, I think not." I was surprised by his words—the child was as awkward with me as I was with him, and I had presumed that was apparent to all.

"You're the closest person to a father he has." Andrews sipped his port. In a house further up someone drew the curtains closed. Christmas was coming to an end for another year, which made me think of the speed of my own passing years; the Yule season would be here again quickly enough.

"You're not getting any younger," Andrews said, as if reading my mind. "When are you going to pull yourself together and propose to her?"

Heat burned in my cheeks. It was true that I often talked of Juliana to Walter during our dinners, but I had never mentioned my feelings for her. I thought I had spoken like a guardian would, rather than a man in love.

"Oh come on, Thomas."

I busied myself with closing the drapes rather than face the gentle humor in his eyes. "It's clear that you are both very fond of each other."

"I'm nearly thirty years older than she," I said, hoping my tone was indignant, but when I heard my often-thought words spoken aloud, I felt some shame that I had ever even considered that she might think of me and marriage. It was ridiculous. "I'm older than Charles," I added.

"Age is irrelevant in these matters." He sat by the fire, where the flames were crackling merrily. "And Juliana is wise beyond her years. Her illness and her grief have matured her."

I wished he would be quiet, but at the same time I found some hope in his words. If a man like Walter Andrews didn't find the idea entirely preposterous, then perhaps I would one day find the bravery to say out loud the words I had so often voiced silently.

"You've helped her through all of it—and her affection for you is obvious. You were close friends before poor Harrington's murder, and you have been resolutely by her side since. If she were to marry again, who else would she choose?"

"She still grieves for her husband," I said softly. I did not think about the headless baby's corpse in Harrington's trunk. I did not think of the glass in my hand gouging his throat.

"She grieves less with each month that passes. Life is short, Thomas. Harrington is gone, Charles's Mary is gone. My own Amy is gone. If you have the opportunity for happiness, then you should at the very least try to take it."

"Perhaps I shall," I said. "Perhaps I shall." I smiled at him. "You should have just written that down as a Christmas gift for me and saved yourself the cost of those expensive riding boots."

"You're right," he declared, reaching once again for the port bottle. "I shall return them tomorrow."

"Ah, but you did not write it down." I held my glass out to him. "The boots remain mine."

By the time Juliana and Charles returned, we were laughing, and soon Juliana was too. It was a good sound, and there had not been enough of it in recent years. Perhaps things were changing for all of us. I looked at her and felt my fierce love tighten my heart. *Maybe this year*, I thought. *Let Christmas be over and the new year start properly*. Maybe then I'd ask her.

5

Extract from letter from James Harrington
to Edward Kane, dated 1888

... my secretary, James Barker (a rather earnest man who my father trusted implicitly with his business dealings, and I am, when my mind is my own, of a mind to agree with his judgment), seemed confused by my suggestion and then told me that I alone had the key to that warehouse and that I had told him specifically that it was not to be used. As soon as he spoke, the memory of it came back to me, but I could not place why I would have said such a thing. Of course I made light of it, but I admit it plagues me. I can find no record of what I am storing there, and the windows have been painted black.

I have hours missing. My nights are sometimes a blur, and it is always when I'm weak with this terrible fever that fills me with dread. I start by working late, going through my father's paperwork to understand the systems he has in place, but then there are black spaces, and fragmented images I do not want to dwell on, and I wake—if that is the right word, for I am far from sleeping during these episodes—in places where I have no right to be at.

I know what you would say—and I still hope to get replies from you even though my writing is becoming a cathartic process of its own. You would say, "See a doctor." I would, Edward. But I cannot.

I came out of one such fugue several weeks ago and found myself in Westminster, near the site of the new Scotland Yard building site. I had no idea what I was doing there, but my arms and back ached, and I was filled with exhaustion—and yet at the same time the weakening fever was gone, and my face was suddenly clear of the hot red blotches that are the mark of my recurring illness. I was afraid, as any man would be suddenly finding himself so far from home and with no recollection of how he got there.

Yesterday, they found something inside the new building: part of a dead woman's body. It was headless and brutally dismembered, and it had been wrapped in the pages of a newspaper that I myself have delivered. I know these things because Juliana's father is working with the police. I can almost hear you laugh, dismissing the two events as unconnected, but there is yet more strangeness here. When I hear them talk of this poor dead woman, I see her in my mind's eye: a tall girl, full-bodied. I see her walking in the sunshine, and then I see her in the dark, staring at me in such fear. I know that she is foreign, and I know that something terrible happened to her.

There are other memories too: memories of feelings: power, hunger, and a lust such as I have never known.

I am afraid for Juliana. I am afraid for Elizabeth, the girl who was the cause of my travels abroad. I am afraid for myself.

I feel as if I am two men, and the one whose deeds I cannot fully remember is the stronger.

And always, always, there is this terrible weight on my back, of something just out of sight—something that I cannot shake free. Something that is driving me insane.

I know I need to look in that locked warehouse—the one apparently only I have the key for. The one I protect so much from Barker and the other workers. The answers lie in the warehouse, and that is what gives me pause. What will I find in there? Nothing? Therefore proving that I am suffering some madness?

I fear that I will find something worse: that I am not insane.

That I am a monster . . .

6

LONDON. JANUARY, 1897
EDWARD KANE

James had been right about London: it was, like New York, a vibrant and exciting city, and like his own home, it had many areas of filth and excessive poverty. But London was actually more like Paris: the air was thick with history, and its streets were filled with secrets so old that even the worn stone had begun to forget them. But the more he saw, the more he realized that neither was it entirely like Paris. The French capital's recent history might be bloodier, but it was nonetheless a city that oozed seduction. London was all grime and grit and labor. There was no romance here. In London even the river worked. In fact, London was like all the great cities of the world, Edward Kane concluded, entirely unique.

He checked his watch as the waiter poured him some more coffee; then he drank it black as his eyes scanned the newspaper without really reading it. He left the delicate sandwiches and cakes on the fine porcelain stands untouched. Fresh tea would arrive when his guest did; he would eat then. She was due at any moment—if she came, of course. He was surprisingly nervous. He glanced out of the sparkling windows into the darkening busy afternoon, following the hubbub and imagining the hundreds of tiny stories wrapped up in each warm body as they hurried past. He'd been at the Dorchester for almost a week now. In between the meetings with bankers and railwaymen, he had gone to the address on James Harrington's letters, hoping to find him recovered and well, and perhaps a little embarrassed at everything he had poured out onto so many pages all those years ago. Instead, he had discovered his friend's death, pulled out of the Thames as a bloated corpse with a slashed throat, and how his poor young widow had nearly died in childbirth shortly afterward.

He had decided it might be best not to go to the new house but instead, to send a message, leaving it up to her to decide if she wanted to see a man who had known her husband only briefly, and in their youth.

"Mr. Kane?"

She stood a little way back from his table, a vision in rich blue, her hat fashionably tilted on top of her carefully styled curls. Beside her, a small boy standing a little too close to his mother's skirt looked at him nervously.

"Mrs. Harrington." He got to his feet and smiled. "It is truly a pleasure to meet you."

"You're American," the boy said, his eyes widening slightly.

"Yes, I am. And you're a fine-looking little fellow—just like your father."

"I don't know my father," the boy said. "He's dead."

"James, sit quietly, please." She smiled as the waiter held her chair, but Edward had noticed the flash of pain in her eyes at the mention of her dead husband. The years might have passed, but she obviously still grieved for him. "I hope you don't mind that I brought my son with me," she added. "I—well, I don't have a governess for him. I prefer to school him myself."

"The more the merrier," he said, and winked at the thin little boy who was continuing to stare at him with some kind of awe. "Isn't that right, James? Also"—he reached down to the bag at his side—"I brought you this. It's a little late for Christmas, but I thought you might like it."

He handed over the box, and James's mouth dropped open wide at the sight of the model railway, with an engine and several carriages, all made from cast iron and painted in his company's colors.

"From America?" the child breathed, and both his mother and Edward laughed aloud at his reaction.

"Yes, indeed. All the way from New York."

"You really shouldn't have, Mr. Kane. That's very kind."

"Edward, please. And it was no trouble. My business—one of my businesses—is the railroads."

The tea arrived, and he waited until it was poured before continuing, "I'm very sorry for your loss. James was a good man."

"Yes," she said, and once again he saw something cut across her face—a shadow of memory, perhaps. "Yes, he was. He wrote to you, I believe, when he was sick."

"Yes, he did." Edward smiled. "That's how I knew you were expecting a child." Her eyes studied him, dark pools of wary intelligence beneath the warmth, and he knew then that she was still recovering and that he would not share the contents of her late husband's letters with her. He feared that seeing what James had written in his last months would break her.

"Uncle Thomas gave me a train for Christmas," James exclaimed as he pulled the engine free from the box, "but it was not like this one!" His shyness was clearly overcome by his excitement. "Thank you!"

"Make sure you say no such thing to Uncle Thomas," Juliana chided him. "That would be rude, and it would upset him."

"Your brother?" Edward asked.

"Oh no." She smiled and sipped her tea. "Dr. Thomas Bond—a colleague of my father's. He's become a very good friend to us since James died. He is quite part of the family." Her eyes darted away, and Edward realized that perhaps that relationship was more complex than simply friends. He didn't push, although he found that he was curious. She was more beautiful than he'd been expecting, despite being too thin, and sadness and illness leaving lines on her face—or perhaps *because* of those things.

Her eyes caught his, and she was suddenly self-conscious. "Is there something the matter?" she asked, dabbing at her mouth as if perhaps there were crumbs around it, even though she hadn't touched the collation that sat between them.

"No," he said, and it was his turn to flush slightly. "It was just . . . well, I was just thinking how much I would like to paint you. Which probably sounds odd coming from a businessman and one who is a stranger to boot."

Her laugh came in a burst that he thought surprised her as much as it surprised him. He had not expected such sweet richness, the hints of earthly pleasure. He thought perhaps here was a woman bound up so tightly by life she'd almost forgotten how to breathe.

"I'm most flattered," she said. "James did tell me that you dreamed of spending your days in an artist's loft, painting—although he said that your preference was for women *without* their clothes on."

It was Edward who laughed loudly then, and heads at the table next to them turned to smile at what must have looked like a happy family enjoying each other's company over afternoon tea. "He told you that, did he?" Suddenly that Christmas in Venice seemed like yesterday, as if time had folded and now held that day so close to this one that they rubbed together slightly. "Yes, I suppose I did dream of a different life—but the one I have has not been altogether unkind to me."

"It does not always work out as we planned, does it?" Juliana said, her smile soft.

"No," he agreed, "it does not, but we have to make the best of what we are given. I'm sorry if meeting me has reminded you of your loss. That was not my intention."

"It has been several years now, and time does heal, no matter how deep the grief. I am glad of your visit. James was very fond of you, even though you did not know each other for long. I would love to hear your stories of him—I think he aspired to be a little more like you. He always described you as 'carefree.'"

"Well, he would probably be very disappointed to find that I did indeed follow my father's wishes and go into his business—and now it is my business. Thankfully, I am a better businessman than I was a painter, hence my visit to England."

"I'm glad you found time to look for James. He would have been glad too."

She smiled again, and as he watched her lips part slightly nervously over her perfect teeth, he thought that she was the kind of woman who never smiled in the same way twice. He might have changed somewhat from the rebellious young man who had been so keen on a life of freedom, but his love of women had not faded, and her sad beauty touched him. He wondered how she would look with that red hair free over her shoulders, and her body released from the confines of her tight corsetry. How would she smile in the moments after her lust was sated? How would she smile first thing after waking?

Suddenly the formal atmosphere in the hotel tearoom was stifling. "I have an idea," he said, and he leaned in toward James. "If you are both free for an hour or so, why don't we go to the museum? I would particularly like to see the Egyptian Room—what do you say, young sir? Shall we go exploring?"

The little boy's eyes lit up, and any protest Juliana might have been about to make was lost in his reaction.

"That's settled then." Edward smiled across the table.

By the time they had explored a section of the exhibits in the vast building, the atmosphere between them had relaxed. As James called their attention to first this artifact and then that one, Edward made up bold stories to explain them that left the boy almost breathless with excitement and rosy-cheeked, dispelling his normally pallid hue, and even Juliana fell under the spell of Edward's exaggerated tales of pirates and grave robbers as they took new and increasingly outlandish turns.

She was still laughing when they emerged into the evening hubbub of London, and she touched his arm as a hansom cab pulled up for them. "You must come for dinner—tomorrow," she said. "As a thank-you for this lovely afternoon."

"That I would like," he answered, and he tipped his hat to her before ruffling James's hair and picking him up to put him in the cab. "He'll sleep well tonight."

"Yes," Juliana said, "and so shall I." She smiled at him again, and then took his hand to step up herself.

Through her elegant gloves, her fingers were slim and strong, and he wondered how they would feel on his body. James Harrington had done well getting this woman to marry him. She was intelligent and warm and witty, and he was sure that if she ever let her guard down, she would be sensuous and sexual. He was still intrigued to find out more about James's fate—especially after the terrible things he had written in his letters—but that interest faded in comparison with his new need: the wooing of his widow. There had been a lot of women in Edward Kane's life, but none before had intrigued him as much as the very English Juliana Harrington.

He walked back to the hotel, enjoying the sound of the city's streets, and then he had an early dinner before retiring to his suite and examining Harrington's letters again. He wondered how Juliana could have lived with someone going through what must have been fits of madness. What had her life been like then?

When he finally extinguished the lights for the night, he imagined his shy, reserved English friend and his wife in their marriage bed. Could James truly have satisfied her? As his mind wandered, his own body replaced Harrington's, moving over the lovely Juliana and hearing her gasp as his mouth explored every inch of her pale perfection before sliding inside her. It was not long before he brought himself to a shuddering climax beneath the crisp sheets.

He lay in the darkness for a while before sleep claimed him, and as he revisited the events of the day, he realized how much he was looking forward to seeing her again for dinner the next day. He thought of his dead friend, shy, sweet James Harrington, so clearly a troubled soul, and said a quiet prayer to him for forgiveness. However, he didn't wait for an answer: Harrington had been dead a long time, and life was for the living. As, indeed, was love.

7

LONDON. JANUARY, 1897
DR. BOND

Edward Kane was a charismatic man, I had to give him that, if a touch uncouth in that open way Americans could be. Young James had certainly taken to him, and before he went to bed there were piggyback rides and tales of cowboys and Indians, and I could not help but envy how easy Kane found being around the boy.

"Your turn, Uncle Thomas!" James cried, breathless from his games. "Be my horse!"

"I'm too old for that, young man," I said. "I fear my back is not what it once was."

"I don't think mine is either!" Edward got up and stretched. "I'm sure you're heavier than you were yesterday, Sheriff."

James giggled at that and ran to Juliana who was wearing a fine wine-colored dress I had not seen before. Her face, like her son's, was brighter today, and when she smiled, there was definitely the visible echo of the life that used to dance in it.

"Your visit seems to be having a positive effect on Juliana," I said to Kane before we went in to dine. "Thank you for that." The last words sounded more proprietary than I had intended, but I could not shake my own dismay at the American's presence. I had done a good job of burying the past, and now here was an old traveling companion of Harrington's, disturbing the graves as he told us stories of their time together in Venice.

"She's a charming woman, and I'm glad my arrival has not caused her too much pain. I hope I can only add to the good memories of her husband—from the short time I knew him." The sparkle that came so naturally to his hazel eyes faded, and I noticed his jaw tighten slightly before he grinned again. "She seems very fond of you," he added.

"We are very fond of each other," I answered a little mechanically, wondering what had caused that reaction. Did he know something of Harrington that he had not shared?

"So I can see," he said.

"Do come sit down," Juliana called through to us, her voice merry. "The food will be getting cold."

I was pleased that although she was charmed by Edward Kane, it was my hand she touched occasionally throughout the meal, squeezing my fingers affectionately as she told Edward about our times hunting, and she spoke of her father and our experiences working on the infamous Jack the Ripper case.

"The police call on Thomas often, you know," she said proudly, "and not just for his medical skills. He has an eye for analyzing the minds of men from their terrible deeds. He's worked on many celebrated cases, not just that awful one."

"Oh, Juliana," I said, attempting modesty while feeling inordinately pleased that she felt the need to press my importance on this handsome, wealthy younger man. "I am not that different from others."

"Yes, you are—even Father says so. He says you have a gift."

The word almost made me shudder—it was so close to what the priest had said of me and my abilities. He had been talking of more supernatural leanings, however, and I was a little embarrassed to remember it.

"It must have been a terrible time," Edward said. "Even in New York the newspapers were full of it."

A terrible time. Edward Kane would never know the half of it.

"I just wish the police had caught him. The killings may have stopped, but there are good men who still feel frustrated that he got away." I was thinking of course of Andrews, for the case was etched in every line of his face. "I share in Henry Moore's hope that he is dead or incarcerated—perhaps in one of your own cities."

"There's a thought," Edward said, sipping his wine. "The world is certainly growing smaller."

"Enough of this gloomy talk," I said after a moment. "The past is done—the present is where we should reside. Tell me more about your business in the railways, and life in New York. I traveled as a young man, but mainly in Europe. I am ashamed to say I have yet to visit America."

The evening passed more pleasantly after that, and although I felt a little reserve toward Edward Kane—probably, if I am honest, as much only jealousy of a charming and handsome man in his prime whom Juliana obviously found engaging company—I could see that he was a clever and thoughtful individual who had no doubt contributed considerably to the success of his late father's business. He was confident but not arrogant, and there was more than a little grit at his core.

When it was time for us to leave, we said our farewells to Juliana, who insisted Kane call on her and little James again, and at Kane's invitation we shared a carriage back into town. At first I thought he was simply being sociable, but once we were away from Barnes, he leaned forward in his seat, resting his forearms on his knees, and said, "I'm glad we have some time together, for there is something I wish to share with you—something that I had originally planned to show to Juliana, but I can see she is still recovering from her grief, and I fear this will not help her. But I have to share this with *someone*, and you care for Juliana—and you also knew Harrington. And you are obviously an intelligent and respectable man. I trust you to deal with them as you wish."

My curiosity was only slightly larger than my trepidation. The iron wheels beneath us rang out against the cobbles as my heart pounded against my ribs. Harrington was intent on haunting me still.

"What is it that concerns you?" I was glad to hear my voice sounded calm. *Whatever it is*, I reminded myself, *there is no way it can point to my own involvement in Harrington's death.* The only men living who could do that were the priest and Kosminksi, and neither of them could speak without admitting their own guilt. We had formed an unholy alliance in our drug madness, but even without their company I still felt its grip on me—especially now.

Kane pulled a small bundle from his inside jacket. "These letters—he wrote them to me throughout the year or so before his death, but I only found them recently, while I was sorting through my father's affairs after he died. The first one was opened, but the rest remained sealed."

"Your father kept them from you?" Despite the cold air, sweat sprung on my hands. Letters from Harrington—words from beyond his watery grave . . . Harrington was becoming my own Banquo. "Why?"

"My relationship with my father was difficult: he lacked imagination, where I was wild and creative, with a passion for adventure that he wanted to stifle. If he hadn't become a railroad man, he would have been a ship builder. He was a man of metal—iron through and through, in spirit and in heart. My trip around Europe was my mother's idea, and he agreed to it only out of fear that I was destroying my reputation at home—and therefore his—with my unseemly, 'rebellious' behavior." He shrugged, slightly embarrassed. "I was an angry young man, you might say, and I had a taste for wine and women. But on my return, we managed slowly to build a working relationship, and we put my impetuous youthful behavior firmly behind us. I imagine he did not wish me to maintain friendships with those I had met while traveling. I had always remembered James fondly, though, and when I found these, I knew I had to visit him, to check on his well-being." He paused, and then admitted, "The letters, you see—well, they are disturbing. I had expected to find him well, perhaps a little embarrassed at their content—I had hoped that was the reason he ceased writing. But when I found out about his awful death, I began to wonder whether there might be some cause for it within them. Maybe you'll be able to find it. But I must warn you, they make for pretty uncomfortable reading. He was obviously suffering some kind of feverish illness, and in his confused state—well, when you read them you will see that he suffered bouts of memory loss at times, so perhaps he was confusing his own imagined misdeeds with the real events that you and Dr. Hebbert were helping the police with." He paused. "I hope they were imagined, for if not, then my gentle English friend became something of a monster, and that I can't believe."

The word *monster* made me shiver, but I held Edward Kane's gaze. He was looking at me with trust and respect. *If only he knew the madness I myself succumbed to during that time*, I thought. *If only he knew what I had found in James Harrington's possession that drove me to slash his throat.*

I pulled myself together and said gravely, "I am sure they are nothing but the fantasies of a sick mind. James suffered frequently with bouts of illness after his travels."

"And therein lies my own guilt," he said, "for it was I who persuaded him to travel to Poland and see more interesting sights than those to be found in the great cities of Europe. I feel partly responsible for his illness."

He held the letters out, and I had no choice but to take them, though I was glad for the leather gloves between my skin and the paper. The bundle felt heavier in my hands than possible.

"If you could find time to read them," he said, "I would be grateful for your opinion on their contents. Perhaps there is something there that could help catch whoever killed him—although I know that is unlikely, especially after so long. And you knew James then—you will know if the deeds he describes are ones he was even able to carry out. I have business in Southampton for a few days, and then I will be back in London. I know you are a busy man, Dr. Bond, but your opinion— and your discretion—would help me greatly in finding some peace."

"Of course," I said, and I smiled as I tucked the small package into my overcoat pocket. "I shall give them my attention and report back to you."

"And you won't tell Juliana?"

"Of course not." His concern for Juliana rankled me somewhat—as if I did not share that concern, or indeed, have far more, for I had loved Juliana for a long time, and there was nothing I would do to hurt her. I had committed a terrible deed to protect her, and nothing Kane could do would ever match that, for all that my actions of that dreadful night had to remain secret for fear of being misunderstood.

Kane sighed and then smiled, warm and open, reaching forward and squeezing my arm. "Thank you. That is a mighty relief. I am very glad to have met you, Dr. Thomas Bond. I can see why Juliana relies on you so much. You are a good man."

Once back in my house I went straight to my study and poured a large brandy before sitting at my desk and staring at the envelopes: pockets of history waiting to be retold. In truth I wanted to burn them immediately, and I racked my brain for ways I could do this and have a valid explanation to give to Kane, but I found none. Instead, I opened the bottom drawer and threw them inside. But still I felt their presence—*Harrington's* presence—too close to me, and knew I would not be able to work in peace at my desk with the letters inside it. I swallowed the brandy before taking the package into the second bedroom and forcing it under the mattress, as far in as I could reach. I closed the door and calmed myself.

I could forget them now. I had no desire to read their contents. Harrington had been a murderer of women, and that is what the pages would tell me, nothing more. There would be no talk of monsters. Of *Upirs*.

Even if there were, I did not want to read it: I would not unlock the door to that insanity again. The past was done, and I would not allow Edward Kane to bring back the ghost of Harrington to taunt me. My hands were still trembling, and I drank another brandy before going to bed, but even then I did not sleep easily, for my dreams were tormented with flashes of memory. When I woke, I knew I had to get the letters out of my house. I would lock them in a drawer in my office at the hospital. I would not have them near me.

I felt calmer after that. The world was still steady. I was a sane man.

8

COLNEY HATCH LUNATIC ASYLUM.
1893
AARON KOSMINSKI

Assessment

The patient's condition continues to deteriorate. His agitations have increased quite dramatically over a period of six months. His illness presents in the form of delusions that are paranoid in nature, and he sleeps little.

The patient has a fixation with the river. His rants when in the grip of his delusions are difficult to analyze as anything other than the result of a confused mind. When questioned as to what is disturbing him, he says, "It is not in the river. It did not go in the river." He repeats this statement several times, each time with increasing anxiety. Occasionally, he mentions blood. Were he a less pathetic and obviously terrified individual, I would have concerns that he has an unknown violent past, but I conclude that he is suffering some form of disease of the mind.

He continues to refuse to wash unless forced by nurses while restrained, and he resists human contact.

9

The *Times*
Saturday, February 14, 1897

MURDER IN A RAILWAY CARRIAGE

As was briefly reported in The *Times* of yesterday, a shocking murder was committed on the London and South Western Railway on Thursday night. Up to yesterday evening no arrests had been made. . . . .

. . . The deceased apparently sat with her back to the engine. Her assailant probably first hit her a blow on the forehead, partially stunning her. She must have then grappled with the man, for splashes of blood were found on the opposite side of the carriage, and her umbrella was found broken. It was supposed that the murderer then swung round and inflicted a second blow on the left side of the head, smashing in her skull and killing her. She was then pushed under the seat, and when found she was lying on her back with her legs across the floor of the carriage.

———————

The *Daily Mail*
Tuesday, February 16, 1897

Any arguments deduced from the nature of Elizabeth Camp's wounds suggest not that she was murdered for her money— for a robber would not have waited to inflict supererogatory injuries such as those the dead woman's head exhibit—but that she was assassinated by somebody who found a revengeful satisfaction in battering her even after his first blows had killed her.

The postmortem examination was concluded yesterday by Mr. Thomas Bond, the eminent Westminster Hospital surgeon. When seen by a *"Daily Mail"* reporter yesterday, Mr. Bond said that the pestle found on the railway lines between Putney and Wandsworth was undoubtedly a weapon with which Miss Camp's injuries could have been inflicted.

"Miss Camp was killed by five or six blows from the pestle," went on Mr. Bond. "The so-called stab in the forehead was not a stab at all, but the result of a blow from the pestle. I frequently notice that a blow on the forehead or on any portion of the body under which there is a good bone support gives the appearance of a stab wound. The skin is broken cleanly against the bone beneath, and it always looks as if it had been cut. I have even known of an appearance as of stabbing in the cases of people who came to their death from a fall on the pavement, the bruise where the forehead struck the stone being so clean cut." Questioned further, Mr. Bond said that the stomach of the victim showed that Miss Camp had not partaken for several hours before her death of anything more than a cup of tea and a roll. He also said that the fact that the body was warm when discovered at Waterloo meant nothing more, in the case of a stout young woman like Miss Camp, than that she had been killed within the preceding twenty-four hours.

Mr. Bond said that as far as he knew, no analytical examination of the pestle had yet been made.

The coroner's inquest will be opened this morning.

10

LONDON. FEBRUARY, 1897
DR. BOND

"And you're sure she didn't put up a fight?" Superintendent Robinson asked, leaning against the desk. "She was a solid woman. Thirteen stone."

"No," I said. "I know the doctor who examined the scene thinks differently, but with all due respect to him, I would say she had no time to offer resistance, or indeed, to even cry out."

The pestle that had killed the unfortunate Miss Camp sat on the wooden desktop between us, still coated with her blood and strands of her hair.

"There were four blows, perhaps six," I continued. "I imagine the attack was frenzied and took no more than a minute in total. That is a heavy weapon, and the first blow—to her forehead—would have stunned her. Why would he pause, allow her to recover and fight back, and then attack again? That logic aside, the placement of the injuries on her skull would indicate a furious flurry of strikes while she remained in much the same position: with her assailant standing above her. Are you any closer to discovering whom that might be?"

The murder of Elizabeth Camp two days before on the seven-forty-two train from Hounslow to Waterloo had grabbed the attention of the population, which didn't surprise me. She had not been sexually assaulted, and because her jewelry was still present when her body was found—one arm sticking out from under the blood-splattered carriage seat—the motive was obviously not robbery. The idea that this could happen to a respectable woman traveling alone in a railway carriage in the early evening had struck fear into the female population, especially given the fevered nature of the attack.

"We're trying to track down the sister's husband, a fellow called Haynes, but I can't see what motive he'd have. He and his wife have been living apart for several months at least. Miss Camp's fiancé says Miss Camp had never mentioned to him any animosity between her and her brother-in-law."

"She did burn some letters a few days ago, though," Sergeant Leonard, a slight but hardy young man, cut in. "No idea as to what they contained yet."

"And no witnesses?" I did not envy these men their investigation. If they had no clear suspect from within the victim's life, then it was likely a random act of madness, and they would need to have the luck of the devil to catch him.

"You know how it is," Robinson sighed. "One man's word is immediately discounted by another's. A pastry cook called Burgess—also a second-class passenger—said he saw a man dressed in a dark coat and top hat leaving in a hurry, but the porter on the platform remembers nothing of the sort. We've got two barmaids in a pub in Vauxhall who report a pale, haggard man in an overcoat and bowler hat who came in and ordered a brandy, but his hand was shaking so much he could barely hold it; they said he left suddenly and got into a hansom cab." He paused, then added sadly, "So no, really we have nothing."

"You're lucky you found the pestle," I said. "At least we know she was killed before the Wandsworth stop. I know this line quite well myself—I take it to visit Dr. Hebbert's daughter and her son in Barnes. Thankfully, I was not traveling on that day, so I believe you can rule me out of your inquiries. And that is not my pestle." Both men smiled at my attempt at humor, and I turned my attention once again to the murder weapon. It was old and heavy, with the number six or nine imprinted on it depending on which way up you held it. If the pestle did indeed belong to the killer, then I would have guessed it to be a six if the killer, by habit, held it the right way when attacking.

"We're having no luck with that either," Robinson said, "but we're still visiting all the chemists—perhaps that number will lead us somewhere."

"I fear this inquest may last for several weeks," I said, "and it will keep you busier than me. I am only sorry I cannot give you more information, but rest assured, my assistance is available whenever you require it."

We said our farewells, and I left them sifting through the little evidence they had. In truth, although of course I was not glad that Miss Camp was dead, I was happy for the distraction. Edward Kane had returned from his business in Southampton, and he was once again spending time in Juliana and little James's company. Although he had not yet asked me outright for my verdict on the letters he had given me, I could feel his eyes searching mine when we met. I had managed thus far to avoid being alone with him, which meant that I had often declined dinner invitations or I had left early on the pretext of work or a paper to finish, and this in turn had led to a little jealousy on my part over the amount of time Kane was spending alone with Juliana. She remained affectionate toward me, of course, and there were still times when I dined with her alone, but it was becoming clear that something in Kane's nature—perhaps the same natural good humor that had attracted James Harrington to him—was having a revitalizing effect on Juliana. She had begun to laugh more freely, and her eyes sparkled at times, just as they had when I'd first met her.

I was not sure how that made me feel. I was glad that she was happier, but I could not deny that I wished very much that Kane would just go back to America and leave us to be happy together, alone—and perhaps then I would have the courage to ask her to become my wife.

Still, the Elizabeth Camp murder had given me the excuse I needed to avoid any conversation about the letters and to start seeing more of Juliana again: I could tell Kane that I had started them but not yet finished, and now the inquest was taking up so much of my time I could not spare any to focus on the letters right now. It was perhaps a little weak as excuses go, but Kane was a gentleman, and he would not push me. I, on the other hand, might be able to start gently pushing him to one side, to ensure that Juliana's fondness for him did not grow during my absence.

And so it was with a slight spring in my step that I came out of the police station, my thoughts on happier things than poor Miss Camp's battered body.

"Dr. Bond!" Newsmen all had the same tone, I had learned over my years of working alongside the police: a blend of aggression and hunger as they vocally jostled for attention. "Dr. Bond! Just a minute of your time, please. What can you tell us about Elizabeth Camp's death? Do you think the killer will strike again?"

I scanned the street for a hansom cab, but luck was not with me.

"I'm afraid I have to get back to Westminster." I turned, irritated, and stared at the reporter. "You should direct your questions to Superintendent Robinson of the railway police."

"I expect I should." The man grinned. "But I helped you before, Dr. Bond—in the vault at Whitehall, remember? Thought maybe you could return the favor."

I stared for a long moment before suddenly I recognized Jasper Waring, the reporter who had persuaded Henry Moore to let his dog search the vault of the building at New Scotland Yard where the torso had been found. The dog had done better than the police bloodhounds, for it had uncovered an arm and a leg.

"Smoker," I said, the dog's name coming from somewhere buried deep in my subconscious. "How is he?"

"Dead a couple of years." Waring lit a cigarette and offered me one, but I shook my head. "He was a good dog—won't be another like him."

"He did well for us, I won't deny." I looked around once again for a hansom cab, not entirely sure how to continue this conversation.

The past had become determined to engulf me of late, and Jasper Waring and his terrier belonged in my memory and not my present. "But I'm afraid I still cannot divulge any of my findings to you with regard to Miss Camp's death."

"It was worth a try, though." He grinned again, and I could not help but smile back. He had not aged, and I wondered if chasing the news somehow made men immune—it was as if they remained untouched, impartial observers of life.

"Savage, wasn't it?" he continued. "Reminds me a bit of Jack— attacking a woman like that, with no motive, in a public place. No wonder people are scared."

His light tone did not deceive me. He was trying to lure me into revealing something.

"As I said," I commented dryly, "you will need to address your questions to the superintendent, or attend the inquest."

He laughed, a warm earthy sound. "Right you are, Doctor. Right you are. And I don't blame you fellows for not wanting another Jack on our streets. I know how hard you and that other doctor worked."

Finally a hansom cab rounded the street, and I waved him down.

"I worried about him for a while, if I'm honest," Waring continued. "Walking the streets of Whitechapel like that—those dead women must've right haunted him."

I had only been half-listening, but at that I frowned. "I'm sorry? Who was walking the streets?"

"That other doctor—Hebbert. I saw him, scruffed down a bit, but definitely him. Saw him a couple of times. We were always out that way during that time—had to be, really. Sometimes I forget how much you surgeons help the police—and the things you see . . . Well, you must have strong stomachs, that's all I can say."

"Yes," I said, forcing a smile onto my face as a chill settled into my stomach, "I suppose we must." I pulled the cab door open and tipped my hat at him. "Well, I bid you good day, Mr. Waring, and I wish you good luck with the superintendent."

I kept the smile until I'd sat back in the seat and the wheels were rolling underneath me, and then it dropped like a stone.

What had Charles Hebbert been doing in Whitechapel during that time? Had he been taking the opium too? If so, it was highly unlikely that our paths had not crossed, for though the periodicals might imply otherwise, the streets of London were not teeming with dens. I had been a regular poppy smoker myself at that time, and I was sure if Charles had been the same, then I would have discovered it—or at the very least, I would have seen the signs.

Why did my heart beat so fast? Surely it could have been as Waring himself had suggested: Charles was simply scouring the streets to find some clue as to who might be perpetrating the terrible crimes. But I knew Charles—he was curious, but he was no policeman, and nor was he like me, a man with an interest in analyzing the behaviors of others. He was a surgeon, and involved only in the meat of the matter.

As the shadows gathered in my mind, I cursed Jasper Waring for calling after me, for throwing more of the past at my feet—a heavy slab of darkness I wished so badly to forget.

By the time I reached home, Mrs. Parks had my dinner ready, a fine roast pork, but I pushed it around my plate, barely picking at it, until eventually I declared I had work to do in my study and left the table. I could not breathe under her scrutiny. She was a good, honest woman, but she remembered well how I had behaved those few years ago when my sleep failed me and madness came calling. My appetite had vanished first, and I was sure she kept one eye on me for signs of the malady's return.

"I ate a large lunch, I'm afraid," I said as I passed her in the doorway, all too aware of her disapproving eye falling on my full plate, "but the meat will serve for a cold supper later."

"As you wish," she said, and I thought I could hear her disapprobation as I ducked away from her and climbed the stairs, making a mental note to come down before bed and throw the meat out for the cats. I told myself this was so as not to hurt her feelings, but in my heart I knew it was because Mrs. Parks could—with one withering stare—turn me in an instant back into an awkward, ashamed boy.

I sat in my study and gazed out at the gathering night. The glare of my desk lamp on the glass of the window trapped a ghostly, intangible world of reflection, where everything was not quite as it should be.

Charles Hebbert had been walking the streets of Whitechapel during the Jack murders. I did not doubt Waring's words, for he had no reason to lie. Charles had been different then, I recalled that much: he had been drinking and despondent—and what was it he had said to me one night? I glanced over at the window again. He had used a particular phrase, *Wickedness through the windows*, or something like that, and he had talked of bad dreams of terrible bloody things. I thought too of Harrington, as much as I wished not to. Many of the police—Henry Moore and Andrews included—had believed a surgeon could have been responsible for the deaths, even though we had firmly believed that it was unlikely. Could Charles have had suspicions that his son-in-law was Jack the Ripper? Harrington *was* killing women at that time, so perhaps Charles had come to believe he might be responsible for the Ripper deaths? Maybe that was why he had not been forthcoming with information when it was discovered that Elizabeth Jackson had lived on the same street as Harrington's family home when it would have been more natural to mention such a thing?

I poured myself a brandy and calmed a little. That must have been it: he was simply suspicious. There was nothing strange about that, after all.

It was later, in the depth of the night, that I woke sweating and gasping from my sleep. My bedclothes had tangled around me, and I fought free of them as if they were a live thing trying to drag me down into some unknown hell. Perhaps they did. The dream that had woken me had already evaporated, but my dry mouth was bitter with its echo, and my heart pounded.

Two things emerged in my mind from that subconscious wandering in my sleep. The first was that on the night that Alice McKenzie, the last of Jack's victims, had died, I had dined with James Harrington. It was not a night I would ever forget, despite how hard I had tried. It was the night I had taken the strange opium and seen the *Upir* crawling up over his shoulder. Charles Hebbert had not been there. He had been dining at his club with colleagues.

The second thing that crawled, dark and uninvited, to the forefront of my thinking was something the priest had said: that Jack was simply a by-product of the *Upir*, part of the mayhem that followed in its wake.

I turned on a lamp, relishing in the glow of the light that returned the shapes that had hulked threateningly in the gloom to being simply the objects of familiar furniture. I could not allow myself to be sucked back into the way I thought in that time. However real the things I had seen might have appeared to be, I knew that they could not exist. Harrington had been a killer; all else was simply drug-induced madness. There had been no *Upir*, and therefore Charles Hebbert could not have been affected by his proximity to it. The idea was simply absurd. The dawning realization that I was even considering my old friend to be a Jack suspect made me feel as if I was once again hovering on the precipice of insanity.

There was only one thing I could do: I must prove to myself that Charles was innocent of these crimes. I would arrange a dinner at his club with him. That would be my first move. I would not think of the priest or the hairdresser or the *Upir*. I would do what I did best: work with the presented facts.

11

LONDON. FEBRUARY, 1897
EDWARD KANE

"Do you live near a river in New York?"

"Sure I do. The Hudson River runs right around the city—but I've never done this in New York." Edward Kane looked down at the small boy beside him and grinned. "And make sure those pants stay rolled up. We'll both be in big trouble with your mother if those get ruined."

"Maybe it's the same river," James said. His cheeks were rosy in the crisp air as he crouched and rummaged in the wet mud revealed by the low tide. He pulled out a large black pebble to add to the collection of odds and ends he'd put in his small pail. "Maybe it goes all the way from here to there."

"Maybe it does, son. Maybe it does." He took the boy's hand, and they walked further along toward the old steps that led up to the pavement and houses. "We need to head back. I've got to go for dinner with your grandfather and Dr. Bond." He looked down at his own rolled-up trouser legs and muddy shoes and winked. "And I don't think they'd like it if I showed up like this, do you?"

James giggled and shook his head. He sniffed in the breeze. "Why doesn't Mother like the river? Should I not like it too?"

It was a small question, but so heavily loaded. Kane knew how protective Juliana was over her son. He'd seen enough evidence of it—the home-schooling, the distrust of strangers around him, and most definitely her insistence on keeping him away from the river. Given how the boy's father had died, that was no real surprise, but he wondered if she realized how much damage her cosseting could be causing. There were many gifts parents could give to a child, but their own fears should not be one of them.

"Rivers are beautiful. You know why I have one in my city and you have one in yours?" The boy's big blue eyes looked up at him as if he were the font of all knowledge. "Because rivers bring life," he continued. "They link people. Because of the river, products from all over the world can get to London easily. Your family business brings in produce from as far away as the Indies to the very heart of the city. Between the rivers and the oceans, and now the railways, we are bringing the world together." He paused, and then bent down and looked James in the eye as he said seriously, "But water can be dangerous. There are strong tides and currents that can drag you away. Plants grow on the bottom that can entangle you and pull you down. The thing with rivers is that you have to treat them with respect—as long as you do that, there's no reason to be afraid of them. I spent some of the best summers of my childhood messing around on rivers. But I was always careful."

"Did you go out in a rowboat?"

"Sure I did."

"Can we go in a rowboat one day?"

"As long as I can persuade your mother," Kane said.

"Uncle Thomas never takes me on the river. I think he hates it as much as she does." James paused. "Uncle Thomas doesn't play with me very much."

"He's a very busy man," Edward said, "and he works very hard. But I know he loves you."

They climbed the slick steps in a comfortable silence and left the river behind.

*　　*　　*

Edward Kane had never really considered children. They were in his future somewhere, just like a sensible wife was—after all, he'd need a son to leave his business to—but he'd never spent any time with them. He swung James up in his arms, making the boy giggle. He was happy to be able to give him some freedom from the stuffy confines of his London life for a few moments. He had discovered that he enjoyed little James's company. Despite his words, he wasn't sure that Thomas Bond did. The doctor had been busy with a murder case for much of the time since his return from Southampton, but on the few occasions they'd all been together, he'd seen how the doctor avoided the child when he could. It was strange, considering how much he clearly loved Juliana. Kane couldn't help it, but that love bothered him: he had all the respect in the world for Bond as a man and a professional, but the idea of Juliana and him as a couple revolted him. If he was honest with himself, he had to admit that what rankled him was less Bond's feelings toward Juliana than hers for the doctor. She might think she loved him, certainly, but it was surely a love born of obligation and gratitude. They were friends who loved each other, and he feared she was in danger of confusing that with being lovers.

Juliana. If anyone should be her lover, then it should be him. He knew that without doubt. He should have been back in New York by now, but he'd rented some offices and hired a lawyer so he could continue his business while in London, in order to stay longer. His father would be spinning in his grave to know that his son was turning his world around to accommodate his feelings for a woman—but the good thing about graves was that they were final. His father could twist and turn as much as he wanted; his son no longer had to listen to him. Edward Kane was very much a grown man, and he could do as he pleased. However, neither was he still quite the rebel of his youth: he was not ignoring his business, and he had in fact made some sound new investments while he was here. He freely admitted the business had become an adventure in itself, and he enjoyed it. He was also enjoying London in all its vibrancy and excitement.

And the most vibrant part of it was undoubtedly Juliana: Jim Harrington's wife.

As if on cue, she opened the front door to them and sighed dramatically at their wind-fresh faces and beaming grins.

"I got rocks!" James held up his small pail.

"So I see."

Kane put the boy down, and he ran inside.

"I hope he didn't go in the water," Juliana said.

"In this weather? Are you kidding me?" He kept his tone light, and she smiled.

"I had better get you some coffee before you go back into town. You must be freezing."

"Maybe put a little brandy in it too," he said, closing the door and wiping down his feet. He watched her as she walked away, her slim hips moving from side to side behind her bustle. She was not like the American society ladies of New York, who were all so self-aware, conscious of every movement, the social standing of each new acquaintance, and especially of their own attractiveness in comparison with others. They were sharp: even when stripped naked and sweating with lust—and there had been plenty of occasions when that had been the case—there was an edge to them that he could not define. He was sure that such women existed in London too, but perhaps in the part of society that belonged to "old" money. There was no such thing in most of America—perhaps only in Boston. In New York it was the bankers and businessmen whose daughters were got up in fancy clothes and glittering jewels and paraded as examples of their fathers' wealth. He'd found of late that most of them left him cold. Or maybe he was just getting older, and the superficial was becoming jaded.

By the time Juliana returned with coffee, his trouser legs were rolled down, and James had run off to wash and sort the treasures collected on their walk. The boy was happy, but a small shadow of concern had flickered across his face when he'd seen his mother. It wasn't fair on either of them.

"He's a good boy," Edward said, taking the cup and saucer from her, "and he's tougher than you think."

"He's prone to fevers and chest infections as his father was." She sat opposite him. "I hope it wasn't too cold outside. And that water—well, I'm sure you understand why he shouldn't go in it. It's full of filth."

The lines between her eyes that had been slowly disappearing gathered together. Did she even realize the tension she was projecting?

"You know something," he started carefully, "as adults, we have to learn to keep our fears from our children. They're very good at picking up those things that don't need language to communicate. I learned that from my relationship with my own father."

"Your father wasn't murdered and thrown into a river." Her tone hadn't changed, but her back had stiffened, and she held her cup up over her mouth so only her dark eyes could be seen. He wasn't a fool; the angry defensiveness in them was clear. But damn the woman, he was no simpering disciple who would back down to her beauty, not when he was trying to do what was right, for her, and for James.

"This is true," he said calmly, "and if that's all you want James to remember of his father, then you keep gripping him tightly and being afraid every time he wants to do things that are actually just part of normal boyhood behavior."

"How I raise my son is none of your business." She carefully placed her cup down and stood up, ramrod straight.

She looked quite magnificent. Edward smiled and raised an eyebrow. "So this is how we're going to play it, are we?"

A flush rose in her cheeks. "I think you forget your place here."

"Perhaps I do." He stood up and moved closer to her. "But just think about it: one day he's going to grow into a man, and he'll need to know more of the world than what you can show him from behind your apron strings. Let him breathe."

She said nothing, but glared at him.

"Why do you live so close to the river anyway?" he asked. "I don't understand, when it causes you so much pain."

"To keep James close," she said eventually. "So he doesn't feel alone." As her eyes teared up she held her chin higher, and he found himself drawn to her even more. "I don't know if he died before he went in the water or not, but if I don't think of the river as being part of him, then I don't know where he died at all, and that is worse."

"He was very lucky to be loved by you." He watched her as she regained her composure. He wanted nothing more than to hold her, to wash away all that grief with his passion. His words must have resonated with his feelings because she wiped her hands on her dress as if dusting something off and then turned away and picked up her cup. As she sipped from it, he noticed the china trembling slightly. Was that the effect of her grief, or was she too feeling some of the heat between them?

"Enough of this conversation," she said, breezily, "when it has been such a pleasant day. And you must be getting back so you have time to change for your dinner with my father and Thomas." She said Bond's name as if it was armor. Was that it? Was he her protection against being hurt again?

"I'm so disappointed not to have seen so much of him of late. Although it has been very kind of you to keep me company, I hope this dinner means that he will soon be able to find more time for me—and for James."

"I'm sure he will," he said dryly. "I know he's very fond of you."

She couldn't meet his eyes, but her smile was wide, another new smile from a woman with a thousand of them. He thought perhaps this one tried too hard.

"I'm looking forward to seeing him myself," he said, reaching for his hat and returning her smile. "He's an interesting fellow."

His words weren't a lie; he was very much looking forward to seeing Thomas Bond again. He hoped that the surgeon had found time in his busy schedule to look through James Harrington's letters. Although Edward was different in many ways from his late father, they shared a dogged determination, and the deeper in love with Juliana he fell—and although just the sound of her laughter could make him hard, he knew that this was something more than lust—the more curious he became about the torments Harrington had suffered at the end of his life. He wanted to lay him to rest. He wanted to allay his own guilt. He wanted them all to be able to move on.

* * *

It was a strange dinner. Charles Hebbert was in a fine mood, and he ordered far too much wine, which they all made a valiant effort to consume. Edward noticed that Bond wasn't matching them glass for glass; he was sure that the doctor often raised his glass to his lips but didn't swallow. It was entirely possible that he could not afford to start the next day with a hangover, or perhaps he didn't have the head for wine that Kane himself had cultivated over the years, but by the time they had lit their cigars and relaxed with brandy, he was certain that Thomas Bond was not in the same convivial frame of mind as the rest of the party.

It hadn't been noticeable at first. The conversation had flowed as they discussed Kane's British business dealings, and then, satisfying Kane's curiosity, the doctor had shared details about the death of the woman on the train that he had been investigating—perhaps more information than he should, but then, he was among friends—or maybe he had been speaking just to fill the space between them? He certainly had not mentioned Harrington's letters, nor dropped any hints about their contents. Kane was itching to have a moment alone with him to ask, but thus far, that chance had not arisen.

Charles Hebbert waved away the conversation of Elizabeth Camp's death, declaring that too much time had been spent digging into corpses, and instead he started sharing anecdotes of Juliana and little James in the way that fond grandfathers—though not something Kane had ever experienced for himself—were wont to do.

"I cannot believe we haven't dined here before," Bond said as they leaned back in their fireside seats. "In all the years of our friendship, I have never been to your club. Fancy that."

"It is very remiss of me, that is for certain. But"—and Charles smiled, his eyes twinkling merrily—"you have often dined in my home and with my family, and surely that is preferable."

"Of course." Bond sipped his drink. "You must be happy that you had so many dinners here with young Harrington before his sad demise—some time away from your wives to just talk business . . ."

From behind a haze of cigar smoke, Kane watched Bond carefully. His head buzzed slightly with the alcohol, but his misspent youth had served him well in that regard, and he was far from intoxicated. Was Bond trying to discover something about Harrington? He scanned his recollection of the letters for any relevance, but he couldn't recall anything useful. Most of what was burned in his mind were the gruesome revelations and madness, not the day-to-day details. He wished he'd made copies before handing them to the doctor so that he could reread them himself.

"Yes, yes." Charles's face darkened in the memory of grief. "A bittersweet pleasure, to have had those times. Although now, of course, I would far rather he had spent those hours with Juliana, given that their time together turned out to be so short. He was a fine fellow, young Harrington. It is so sad to lose someone so young, someone who had such a bright future ahead. And such a terrible end."

"Did he become a member here? I don't recall," Bond continued, ignoring the emotional content of Charles's words.

"Are you considering it yourself, Thomas, dear fellow?" Charles said, not answering the question. "If so, I would be more than happy to make the recommendation. Every chap should have a club—a sanctuary. Are you a member of any club in New York, Edward?"

"I most certainly am," Kane answered, "although the Union Club does not have quite the heritage you have here. Not yet, anyway. We're a little behind you with our history." He laughed with Charles, whose face was glowing with the effect of the brandy on top of the wine, but his attention was still focused on Bond. He looked for some sort of signal from him, but none was forthcoming; instead, Bond stared into his glass for a moment and then excused himself. Kane was tempted to follow him, but Charles Hebbert leaned forward and slapped him on the thigh.

"Glad to have you alone for a moment, young man—wanted to thank you for the efforts you have made with young James," he said as Dr. Bond disappeared out to the foyer, no doubt seeking the bathroom. Kane was trapped where he was. His conversation with the good doctor would have to wait.

"It's not a chore. I like him—and Juliana." He sipped his brandy. "I think Jim was a lucky man to marry her."

Hebbert chuckled. "I did wonder why you hadn't yet returned to New York."

"I meant nothing untoward," he said quickly. The last thing he wanted to do was talk about Juliana with her father. If the growing attraction between them became the subject of discussion with her parent, she would withdraw from him; of that he was certain. Her defenses were too great, her grief still too raw, and she was still nervous about him, and probably of what might happen between them. He would work his way through her barriers, but he had not yet done so, and he would not risk losing her for the sake of a precipitate conversation with a doting father.

"Thomas is very fond of her too," Hebbert added. His eyes drifted toward the door through which Bond had gone, and for a moment they were thoughtful. "Although I fear he is not very fond of my grandson."

"Why would you say that?" Kane asked, although he had also noticed Thomas Bond's coolness around the child. "He's probably just not used to children."

"Yes, perhaps that is it," Hebbert conceded. "He has always been a more reserved man than I. And I cannot deny that he has been a fine friend, and he has looked after Juliana well over the past few years. She was very ill for a long time after James was born. We nearly lost her too."

"Maybe that's why he struggles with the boy," Kane said. "Because of her sickness?"

"Such resentment isn't in his nature. He's a good man." This time the intent gaze was on Edward. "He really is good for her."

"I'm sure he has been." Edward wasn't sure if his own shift in tense had been intentional or not.

They sipped their brandy, and the fire crackled between them, punctuating the background hubbub of male voices.

"But I do wonder," Hebbert said, "if a younger man might not be better for her. I fear were she to marry Thomas, as fond as I am of him and knowing how deeply he does love her, that she would be achieving the wrong type of security."

"She would feel safe with him," Kane said, "that is for sure." If he could not derail the conversation, at least he would not stoop to trying to discredit Thomas Bond's credentials as a suitor. For a start, he liked and respected the man. And it was becoming clear that Hebbert already had doubts about that possible match, if Bond ever got up the nerve to ask her to marry him, so there was nothing to be gained by sticking the knife in here. If he were going to win Juliana, then it would be through his own efforts, not by trying to malign his rival. It was hard to consider Bond a rival—how old was he? Late fifties? Not that much younger than Kane's father had been when he had died.

"Yes, yes," Hebbert agreed. "Thomas is a fine man. But he is nearing retirement, and she is still a young woman. London can be a hard city to live in—I often see the very worst of its actions—and no doubt worse as a widow of means."

He left the rest unsaid, but the message was clear. If Edward Kane were to win Juliana's affections and take her to New York to live a wealthy and privileged life, he would find no argument from her father. He felt a moment of guilt for Bond. He had taken the doctor into his confidence about James Harrington's letters, and if he were a true gentleman, he would back away from his growing relationship with Juliana. Where affairs of the heart were concerned, however, gentleman or not, he'd learned that people invariably did what they wanted to. Fighting it only delayed the inevitable. Even for those less carnally driven than himself.

"She's a strong woman," Kane said. "Whatever she chooses for her future, I'm sure she'll do just fine." He was careful to say what and not whom. He'd seen his father tell a thousand faux truths in boardroom meetings to know the power of choosing the right words.

"We should play cards," Hebbert announced suddenly, changing the tack of the conversation. "There is normally a game or two going on, and I don't feel quite ready to retire yet. What do you say?"

"I'm always in for the tables," Kane replied.

"Excellent!" Hebbert was back to his jovial self. "Then we shall—Ah, Thomas! There you are. Cards?"

"Sadly not." Bond finally returned to join them, but he didn't sit. "I have only just realized the time," he said. "I fear I must go home. Otherwise I shall be of no use to the police in the morning. Nor to my patients at Westminster."

He appeared slightly flustered, his smile tight.

"Damn shame," Hebbert said. "It's been a most pleasant evening. No doubt we shall meet again soon enough though."

Bond nodded and shook both their hands. His fingers felt cold in Edward Kane's grip. What was Bond hiding? Anything? Maybe it was just his own imagination at work, looking for signs that weren't there. Always possible, he concluded, as he picked up his brandy and followed Charles Hebbert toward the cards room. Possible, but unlikely. He'd learned to trust his instincts, and they were telling him that Dr. Thomas Bond was onto something.

12

LONDON. FEBRUARY, 1897
DR. BOND

I did not sleep well that night. At first I had thought my investigations would be easy. On arrival at the club, Hebbert had signed us all into the Members' Ledger before we handed in our coats and hats. It was as I had hoped: a record of each visit was made, and I imagined that the club was quite prestigious enough for the expensive leather-bound books to be kept for posterity.

I ate a good dinner, and I entertained Edward Kane with stories of the inquest, glad to be able to avoid the subject of Harrington's letters. When we had retired for brandy and both of my companions were pleasantly merry from wine, I excused myself and hurried to the entrance. With the list of dates of Jack's murders in my pocket, I had hoped to be able to quickly scan the right pages and confirm whether Charles Hebbert had been there those nights—even if I only had time to check the date of the Alice McKenzie killing, the one date he'd claimed beyond doubt to have been dining at the club.

I was not in luck: despite my entirely plausible excuse of wanting to check some personal dates of attendance to clear up a matter with a friend—banking on the fact that the man in charge would not know whether I had visited there before or not—he could not provide me with the books, for they were stored elsewhere, and in any case, members' records were a private matter. I could, however, leave a note with my name and the date in question on it, and someone would check on my behalf and send a message to me. All of this was explained on the presumption that I was a member and not simply a guest, and so I smiled and I told him I might well do that if I could not find the details in my own papers, and I wouldn't want to put anyone to such trouble until I was certain it was necessary.

After that, I made my excuses to my companions and left. I could not risk that the gentleman at the desk would change his mind and come to find me, for there was no story I could conceive that would explain to Charles my needing to see the club's records. As I was quite sure he was innocent of the suspicions I needed to allay in my mind, it would make me look a fool, and it would also damage our relationship—and thus my relationship with Juliana.

My sleep was fitful as my mind dragged images and memories I thought had long since faded to the fore of my nightmares and then twisted them with images of Hebbert and Juliana and of course James Harrington until I woke, sweating and terrified, a little after four. There was no laudanum in the house, and I was glad of that, for I am sure I would have swallowed half the bottle to calm myself.

I needed to check those records. It was the only way I would find peace for myself again. The kernel of suspicion I held about Hebbert was like a gateway to all the horrors of the past I had worked so hard to put behind me.

After Mrs. Parks's breakfast, which, though I was in no mood to eat, I managed anyway, I took a cab to Walter Andrews's offices and asked if I could engage his private investigation services to get the records for me. To his credit he did not press when I told him I would rather not share why I wanted them at this stage, but I did say it had something to do with young Harrington. I was simply trying to clear up a small matter, nothing important.

When he arrived that evening with the Members' Ledgers for 1888 and 1889 in his hands, he was more curious. Although I was desperate to check the entries, I put the books on a side table and offered him a drink, which he accepted.

"I must have them back early tomorrow morning," he said. He hadn't taken his coat off, and the heavy raindrops caught in its folds dripped on the rug, marking out the seconds. "And there is a small sum to be paid to the employee who provided them—no fee on my part though, Thomas. Consider it a favor to a friend."

"Thank you." I handed him a small glass of brandy—an ungenerous measure, but I didn't want him to linger. "I shall return them first thing."

"You could of course check what you need while I wait," he said. "And then I could return them tonight." I did not miss the curious look in his eyes. I knew Andrews well, and his eye for detail was as acute as mine. We also trusted each other, and I had no doubt he was wondering why I was being so reticent about this.

"I need to look at these in conjunction with some other documents that aren't in the house, I'm afraid," I extemporized. "But have no fear: I shall have them back to you by breakfast time, I assure you."

"That's fine." He drained his brandy. "Then I shall leave you to it."

"Thank you once again," I said, trying not to look overeager as I edged him toward the drawing room door. "I really do appreciate your help."

He paused in the hallway and studied me in the dimmed light. "I could not help but notice the years of the ledgers: eighty-eight and eighty-nine. Jack's time."

I forced a laugh. "Sadly, this is not related to our missing killer but a far more mundane matter of spending. Something I would rather keep quiet for others' sake."

"Well, if you need any more help, then just ask. And you know you can talk to me about anything that might be concerning you."

"And I would, Walter, I would." I shook his hand firmly, hoping my palm wasn't sweating in his. "Now I'm sure you have supper waiting for you at home. I've kept you out long enough."

Finally, he left, and I heaved a sigh of relief as the door closed behind him. I gave it a few minutes until I was sure he was truly gone, and then I grabbed the ledgers and ran up the stairs to my study. I had already drawn up a list of the dates of the Ripper killings, and I placed it next to the books. I'd start with Alice McKenzie. If Hebbert had been in the club as he'd said, then the rest was of no consequence and I could sleep easy in my bed once again, all the while laughing at my own foolishness.

July sixteenth. I scanned through the months until I found the date, and then I ran my finger down the inked names. I reached the last entry and paused. With a sickly knot forming in my guts, I went back to the top and started again. Three more times I searched, my eyes moving faster and faster over the names as dread crept into my limbs.

Charles Hebbert's name was not there. I looked to my list and reached for the 1888 books. Martha Tabram, Polly Nicholls, Annie Chapman, Elizabeth Stride, Catherine Eddowes, and lastly poor Mary Jane Kelly, the wreck of whose body I had studied in her room. Hebbert had not been at his club on the nights of any of their murders.

I sat back in my chair, a boulder settling on my chest. Could I really be suspecting Charles Hebbert of such crimes? And if it was Hebbert, why had the killings stopped so suddenly?

Because Harrington had died. My mind's whisper was like a worm burrowing deep into my head. *And Harrington was the* Upir, *and the* Upir *had brought the mayhem. Without the* Upir *close by, Hebbert was saved from the dark urges and fantasies that had lived inside him.*

It was preposterous—it had to be. I poured myself a brandy and drank it quickly, hoping to stop the trembling in my hands. Then I flicked through the pages of the books once more. Even where Hebbert was present, I could find only two occasions when he had taken Harrington with him—and yet Juliana had complained to me at the time that Harrington and her father were always at his club. Why would Hebbert lie about that? Surely one or the other would have revealed the truth at some point—so was this lie complicit? Had they known of each others' awful secret deeds?

I needed to look at Harrington's letters. The thought filled me with a terrible fear, but I knew my curiosity would drive me to madness otherwise. I would not read them all, I vowed, as I went downstairs and pulled on my coat and hat. I would simply scan them, looking for references to Hebbert's club, no more than that. I would not be pulled into the insanity of the supernatural again. I had to go to my office at the Westminster and see what the letters held.

As I stepped outside, the freezing night gathered round me like a shroud, and in my wake I could feel the ghosts of dead women reaching out to cling to me. They needed answers. And, God help me, so did I.

13

Extract from letter from James Harrington
to Edward Kane, dated 1888

. . . I have been so wrapped up in my fears for my sanity that when she said she was upset about my behavior, I was expecting some revelation that she knew of my blackouts, or perhaps something worse, some confirmation of the things I fear I am doing in those times. But it was none of that. She said only that she felt lonely. I had promised her she could come help me with some of the books, and she said she did not mind that the opportunity had not arisen (although it was clear that had upset her too, but how could I let her near the wharves? How could she see how little I concentrated there and how my mind was focused on whatever was behind that locked door that I trembled to open?) and that she was glad her father and I clearly found each other's company interesting, but she was tired of spending evenings alone while we dined at the club.

I did not know how to answer that. As far as I was aware, I had dined with Hebbert at the club only once, maybe twice; it certainly was no regular occurrence. I did not say this though; I opened my mouth to deny it, but I found I could not speak the words.

I know what you're thinking, Edward—if you're thinking anything other than I should be in an asylum by now—and that is that if I am suffering blackouts from my fever or something worse, then perhaps I am dining with Dr. Hebbert and simply not remembering it.

The vague spaces I sometimes occupy don't work like that. And my strands of memory related to them are always grim. Surely if I were dining so frequently with her father that it was upsetting Juliana, then I would remember at least some of it? I wondered if it was a lie I had told her at some point and forgotten, but it was not something that it would strike me to say. I know that when I returned from wherever I found myself late at night, I would tell her I had been working late (another reason I could not allow her to come to my offices to help me), but I could not recall ever including her father in my terrible deceptions. Why would I? It would be so easy for her to prove wrong.

I mumbled an apology, and I did my best to make her feel better. She loves me very much, and it hurts me terribly to see her so distressed. It is not the grand passion I had with Elizabeth—that was a first love, and I was different then—but I do love her, and I wish that this terrible weight on my back and in my soul did not plague me so, that I could be a good future husband to her.

At times, when the dream-like visions of what I am coming more and more to believe are recollections of my own actions overwhelm me, I think I should break off our engagement. Surely it is wrong of me to marry her knowing how troubled I am, but the idea of being alone—more alone than I feel already—terrifies me even more. It is as if Juliana and the normality of my life with her is the only anchor I have against this growing madness. And when the fever passes and my mind clears, it is easier to dismiss all my terrible misgivings as flights of fancy. Then I think myself foolish for even considering giving her up.

I ramble once again, but these letters are a comfort to me, perhaps as much because you do not answer them (although I hope you are well and there is no sinister reason for your lack of correspondence). They are like a confessional. If you are not receiving them, then whoever is reading them—if anyone at all—is simply a stranger in another country, and I care not what they make of my strange predicaments.

I mentioned our visits to the club to Charles over dinner, a brief throwaway remark, even though beneath my hopefully calm surface, I was trembling. He simply paused, and for a second I thought he was as confused as I was, but then something shifted, and he smiled at me before saying that men must have their pursuits away from womenfolk, and then he moved the conversation on. I could barely eat after that. I know that it sounds strange that I am so certain I have not been spending several evenings with him this month, but I know in my bones I have not. But why would he lie? And if he had his own secret—a mistress, perhaps?—why would he involve me in his lie if he did not know me to have secrets of my own? Perhaps he knows that I would not expose him, but it seems to me a great risk. Deception, which has never been part of my nature previously, is becoming something on which I am an expert. I am so tired of the doubts that surround me. I am so tired of my fears and the thing always out of sight that I fear is driving me to a terrible end.

I have not yet opened the warehouse door. I will. I promise myself I will.

14

COLNEY HATCH LUNATIC ASYLUM.
1894
AARON KOSMINSKI

Assessment

Since his last visitor two weeks ago, the patient has become violent when approached, and it has become necessary to separate him from other patients for their own safety. Staff maintain a minimal contact policy at all times, and Mr. Kosminski spends most of his hours alone, which calms him slightly.

I believe that the visitor he received has in some way fed into Kosminski's complicated paranoias. The report from the doctor and nurse on duty who supervised the visit can shed no light on why it affected the patient so badly. The gentleman who called on him was a foreign priest. The two men spoke intently for some time, during which the patient was entirely calm. The priest, notable for his missing hand as well as his accent, embraced the patient, and then after a short while, he left.

He told the doctor that he had been sent by the patient's older sister, Matilda, but she has since stated that she did no such thing. She did say, however, that her brother did have two friends with whom he spent many hours, but she did not have their names. She thought that one was foreign.

One week ago Kosminski was violent toward himself, beating his head against the wall of his room. This was perhaps a suicide attempt, but before he could cause himself any sustained injury, he became tearful and would say only, "It won't let me."

He masturbates frequently and aggressively and with no care if he is observed. He mutters to himself almost constantly and eats and drinks the bare minimum to survive.

My recommendation for this patient is to move him to Leavesden, where they are better accommodated for the treatment of excitable patients.

15

LONDON. MAY, 1897
DR. BOND

"Does it feel strange to be taking this train back into town after your recent case?" Edward Kane asked. "It must be far more real to you than it possibly could be for the rest of us, who just read the details in the papers."

Charles Hebbert, tired from playing with James and Edward in the garden while we all enjoyed the sudden breath of summer in the air, had taken a carriage from Juliana's earlier in the day, but Edward Kane insisted on taking the train. It didn't surprise me; the railways were his business, after all. However, I could find no excuse of my own not to travel with him, and so here we sat, facing each other, as we rolled from station to station toward Waterloo.

"Sadly, if that were the case, then there would be very few places left in London where I felt comfortable. I would probably never leave my house." I smiled and then returned my gaze to the window, hoping we would be able to travel the rest of the way in relative silence.

I thought once more upon Charles's enthusiasm as he acted like as young a man as Kane this afternoon. He had piggybacked James up and down the garden at a fair old pace, then let him climb on his back and ride him like a horse before playing catch with both of them. Had this been just a surge of grandfatherly affection, or had he been avoiding my company?

Apart from my discovery of his lies about his visits to the club, I had been able to find nothing concrete in Hebbert's behavior or habits to give ground to my doubts about him. When not immersed in my work at the hospital or with inquests—Elizabeth Camp's had run into April—I had followed him and studied him whenever in his company. But there was nothing, no sign of anything untoward. He worked, he went to his club—no lies about that anymore—and he visited Juliana, and those three activities took up most of his time. Even when he was drunk and I engaged him in discussion about our time on the Ripper case, there was never any flicker of guilt about him; he remained as cheerful as ever, that very disposition which had drawn me to him so early in our friendship. The more that winter faded, giving way to the scents of early summer in the air, the harder it was for me to find darkness in him.

But still I could not shake my curiosity.

"You seem tired lately."

Kane's words broke my reverie, and I looked over at him to find his dark eyes resting thoughtfully on me. "And preoccupied," he concluded. "If you don't mind my saying so, you look like a man in need of a vacation."

"Perhaps I am a little tired," I admitted. "I sometimes find it hard to relax at night."

And that was no lie, for sleep was once again evading me. Although I wasn't being troubled by that awful sense of dread that had plagued me during those terrifying months when blood seeped into every stone of London's streets, my mind would not rest. At night, when the inner world had a tendency to become as dark as the outer one, scorpions of doubt and suspicion skittered wildly within my skull. I had done my best to push the priest and the *Upir* from my thinking, but if Charles Hebbert *was* Jack, then it was strange that two such terrible killers had come to live under one roof.

Was my suspicion of Hebbert based solely on my subconscious still believing in part that the *Upir* affected those around the host?

Or could it be that Hebbert and Harrington had been drawn to each other, each recognizing some unspoken bloodlust in the other? Juliana had said that Harrington had been friendly to her when they first met, and it was only after being introduced to Hebbert that his intentions became romantic. Or perhaps I was making links where there were none; there could be a far more mundane explanation for his lies about dining at the club.

It was entirely possible that Charles Hebbert had been lured by the call of those unfortunate women of Whitechapel and had sated his lusts on them in ways that left them a few pennies richer but very much alive. He wouldn't be the first or last gentleman to wish to experience such a thing. Distasteful as I might find it, that could easily be the cause of both his nocturnal visits to the East End as witnessed by Waring and his lies about his visits to his club.

But I had to admit that I found it harder to accept this explanation, simply because he'd involved Harrington in it—that seemed unnecessary to me, and it laid him open to discovery. Had he perhaps had a conversation with Harrington, possibly that the young man had forgotten while in the grips of the fever? Perhaps he had seen Harrington with a woman—one of his victims—and had mistaken the meeting for some sexual indiscretion, and so he knew Harrington would not challenge him; instead, Harrington provided cover for both of them. But knowing how much Charles loved his daughter, that too did not ring true to me. I was certain he would not have tolerated that behavior from Harrington, especially before the young people had wed.

It was a knotted mess, and I could make no sense of it. Although much of the time, especially now that the days were longer and the air warm, I ridiculed myself for my suspicions, I still knew I needed to find some logic that would allow them to be shaken away, for my own sanity as much as for my sleep. If Hebbert had been our frenzied Jack, then why had he stopped killing so suddenly? The only event I could link it to was Harrington's death, and that brought me straight back to the *Upir* and the legend of the wickedness it brought in its wake, and I would not—*could not*—entertain that.

Once again I cursed Jasper Waring for his idle remark, and Edward Kane for bringing the past back to London.

The latter was still watching me patiently, and I turned my mind back to his question.

"I am perhaps getting a little old for such long-winded inquests on top of my responsibilities at the hospital," I admitted at last.

"I apologize if I have added to that," Kane said, "by asking you to look through Harrington's letters."

"No, not at all—and I am sorry to have taken so long. But I have used my sleepless hours to browse them." This was not entirely a lie; I *had* browsed them, albeit swiftly, without lingering on any detail of superstition or fantastical monsters, but rather just trying to find any references to Hebbert's club during the nighttime hours.

He leaned forward. "And what did you make of them? Can you understand my concerns?"

"Oh, indeed," I said, "and I would have been equally disturbed in your position. But let me put your mind at rest. As terrible as the things he wrote to you are, I truly believe they were simply the effect of the fever on his mind. He was often very ill, and I think he would have been in no condition to carry out such deeds."

"You think it was just some kind of hallucination?" He looked relieved, but the conversation was not yet over. I was beginning to think that Edward Kane's mind was as meticulous as my own. He had clearly not been able to put the letters behind him, and he wanted to understand Harrington's motivations—perhaps because he had not been there to offer his help at the time. "But what of the warehouse? The women?"

"He heard so much about those cases from Charles and me—if he had been experiencing periods of blackouts during his fevers, then it is not a great leap to wondering what could have been the worst acts he could have committed in those missing hours. The imagination is a very powerful thing, after all."

"And his talk of a monster on his back? This *Upir*?"

Hearing the word aloud from another's lips startled me. Harrington had written about the *Upir* in his letters? I had not seen that, and I had no wish to. Although the very word made me shudder, I could find an easy explanation for Harrington's mentioning it: the priest had said he'd been sent by the village. When Harrington was ill in Poland, he must have heard about their suspicions, and the legend lodged in his mind. Perhaps it even gave him an excuse to allow the killer inside him to get out.

I turned my shock into a forced laugh. "Do you believe in such things?"

"No, of course not," Kane said promptly, "but from the letters it appears clear that Jim did."

"I imagine he heard of this legend while traveling and it embedded itself in his subconscious," I said calmly. "James suffered badly from repeated chest infections, which could indeed create the sensation of a weight on his back. If he was already suffering some delusions, it would not be a great leap for him to believe that perhaps there was something there controlling him." I hoped I had not spoken more of the nature of the *Upir* than was written in the pages, but I wanted the conversation to be over. I wanted to burn those letters and never think of that time again.

"And so you think it's all just fantasy? I hoped as much, but with the violence of his death—and with no one knowing where he had been that night . . ." Kane looked embarrassed as he finished, "I wondered if he had tried to take another woman and it had gone wrong." He tilted his head slightly, then dropped his eyes. "Although that sounds just as crazy out loud as the thought of him actually murdering women is."

I was struck by a moment of genius, and I leaned forward so our faces were only inches apart. "Where did Harrington say he killed these women?" I posed the question in such a tone as to suggest I already had the answer and this was a test. But in fact, I needed to know just how much information Kane remembered from the letters so that I wouldn't inadvertently reveal too much.

"In one of his warehouses," Kane said promptly.

"Well then, apply the logic," I said. "If Harrington had indeed been killing women in a warehouse at the wharves, then surely when he died and the inventory of the business was done, evidence of his terrible deeds would have been discovered. He did not know he was going to die that night, so all the tools of that gruesome trade would have been there. And even if there had been no bodies, then there would most certainly have been bloodstains." I paused. "And no such evidence was found."

The priest had cleaned it up well, especially for a one-armed man. All evidence of Harrington's guilt had been erased, and although I had not been near that warehouse since, no alarm had been raised.

Kane leaned backward, his shoulders slumping slightly as he smiled. His relief was evident. "Of course! Why didn't I think of that?"

"You were worried, whereas I was analyzing," I said with a smile. "Also, I am quite sure that on the dates during which those women were murdered, James Harrington was quite ill." Now that he was relaxing, I felt more confident. "He was more than likely bed bound, or at the very least, far too weak to have mutilated their bodies. Having read these letters, I can't help but wonder if the infection had spread to his brain. It could easily have caused all this anguish he was suffering. It might turn out—although I would never say as much to Juliana—that his quick death was a mercy." By the time I'd finished the sentence, I'd almost succeeded in convincing myself.

"I am mightily pleased to hear you say this," Kane said. "The idea that someone I knew could be capable of all that and I hadn't noticed— well, I won't pretend it didn't disturb my sleep for a while there. But you've given me some peace, Doctor. Now I owe the memory of my friend an apology. Suspicion eats at the soul, doesn't it?"

My small moment of victory soured with his words, and I thought of Hebbert and the doubts that refused to leave me. He was a good friend, one who had shown me nothing but kindness over the years, and yet now I veered between thinking him innocent and believing him to be a monster. My lies had given Kane peace, but I had none of my own. I ached to get home to the laudanum bottle, and that in turn made me feel ashamed. It was too much of an echo of darker times.

I need to get myself back under control. If I could not prove Hebbert guilty of anything, then I was going to have to try and find a way to let the matter go. I could not be dragged in to madness. My life ahead should be peaceful old age with Juliana by my side. That was all that truly mattered.

16

The Lloyds Weekly Newspaper
April 10, 1896

THE READING BABY FARM

SIX BODIES IN THE THAMES

STARTLING REVELATIONS YESTERDAY

Within the last few days the bodies of five babies have been found in the Thames at Reading, and the discovery of a sixth dead infant yesterday has caused such a sensation as the district has not known for many years. Last week the body of a child about 18 months old was found, and the evidence went to show that the infant had been strangled—a piece of tape being tied round its neck—and then wrapped in some material. A verdict of "Willful murder against some person or persons" was returned at the inquest. Last Wednesday a second body was discovered, the police having engaged men to drag the river, believing other children had been similarly disposed of. At the inquest held on Friday morning, the jury returned an open verdict, the doctor being unable to say what was the cause of death, the body being so decomposed. A third body was brought to land the same day.

In each case a piece of tape was found tightly tied round the neck, and death was evidently due to strangulation. The bodies were enveloped in linen and other materials; a brick was placed in each parcel. On Friday night, when dragging the Clappers Pool, the police hitched on a carpet bag, which was proved to contain the bodies of a girl and an exceptionally pretty boy. Two bricks were also placed in the bag. Yesterday information was given to the Reading Borough coroner that a sixth child had been found in the river Kennet, in Reading, which had every appearance of having been killed in the same manner as the five infants already mentioned.

Two arrests have been made. A woman named Mrs. Annie Dyer went to live at Caversham a few weeks ago, and in her lodgings w found tape, &c., corresponding with that found on one child and in the parcel, while a piece of paper, with an address, found with the body, referred to the woman's address.

The *Times* of London
Wednesday, June 9, 1897

INQUESTS

Yesterday evening at the Coroner's-court, Mortlake, Mr. A. Braxton Hicks held an inquest on the body of a male child, of unknown parentage, which was found enclosed in a box in the Thames on the 2nd inst. George Spansfield, a labourer working on a coal wharf at the Queen's Head, Mortlake, said the tide was ebbing when he found the box on the foreshore. It was not there on the previous day. The box was produced by Sergeant Oliver, the summoning officer, and the coroner said it was evidently made for the purpose to which it had been devoted. Dr. James Adams, the divisional surgeon who was called to examine the body when it was found, said it was that of a well-developed child. Curiously enough, a postmortem examination had already been made, and all organs had been examined, no doubt by a fully qualified medical man. The child had certainly been dead two months, but he was unable to say that it had unquestionably lived. He was unable to ascribe death to any particular cause . . .

. . . The coroner said it was one of the most extraordinary cases he had ever investigated. All the London coroners had been asked whether they had held an inquest on a child during the past two months whose burial might not have been accounted for, and he could only think that some midwife or undertaker had disposed of the body in this way. It was a scandalous state of affairs.

17

LONDON. JUNE, 1897
DR. BOND

"But it's so awful," Juliana said, fanning herself and squinting slightly in the bright sunshine. "Who would do that to their child?"

"Funerals cost money," Charles said. "Something the poor, by their very nature, have very little of."

"But to put the little thing in the river where you could not even visit the grave? That's so heartless."

"You can never understand what is going on in others' hearts, my dear. It is often better not to wonder about it."

It was a warm day, and the air was thickening, the damp from the nearby river weighing it down and making me itch under my shirt collar. Tiny flies hovered just over our heads, a portent of the rainclouds that would likely gather later in the day, and every minute or so, they would drop and buzz around my head, enjoying my muttered irritation, before darting just beyond reach of my swatting hand.

Hebbert had no idea of the irony of his words. I watched him as he poured more lemonade from the jug. In my daily life I had done my best to purge suspicion from my mind, but it reigned in my dreams where the past came to haunt me. Last night I had nightmares of the two of us in his study, and an awful look of despair that filled his eyes as he spoke of terrible dreams of his own and the wickedness in the city. In the version with which my subconscious chose to fill my sleeping hours, the terrible creature I had seen attached to Harrington's back hung in every shadowy corner of the room above us.

Needless to say, I had not awakened in the best of moods, but I had hoped that a day at Juliana's would restore me to some form of good cheer. It was not to be, however, and I wished we could at least go inside, away from the stifling warmth and the stench of the river that appeared to bother no one but me. There were also more visitors than I had expected.

Edward Kane—who, it was becoming quite clear to me, was indeed a rival for Juliana's affections—had been here all morning apparently, and he had taken little James out for a few hours for a birthday surprise. As well as Charles Hebbert, Walter Andrews was also present. I had dined with him two or three times since returning the club's registers, and on more than one occasion I had seen curiosity in his sharp eyes. I had been tempted to share my thoughts with him—but I could not. I did not know where such suspicions would take him. He would either laugh at me or investigate, and neither of those was an appealing thought.

"I am very much looking forward to the Jubilee celebrations. If the weather is fine, it will be quite a day."

I sipped the lemonade, though it was a touch tart for my taste, and I looked over at the man politely trying to shift the direction of the conversation to something more pleasant. When I had arrived, Juliana had told me she had invited Barker and his wife, and I am quite sure my mouth dropped open in shock. James Barker was Harrington's secretary at the wharves. The last time I had seen him was that fateful moment when we had bumped into each other in the street and he had told me about the amount of time Harrington was spending in the small warehouse. He had also told me he had left Harrington's employment. It appeared now, however, that once his employer had died, he had been sought out and rehired. More of the past was coming into my present to haunt me.

"Yes, it shall," I said. I had no desire to speak to him, but at the same time I had no desire for the topic to veer toward anything that might cause me trouble. I could not relax with him here—what if he mentioned something to Edward Kane about Harrington's strange activities? I was sure I could provide some explanation, and I would once again blame his fevers—but Kane might then mention the letters to Barker, and where would that lead? It was as if I were standing in the center of a net and the slightest movement would cause it to close up around me. Regardless of Harrington's deeds, I too had committed a terrible crime, and each day I felt more and more as if the world was conspiring to never allow me to be completely free of it.

Juliana joined in, talking of her plans to take little James to watch the spectacle, and as her words washed over me, I realized sadly that if I were not careful, she would slip away from me. When I had asked her why she had invited Barker, she told me that Kane had been encouraging her to take a more active role in the business—it was James's inheritance, after all. Her eyes and smile had been all light, and there was an air of excitement about her that I had not seen in years. She had always wanted to be more involved in James's business—and when she said she thought that her late husband, God rest his soul, would be proud of her, it was the first time I had seen her mention him without sorrow tightening her expression. I had always hoped I would be the one to make that change in her, but apparently it was not to be.

She told me that Kane had been trying to persuade her to get a private tutor for James, and then, if she found she was happy with that arrangement, perhaps it would be time to find a good school for him. That in turn would give her more time to spend learning more about the import and export business. Kane would help her, she said, by introducing her to some of his contacts.

I had felt impotent listening to her, and I could not help my jealousy escaping in a small barbed comment about Kane's making her decisions for her, and that I had thought her stronger than that. Juliana had looked shocked—as had Andrews—but Charles

Hebbert had laughed merrily, and he told me not to be so dour. "I think Edward Kane is a fine young man," he said. "He's a good influence on Juliana. The young bring out the life in each other."

He had slapped me on the shoulder and gone out into the garden, where we all now sat so politely waiting for Kane and little James to return.

His message was clear: Kane was a far more suitable husband for Juliana than I. His words stung most because I could not help but agree: Edward Kane was younger, wealthier, and certainly more full of life than I—but I could not believe he loved her more. It was I who had been with her through all her dark times; he had not arrived until the butterfly was emerging from the chrysalis.

I must admit that it hurt to think that she might prefer him to me. I was an old fool, perhaps, but an old fool in love for the first time in so many years.

"Thomas?" She was looking in my direction. "Are you all right? Mr. Barker was asking if you were going to the parade."

"I'm sorry," I smiled. "This infernal heat is making me drowsy— and the river is more pungent than usual today."

"All I can smell is honeysuckle," Andrews said, "but it is indeed warm."

The mention of the river caused a small crease to momentarily furrow her brow, but then she shrugged it away. I wished I found it so easy. My dreams had left me with a trace of my old madness, and in this tense atmosphere and stifling heat, I found it hard not to think of the Thames without remembering the priest and his struggle with the *Upir*, and particularly the splash of the water on that grim night of Harrington's death.

"But perhaps we should go inside," Charles said. "It is rather sticky, and no doubt Edward and James will be back soon from their mystery adventure."

"Oh, no mystery there," Barker said gaily. "They looked as if they were having a very jolly time when we arrived."

"You saw them?" Juliana said. "Where?"

"They were fishing—in a little rowboat in the river. I'm sure it was them at any rate. It certainly looked like Mr. Kane."

The poor man could have had no idea what he'd said, but before he had even finished his sentence, Juliana had leapt to her feet and was running inside. Hebbert and I immediately followed, all politeness forgotten, and by the time we had caught up with her, she was through the house, the front door was wide open, and she was halfway across the road.

"James!" she shouted, her hands gripping the thick stone wall. "James!" She turned to run down the damp steps to the bank, but Charles grabbed her.

"Juliana, stop it!"

She called her son's name again and struggled against her father. "Let go of me! I want him away from the water! *James!*"

"You'll scare him!"

Charles was right. The little rowboat was not far from the bank, and it was tethered to a sturdy post with a thick rope to stop it from drifting as the man and boy sat and dangled rods over the side. I imagined that before we had arrived, it had been a picture of serenity, but James, hearing his mother shouting his name in such alarm, stood up in the boat and spun round. Edward Kane, surprised, twisted too, and the boat rocked with the precipitous movement. As the boat tilted, James, unused to being on the water, started to lose his balance. With his focus on his mother's anxiety rather than on where he was, he took a step forward, and his shoe caught on his fishing pole and he tripped. Kane grabbed for him, but James had leaned too far forward, and Kane's shifting weight sent James tumbling over the side and into the water.

Hebbert thrust his daughter into my arms and ran down the slick stone steps. I held her tight, expecting her to start screaming hysterically, but all I felt was a dead weight. She had not fainted, but all the life had drained out of her in the single instant.

Edward Kane had wasted no time. He had stripped off his jacket and shoes and now plunged from the rowboat into the murky water to where James had briefly splashed before sinking below the dark surface. The boy had never learned to swim, and even though it was a warm day, I had no doubt that the water was cold enough to shock him.

Andrews and the Barkers had joined us, but I barely noticed them. My heart raced, and I knew I was muttering some words of calm to Juliana, though I have no memory of what I said. Below us Charles Hebbert was standing at the water's edge, one hand gripping the post to which the small boat was moored, calling both for Kane and James. A dark head broke the surface for the briefest moment, and then Kane was gone again, searching the depths. Although they were close to the bank, the river's currents were not gentle, and the bed was full of weeds to snarl a boy's legs in.

As we waited with baited breath, I could not help but think of the fantastical *Upir*, thrown back into the river after Harrington's death. It did not exist. *It did not*—and yet I felt a shiver of dread that left me trembling almost as much as Juliana was.

"He has him!" Hebbert shouted up from below. "*He has him.*"

Juliana broke free of my arms and ran down to the bank, Andrews right behind her. Kane was swimming toward Hebbert, dragging the boy on his back behind him. He staggered onto the filthy mud and lay the boy down, and Hebbert and Andrews were on their knees instantly, pumping at his chest and blowing into his small mouth.

I did not move. I knew I should. I was a medical doctor—I had served on battlefields. It should have been me there in Andrews's place, fighting alongside Hebbert to get the stinking water from the boy's lungs, but I could not bring myself to go to the river's edge.

Even from where I stood, I could see that James was deathly pale. Strands of green slime colored his blond hair, and I could not help but wonder how far he had sunk into those murky depths. The idea of placing my mouth over his revolted me. The river had been *inside* him. What else had reached for him as he sank? I could not help myself: I thought of an ancient creature with red eyes and sharp teeth waiting on the riverbed for a new host.

James finally retched and coughed, and a blast of water ejected itself from his lungs. As he opened his eyes, he looked dazed, struggling to remember where and with whom he was. His mother fell to her knees and smothered him with hugs and kisses, her tears washing away the stench.

Beside me, the Barkers gasped with relief and clutched at each other. I alone remained unmoved.

Kane, drenched and filthy, scooped the boy up and brought him up the stairs as Andrews pulled the boat to the bank and retrieved the American's coat. It was only now, as the group hurried back inside the house, that I was able to shake off my stupor and join them, trying to ignore my overwhelming disgust and fear.

The Barkers departed shortly after that, having ascertained that little James was alive and would be well. They were not part of the family like the rest of us, Kane included these days, and they let us get on with looking after James. The housekeeper started boiling water for a hot bath as Juliana and Hebbert stripped the shivering child of his sodden clothes. Within an hour he was tucked up in bed and trying to eat the beef broth his mother was forcefully feeding him. I loitered in the doorway and watched for a moment before heading downstairs. Was it my imagination, or had red blotches begun to appear on his pale cheeks? Or was it simply my tiredness playing tricks on me? I had never liked the boy, but I could not help that, for I knew what his father had become and that his birth had been so difficult as to be almost unnatural. It had always been hard for me to put those things to one side in my mind.

"He will be just fine," Hebbert said, handing Kane a brandy. The American was wrapped in a blanket himself and sitting by a hastily lit fire. "Children are hardy. His mother thinks he is fragile, but I've seen children with far more serious complaints than his occasional coughs and colds. His father had a weak chest, and I don't doubt he's inherited it, but more fresh air will no doubt sort that out."

I poured myself a brandy and saw my hand was shaking slightly. What else had the boy inherited from his father? Could it be Fate that had forced him into the water? Had something been waiting for him under there? My jaw tightened, and I cursed my dreams and my memories. *There were no monsters.* I would not believe it.

"What happened to you?" Andrews said quietly. "You didn't so much as move an inch."

"I'm afraid I do not know," I said. "My reactions are not what they were when I was a young man—perhaps it was shock?"

My friend did not look convinced, and I am certain I saw more than a little disappointment in his eyes. What could I say? That I was terrified of the river on some deep subconscious level, of what might be in it? That the thought of pressing my mouth to the boy's and *tasting* the river filled me with dread? For even if there was no *Upir*, the memory of my own madness had been thrown into that river, and I was becoming more and more fearful of its resurrection. Everywhere I turned, pieces of the past were gathering around me.

"I feel some shame at my inaction, Walter. I truly do, but James will be fine."

"Thankfully."

"He should not have been out on the water anyway," I said, suddenly feeling the need to defend myself. "Juliana would not have allowed it." I spoke louder than I had intended, and Kane looked up, guilt filling his dark eyes.

"He wanted to go fishing. I thought it would be harmless."

"Come, come, Thomas," Hebbert interjected, "we swam in worse when we were boys, surely? I know I certainly did. And the boat was securely fastened and close to the bank. Let's not make too big a fuss of all this, eh? Edward's company has been good for the boy. None of us can doubt that."

Outside the sunshine was fading, and heavy gray storm clouds had gathered, hanging low and pressing against the glass as if to watch us all growling at each other.

"You're very calm about what could have been a terrible accident," I said. "Your grandson could have died. Perhaps you are more *laissez faire* about death than I." The words came out in drops of acid.

"Thomas!" Andrews exclaimed, as Hebbert's eyes widened. "What a thing to say! At least he ran to help."

"Yes—where were you?" Hebbert bit back. "It's obvious you care little for the boy, but to stand at a distance and watch? That is colder than I imagined even you were capable of."

And so the gloves were off. We glared at each other, Charles Hebbert and I. In the history of our friendship, we had never had a single angry exchange—but perhaps I had never really known the man at all. He was, after all, a man who had had terrible dreams of blood as Jack murdered on our streets, and a man whose whereabouts could not be accounted for during those times.

Or perhaps it was I who was sinking back into madness after my paranoid delusions of years before.

Either way, I felt the heat rise in my stomach. "Whatever you believe of my feelings toward the boy, I would not have taken the child out onto the river, not without his mother's permission. And neither will I excuse or laugh off such an action. James is Juliana's son, and it is her place and her place alone to decide these things."

My suspicion of Hebbert and my jealousy of Kane were rolling into one mass of emotion, and I was too tired to watch my tongue. But still I asked myself, *What is happening to us?* Ever since Kane's arrival my world had started changing again, and pleasant as he might be, I was beginning to hate him for that. I wanted to get home to my laudanum and brandy and the quiet of my study and forget for a while that the normality I had worked so hard to rebuild was crumbling.

"He's right," Kane said quietly. "He's absolutely right. I didn't think—but James was so keen, and I took such care with the boat . . . I thought maybe if I presented it as something already done, she'd realize he would be safe."

"He's not your child," I reiterated, all the while squirming inside at the sanctimonious tenor of my voice. "His father is dead." The image rose up unbidden of Harrington's face as I slashed at him with the broken glass. "Whatever your feelings for Juliana, do not confuse them with having rights that are solely hers."

"Thank you, Thomas."

I turned to find Juliana standing in the doorway. Her back was stiff and her face was drawn and pale.

"Juliana." Kane got to his feet. "I'm so sorry—"

"Thomas is right," she said. Her voice was as cold as her eyes. "It was not your place to put my son in danger."

"My dear," Hebbert started, "you—"

"'I' nothing, Papa." She turned to Kane and said quietly, "It is not that you took him out on the boat, Edward. I know that I have perhaps allowed too many of my own fears to color how I raise my son. Had you asked, I might well have said yes." She drew herself up tall, and I think I had never loved her more than I did in that moment. "But you did not ask. And now I would ask that you leave." Only then did she take her eyes from the somewhat cowed Edward Kane and glance at the rest of us. "All of you. Thomas, if you would call tomorrow to check on James, I would be most grateful."

"Of course," I said, some of the darkness lifting. I might not have helped bring the boy out of the water, but suddenly I was back in favor—and more importantly, Edward Kane was apparently out, at least for now. I knew Juliana to have a generous and forgiving nature, and I was sure that when James was fully recovered, she would calm toward him, but for now, he had broken her trust.

Outside, I walked with Andrews toward the train station. I tried to make idle conversation with him, but he was singularly unresponsive to most of what I said, emitting only one-word answers here and there and refusing to be drawn into more. A hansom cab appeared at the end of the street, and he flagged it down.

"Shall we travel together?" I asked.

"I think I had rather go alone," he said. He turned to me, and his sharp eyes narrowed. "I think perhaps you need some rest, Thomas. How you spoke to Charles was both rude and unwarranted."

I opened my mouth to protest, but he talked over me.

"You implied that he did not care if young James died—how could you say that?"

"That was not what I meant!" Walter Andrews was my friend and a clever man. While it might be true that my words had been a little too aggressive, surely he would wonder what my reasoning was, rather than just thinking me rude? "Perhaps none of us know Charles Hebbert as well as we think," I snapped.

"What on earth do you mean by that? Hebbert is a good man—a good doctor," Andrews protested.

"He lies," I said, turning on my heel, my teeth gritted. "The man lies."

I strode away as the first rumble of thunder overhead echoed my fury.

"What do you mean by that?" he called after me. "Thomas?"

"Forget I said it." I barely broke my pace, but I turned so I could face him even as my feet carried me backward. "And I am truly sorry if I offended you, my friend. You are right: I am very tired."

I was still shaking by the time I got home, and as I poured myself a brandy, the storm rattled the house as if my inner conflict were exploding outward. What was happening to me? Had the paranoia that had gripped me years before left a seed in my guts that was now growing like unkempt summer weeds? Did it really take so little to reignite my fears? It is true that I have always found it hard to warm to little James, but my body's refusal to run and help him had nothing to do with any possible inherited wickedness and everything to do with what the priest believed he'd thrown into the river on that bleak night, the last time I saw him. We had *all* believed at the time that he had consigned the *Upir* to the Thames.

I shuddered, catching my own reflection in the glass as lightning seared across the sky and seeing a fearful old man. Where was the notable surgeon Dr. Thomas Bond? How had he become this person, a man who distrusted a long-time friend simply because he had lied about where he was on a few occasions? I thought of how I had snapped, and how Andrews had looked at me when we left Juliana's house.

This would not do. I could not become obsessional again.

Despite the storm outside making the house feel damp and chill, I did not light a fire. My face burned as my head raced and I felt anxiety trying to grip me. I would not allow it. I would not be dragged down after all this time. It had to stop, and it had to stop *now*.

At my desk, I pulled out my notepaper and began to write to Andrews. I was not sure what I intended to say, only that I needed to make reparation for my actions and words of this afternoon. But once the words started, they flowed. I told him I had suffered a fear of deep water since a boating accident in my own childhood, and it was that experience which had frozen me. I told him that my own embarrassment had made me snap at Hebbert and that I was feeling resentful as he was clearly favoring Kane over me as a suitor for Juliana's hand. I told him that a fall I had taken a month or two before at the hunt had left me with back pain (of everything I wrote in the letter, this was the only completely truthful part), and the pain was making me irritable. Finally, I asked his forgiveness. I sealed the letter and addressed it before starting immediately on another for Hebbert, in which I apologized for my unforgivable rudeness, blaming my behavior on my jealousy of Kane.

Normally I would feel ashamed at being so open with my emotions, but my desire to restore the balance of my friendships—and myself—overwhelmed any such considerations. By the time I had finished and both envelopes were ready to be sent the next day, the brandy was gone and I was calmer.

If I said that such simple actions had removed all my dark woes, that would be a lie, but I was more at peace, and I was determined not to return to the bleakness of soul that so nearly destroyed me before.

I lay in bed and listened to the rain beating at the house, and I tried to think of nothing else but the rhythm of my heart and the ticking of the clock, filling my head with sounds rather than thoughts of dead women and old legends and drug-induced bouts of madness that never quite let go.

I slept fitfully, waking several times in a sweat with my sheets tangled around me, but when morning finally came, although I was tired, I did not remember my dreams, and for that I was grateful. I sent my letters, and I went straight to Juliana's to see how James was.

I was happy to find that although Juliana was sure he had a slight fever and had confined her son to bed, James appeared to be well and happy, unscathed emotionally by his fall into the river. I agreed that he was perhaps a little hot, and although I was drawn to them, I did not focus on the faint red blotches high on his cheeks and on his neck. They were nothing, I told myself, simply the effects of a mild sickness brought on by falling into the water. But still I stayed with him throughout the day, playing cards and reading to him while Juliana watched us both—I like to think with a considerable amount of affection.

As much as I was enjoying Juliana's appreciation of me, my feelings toward her child had not changed. That I could not help, but I did need to help myself after the previous day's fiasco. I refused to allow my paranoias to root inside me; I knew I must allow them no room to grow during the long, dark nights. I would stay with the boy until he was well, watching him for anything unusual, for only that way could I prove to myself once and for all that no trace of the *Upir* existed in him.

18

The *Times* of London
Monday, April 20, 1896

THE CHILD MURDERS AT READING

Annie Dyer, whose name is now said to be Amelia Dyer, alias Thomas, Harding, Stanfield, &c., described as a nurse and age about fifty, was charged on remand before the Reading Borough Bench on Saturday with the murder of a child named Fry, the first of the children picked out of the Thames and now identified by its mother, and with the murder of two infants named Doris Marmon and Harry Simmons, found strangled in the carpetbag that was dragged from the Thames at the Caversham Weir head. Arthur Ernest Palmer, the other prisoner's son-in-law, was charged with being an accessory after the fact . . .

. . . The doctor would give evidence that the cause of death was strangulation by the tying of a ligament, supposed to have been tape, round the necks of the infants. In the case of the female child the tape had been removed, but in the case of the other child the tape was still around the child's neck. The appearance of the body was such as to show that it had been in the water about ten days.

19

LONDON. JUNE 22, 1897
DR. BOND

Even though the summer's weather had been notably terrible thus far, as the cannon fired in Hyde Park and the sound boomed across the excited city, the clouds finally broke and bathed us in sunshine. That morning, bells had rung out in all the churches of England to celebrate Her Majesty's sixty years as our monarch, and the day was a holiday for all. The celebrations were planned to run for most of the week.

Once I had met up with Juliana, little James, and Hebbert, we wove our way through the busy throngs to find a suitable vantage point from which to watch the procession pass by. I thought the jubilant mood of the city was very much a reflection of my own good spirits. I even held James's hand, and later I carried him for a short while so he could see more over the heads of those around us. He had shaken off the cough and fever resulting from his tumble into the river, and Hebbert had declared him healthier for the experience. I had managed to shake off—very nearly—my dark thoughts and doubts, and then, two nights previously, light bloomed in my heart, for Juliana agreed to become my wife.

We had dined together in one of London's finest restaurants, sharing both good reminisces and a fine claret. When I finally summoned up the courage to make my proposal, Juliana told me that though she was not yet ready to go forward, in principle yes, when she was ready, she was certainly not opposed to the suggestion—but she would prefer we keep our agreement between us two for now.

It had taken all my natural reserve to stop myself from scooping her up in my arms and kissing her on the spot. I did not, of course, for that would have been most ungentlemanly, but since that moment I had felt as if years had been lifted from me. The ache in my back subsided, and I walked on air. There would be no more laudanum. There would be no more suspicions, no more paranoia. I would be simply Dr. Thomas Bond, eminent surgeon, with a beautiful woman who was prepared to be his wife.

Now walking beside me, Juliana laughed merrily, swept up in the mood of the crowd. I had been surprised that she wanted to bring James into the heart of the celebrations, but she had said she was determined to be less protective of him, and this was an occasion that he was unlikely to see again in his lifetime.

We took in the Union Jacks that hung from every window and available space, her eyes sparkling, and she squeezed my arm to point out something or other as we found ourselves a space near the National Gallery. Around us vendors hawked their commemorative wares—souvenir flags, mugs and programs—and Hebbert waited in turn and bought us each a mug and a flag for little James to wave. I did not know if Juliana had told him of our agreement, but I had made every effort to restore my friendship with him to how it had been before, and such was Charles's cheery disposition that he had made it easy.

An added source of joy for me was the continued absence of Edward Kane from our lives. Juliana did not talk of him, and I did not raise the subject. Although I was certain he would have apologized sincerely—and more than once—for his actions, Juliana had clearly not forgiven him yet. I was sure that she would—she was not a woman to bear grudges, and now that James was fully recovered, the fear she had felt that day was fading—but I hoped that when she did, she would keep him at a little distance. Though I had to admit, grudgingly, to liking and respecting the man, I was very conscious that he was a rival for Juliana's affections, and I was far happier when he was not present. I was fearful of losing Juliana to him, and I was also fearful of the past's grip, made stronger by his relationship to James Harrington. The sooner Edward Kane returned to New York, the better it would be for all of us.

The day was wonderful. We watched the parade, with people and nationalities from all over our great empire taking part, and to my pleased surprise, I found myself taking pleasure in James's delight. He was simply a little boy, and I had been wrong to let my feelings toward his father influence my reaction to him. I would strive to be a better man, I vowed—I was a scientist, after all, and as such I, more than other people, should not believe in hereditary evil. Watching the boy laughing, I wondered if he might soon have a little brother or sister to play with—a child of mine. It had been a long time since I had felt so happy, and when at last Queen Victoria drove past us in her open carriage pulled by eight cream horses, I cheered with the crowd until my throat was raw.

We were a happy party as we wandered away in search of food and liquid refreshments. The pubs were very busy, with people spilling out onto the crowded streets to wish Her Majesty a long life and many more years reigning over us, and although plenty were past merry, there was no aggression or poor behavior to be seen. Just a few years ago, London had been in its darkest place; today it was at its best, and men from all walks of life tipped their hats to each other as they passed as if we were truly all friends. Perhaps, on this unique day, we were.

We picnicked in the park, and then, as the late afternoon crept toward evening, James suddenly grew weary, as children do, and Juliana and Charles took him home, leaving me to head contentedly back to Westminster. As night fell, bonfires were lit on all the hills across the country, and even from my house in the heart of London, I could see dots of light stretching into the distance. The streets remained loud, and no doubt would throughout the night, but I did not mind. This was the London I loved.

I closed the front door behind me, and for once I enjoyed the emptiness, the luxury of being alone in my home, Mrs. Parks having the day to herself. As I took off my hat, I noticed the white envelope waiting for me on the floor, written in Henry Moore's hand. I opened it to find an invitation to dine with him and Walter Andrews the next night, as he wished to discuss something that might be of interest. As with his speech, his writing was direct, but gave nothing away.

Perhaps he wished to pick my brains on a new case? I looked forward to the dinner regardless, for it would be an opportunity to once again apologize to Andrews. I had seen him since—he too had called on Juliana to see how James was—but he remained somewhat distant with me. Perhaps now that my mood was so obviously elevated, he would be able to understand that my outburst—indeed, my behavior that day—had been a result of a temporary woe, and quite out of character.

I poured myself a brandy, simply for the enjoyment of the drink this time rather than to soothe my nerves, and I went into my study to select a book. I left the curtains open to enjoy the light and life outside, and when I finally turned the lamp out and settled back on my sheets that night, I was a contented man. Life was good.

20

The *Standard*
Wednesday, October 24, 1894

THE STRANGE DEATH OF A PRIEST

No order has yet been issued for the exhumation of the remains of the Argentine priest, Father Gabriel T. Segni, who was found dead in a Soho hotel on the 7ᵗʰ inst. After the inquest the body was interred as that of Louis Caccres in a pauper's grave in Woking Cemetery, at the cost of the parish of St. Anne, Soho. The real name of Father Segni's companion is believed to be Rabellot, and there is reason to suppose that some years ago he was employed as a "sauce and soup chef" at a first-class restaurant near the Criterion, Piccadilly. The silk handkerchief by which the body of Father Segni was fastened to the head of the bedstead was a new one of Macclesfield manufacture, and apparently had only recently been purchased. Late last evening Chief Inspector Moore and Inspector Greet, of Scotland Yard, were put in special charge of the case, and one of these officers will probably proceed to Havre and make investigations there.

21

LONDON. JUNE, 1897
EDWARD KANE

In the end he hadn't been able to stay away. The only message she'd answered was a letter he'd sent asking if little James was okay, and she had sent only a brief reply saying that, thankfully, he was fine. She had not asked how he was, nor had she mentioned any of his other letters full of apologies and stating quite clearly how he felt about her *and* young James. He had spent the Jubilee celebrations in his hotel room, staring at various papers to do with his work and watching the words blur in front of him as his mind refused to focus and his stomach twisted in knots. Of all the things that he had expected from his visit to London, this had not been one of them— women, perhaps, but not one woman.

"I suppose you had better come in," she said, when she found him waiting outside her house like some lovesick fool, his hat in his hands as he paced nervously up and down the pavement carrying chocolates and a toy. James had broken away from her and run to him, laughing and calling his name, and he had had to resist the urge to pick him up and hug him, knowing that Juliana might see their bond as a betrayal of her.

"We've been to a parade with horses, and a man is going to tutor me!" James said excitedly. "I'm going to go there every day, and then I might go to school!"

"You really must watch your manners, James," Juliana said, ushering the child inside. "What have I told you about speaking before spoken to?" She closed the door behind them, and Edward stood back awkwardly as she took off her hat and gloves.

"Sorry, Mother," James said.

A young girl in a maid's uniform hurried into the hallway, and Juliana asked her to take James and put him to bed, after bringing tea to the sitting room. She bent to kiss him, promising to read him a story when he was all tucked in.

"A new addition to the household?" he asked, returning James's sneaky wave good-bye over her shoulder as the girl led him away.

"I intend to start taking more of an interest in the business," she said. Her chin was high, and the lowering sun cut through the stained glass at the top of the front door, bathing her beauty in fractured colors. She looked like a dark angel, a mystery wrapped up in soft skin, and he wanted so much to slide inside her and feel her enveloping him. He also wanted to throw himself into the river for having such thoughts. What had happened to him? When had one woman been able to control him like this? He hadn't been able even to think of another, let alone touch one, since meeting Juliana Harrington.

"So not all my ideas are bad ones then," he said with a smile, walking into the sitting room. He might be nervous as all hell on the inside, but he was damned if he was going to show it. He'd groveled enough. Away from her all he'd felt was the fear that he'd never see her again, but now that she was close she brought the fire back into him. "And I see James is looking well."

"You should never have taken him out on the river!" Her façade of coolness fell away, and her face flushed as she turned on him. "How could you *do* that? How could you? I trusted you!"

"He was safe, Juliana—and he would have stayed safe if you hadn't panicked him."

She opened her mouth to protest, but he continued to speak over her. "And I've apologized as much as I can. If I had the time over, I would have spoken to you about it. It was foolish, I know, but I wanted the boy to have some *fun*. I don't want him to grow up and resent you the way I resented my parents. You can't smother him, and I know you know that. I have written and said I'm sorry, and I have begged for your forgiveness to the point of shamelessness. I have told you everything I feel, and—goddamn you, woman, I think you feel the same way too! So why can't we just put this behind us?"

She stared at him, and he was sure she was trembling slightly. "I cannot," she said. "I just cannot. It's not that simple."

"Why isn't it? You know how I feel, Juliana: I love you. And I know women well enough to know you are not immune to me either."

Light and dark shimmered in her eyes, and her mouth twitched. She looked like a cornered animal. "I have spoken with Dr. Bond about marriage," she said quietly.

The sentence was like a punch in the guts, and he prayed he had not heard her correctly.

"You've done what?"

There was a light knock on the door, and they stood in silence as the young maid brought in the tea tray and placed it on the table before scurrying out again.

He stared at Juliana, and her eyes slipped past him.

"I said—"

"I heard what you said. Are you crazy? He's old enough to be your father! You can't possibly love him—"

"Do not presume to tell me what I feel!" Juliana cried. "I *do* love him. He's been very kind to me—he always has been. Even when James was alive and sick and I was lonely. Thomas is a *good* man."

"Yes, he *is* a good man," he agreed. "He's decent, and I like him. And, sure, you love him—like you love a good friend—but that cannot be enough to tie yourself to him for the rest of your life."

The idea of Juliana in bed with Bond was making his stomach turn. She was young and beautiful, and yes, it was quite clear the good doctor loved her—but that would not be enough.

"You think you'll still love him after a few years of marriage? You think you won't begin to dread his touch? Or will you make arrangements so your marriage bed remains as dead as your heart? I am sure he would put up with it, for you. But what kind of life is that? What are you so afraid of?"

His voice was rising, and he could see he was upsetting her, but he could not help himself. This was *madness*. She was just afraid, and she had been afraid for too long.

"You can't marry him," he said firmly.

"Yes, I can. Why shouldn't I? He is safe, and he'll look after us."

"I can do all that," Edward growled. He stepped closer to her and gripped her arms, pulling her to him. "And I can do this too."

Before she had time to protest he pressed his mouth on to hers, and one hand slid up to gently stroke her face, and then his fingers entwined in her hair. After a second, her lips softened and she wrapped her arms around his neck.

The first kiss was everything he had hoped it would be, and more. Life was going to be good.

22

LONDON. JUNE, 1897
DR. BOND

The good weather continued along with the celebrations, and it was through a London in fine spirits that I weaved my way for dinner with Walter Andrews and Henry Moore. The city's cheerfulness buoyed my own already good mood, and I wondered if I had ever been so happy or free of worry in all my adult life.

I had dined with Moore on several occasions, but never before at his house, and I wondered if this was perhaps a conscious decision to separate his work from his private life, a sensible move. I was still curious about what kind of wife and home the down-to-earth policeman must have, what side of himself he kept just for them—or was he the same gruff, clever practical thinker when away from the grime of the city's criminal life as he was when immersed in it?

The restaurant he had chosen was perhaps less formal than somewhere Andrews or I might have picked, but the food was hearty and more than agreeable, and the tables were full of life and laughter amid the clatter of cutlery and the clink of glasses. I presumed he had called us together to discuss a case, maybe wanting Andrews to investigate something for him and needing my forensic insight, but as we chatted about the jubilee, he said nothing of the sort. But his eyes sparkled as he ordered us more fine wine and declared that he would be paying the bill.

After we had exchanged several quizzical looks, Andrews finally broached the subject, demanding to know the cause of Moore's excessive good cheer, delighted as we were to be there to share it with him.

"Not until the cigars and brandy," Moore said. "Let's do this like gentlemen." He winked then, a gesture of lighthearted humor I had never previously associated with him, and both Andrews and I, despite our curiosity, became infected with his cheery excitement. The wine flowed, and whatever dregs of bad feeling there were left between Andrews and me evaporated as we tried and failed to guess what Moore's news might be.

Eventually, Andrews frowned slightly and said, "Have you heard that I am retiring from private investigations? I have told very few people as yet, so if you have, I would like to know the source of your information."

Moore and I both stared at him, and it was clear from the chief inspector's expression that he, like me, had not heard such a thing.

"Why?" I asked at length.

"We are none of us as young as we were, Thomas," he said, "and I am done with the seediness of the city. I do not thrive on it as you do, Henry. I think I would like some quieter time while I am still healthy enough to enjoy it."

"Then I think," Moore said, "that what I have to share with you will be a fitting retirement gift." The brandy and cigars had finally arrived, and as he leaned toward the waiter lighting his, he winked again before becoming momentarily lost in a haze of smoke.

"You may finally be able to put some of the past behind you," he announced, and with his mention of the word "past," I felt the first trickle of something cold running through the warmth of my good mood. *The past.* What more of the past could come for me?

"Well go on then, man," I said, praying it would be nothing of import to me. Of course it wouldn't; I was sure of it. Still my palms had started to sweat.

"It began with the strange death of a crippled foreign priest several years ago," Moore started. "The man, an Argentinean, we thought, was found dead in a Soho hotel back in the winter of '94. He'd been strangled with a silk scarf—most likely murdered by a recent companion of his."

I gripped my glass more tightly, and heat rushed to my face, leaving the pit of my stomach cold. He surely could not be talking of the priest I had come to know at the end of the last decade, could he?

"The case led us on a real wild goose chase—all the way to Le Havre, in fact—but all we found there was some missing money and a series of false identities. Whatever name the dead man had been given at birth, it was long lost."

"And what does this strange case have to do with us?" Andrews asked.

"On first sight, nothing—in fact, I had forgotten all about it," Moore admitted. Then he smiled and added, "Well, I had, until this new development."

"What new development?" I asked. My throat was dry, and the laughter in the restaurant around us was suddenly ringing too loudly in my ears.

"I received a message from the hotel yesterday. They have been renovating some of their rooms, and one of the workmen found a letter tucked behind a loose skirting board in the room in which the priest died. The original intention perhaps had been for it to stick out far enough to be seen by the police, but even if it had been, we did not notice it at the time. I like to think that it had dropped into the gap before I attended the crime scene. The hotel manager waited until yesterday to pass it on to me—no doubt worried about a scandal affecting their Jubilee holiday bookings—but at least he passed it on rather than just throwing it out with the damn trash."

"So? Don't keep us in suspense! What was this letter?" Andrews asked.

Moore smiled. "It was addressed to Thomas." He pulled the envelope out of his pocket. "Look." He slid the small envelope into the middle of the table.

I stared at it. *Dr. Thomas Bond* was scratched carefully in black ink.

"A crippled priest?" Andrews asked suddenly. "How was he crippled? A strange arm?" He turned to me. "Did you not see a man like that? During our investigations? I could swear you mentioned such a man watching at Whitehall."

"Perhaps I did," I said, trying to keep my voice light and cursing Andrews's eye for detail. "It was a long time ago, and I don't recall too clearly." I picked up the envelope, hoping my clammy fingers weren't trembling too much. *So the priest is dead*, I tried to reason with myself; *surely that is better than his being alive and returning perhaps to blackmail me?* If he was dead, then perhaps the past truly was finally being laid to rest.

I unfolded the paper, and despite wishing to clasp it to my chest and read it privately, I placed it in the space between Andrews and me. I could not afford to let him get any more suspicious.

The words were written in a surprisingly elegant hand.

> *I beg your forgiveness. I thought I could stop it. I thought I was strong. I have failed. I have fed the river with the piecemeal products of my abhorrent deeds. Women have died at my hand. They will come for me now, although I have done what I can do to put things right. Let us hope the weak man is the strongest of us all.*

"The river?" Andrews gasped after a long moment of silence. His eyes were wide. "The Torso killings? *Elizabeth Jackson*—? You think this man was—? But his crippled arm—?"

"Madness can give men strength," Moore said. "And we don't know *how* he killed them, just that he cut them up and disposed of their body parts. But yes, I think this might have been our man." He looked at me, grinning like a wolf. "What say you, Thomas? You've a mind for these things?"

"I think you may well be right," I said, nodding too vigorously as my mind raced, trying to both decipher the meaning of the letter and also to react appropriately in front of my companions. "His arm was damaged, yes—but he might still have had strength in it. And if he *was* the man who was watching me—and given that the note has my name on it, I think we can safely presume he was—and with the mention of the river . . . well, I can only conclude that you are right: this dead priest was indeed our Torso killer."

"It was hard to judge how crippled he was," Moore said. "One hand had been crudely amputated. The doctor who carried out the postmortem examination thought it had happened within a year of his death."

"To stop himself from killing?" Andrews asked. "A madman, no doubt." His face was alive with excitement, and I realized his back was straight for the first time in years. This news was giving him palpable relief—it might not have been the identity of Jack, but it was the next best thing. And I had no doubt that Andrews would be able to convince himself that the same man was responsible for both sets of murders if he really put his mind to it.

For my own part, I could feel my world crumbling.

"More brandy!" Andrews shouted to a passing waiter. "My heavens, Henry! This is incredible—we must thank God they found the letter and passed it on to you."

"I am glad it has made you happy," Moore said, grinning. "We may not have caught the bastard, but at least we know he can't do any more harm."

"What about the others he mentions in the letter?"

"The imaginings of a disturbed mind? Perhaps this man who killed him—another priest perhaps?—realized what he had become? Whatever the meaning, this is a truly remarkable turn of events," I said, and I raised my glass to them. "To Walter's happy retirement, and to the closing of cases." Our glasses clinked and we drank.

I drained my glass almost in one, my head a swirling mass of doubt and the ghosts of the past. My happiness with Juliana now felt like an insubstantial light trying in vain to pierce a fog that was determined to lose me forever within it.

I laughed loudly at everything my companions said and wished for this interminable evening to be over. When finally we came out into the warm night, Henry Moore stood between us and seized us both around the shoulders, almost as if we were sailors heading back to our boat after a night of carousing. I said my farewells, promising to stay in touch more frequently with them both, and climbed into a hansom cab.

I waited until I was several streets away from them before signaling the driver to stop and set me down near a quiet alley. Once he had moved on, I leaned against the wall and vomited until my stomach was empty of everything but bile and my throat was burning. I wanted to weep. I was snared in the past, and every time I thought I had wriggled free, another hook snagged my skin.

As my skin cooled and my legs grew steadier beneath me, I began to walk, aimlessly, trying to process this new information. The priest had died in 1894—it was about then that my sleep had returned to normal and the vague sense of dread that had haunted me had finally slipped away. Surely that was just coincidence? The words of the priest's note were etched in my mind: so he had killed women. I thought of the splash of the river on the dark night James Harrington had died, the sound of the priest disposing of the *Upir*. But had he? Or had the monster clung on to him? And if that had been the case, where was it now? Why did I no longer feel that same unease? Had whoever killed the priest dealt with the *Upir* at the same time?

No. There is no Upir, I told myself again and again. There was only madness. I sucked in deep breaths of the hot, stinking London air, glad that I could not taste the river in it. Perhaps the priest had been unable to shake the madness he had believed in so sincerely. He must have come to think himself to be carrying the beast on his back, just as Harrington had. Was that it? The fantastic and the logical battled in my mind as I remembered the sight of the thing wrapping around Harrington's neck. I remembered the whip marks on the priest's back as he prepared for his battle with the demon—the battle he had apparently concluded he had lost. Such things could not exist—surely they could not. What had the priest meant in his note about "putting things right"? And who was the weakest man—me? The hairdresser, Kosminski? I had given the odd little man little thought over the past few years, and now I found myself most fervently wishing that he too were dead. But if he was not, was he now killing women? I did not want to think of his visions; I had never been able to find a way to explain them away, not rationally. The way he had led me to the priest's rooms that night, the things he had *seen,* they were not so easily dealt with by my scientist's mind.

I walked until my legs ached, and I found myself where some part of me must always have known I was heading: the dark heart of London's underbelly, where I could find some relief in the poppy smoke. I wanted to numb my mind, to shake away the bitter past that was threatening to drag me down. I wanted to escape the terrible sense I had of Fate at work against me.

I did not speak to this Chi-Chi. I merely signaled him wearily to bring me a pipe as I found a cot in the corner of the room. The day's heat had settled thickly in the air, and now it was weighed down with smoke and sweat and body heat. As I sucked in the opium and lay back on the thin cushions, I loosened my collars and allowed my skin to breathe.

Ah, the opium, I thought, as my mind drifted into a sea of colors and shapes, my skin tingling and my muscles relaxing. *I have missed it.*

23

London. August, 1897
Dr. Bond

The train journey was interminably slow, and as the heat made my mustache and the skin under my collar itch, I wondered once again what I was doing here. There was no turning back, however. A driver was waiting to pick me up at the station to take me the last mile or so, and if I were to cancel my visit and regret it, I would most likely be met with hostility or suspicion should I try to rearrange it, regardless of my eminent position in the medical world.

Over the past month I had tried to force the news of the priest's letter and his demise from my thoughts as much as possible, but it had proved difficult. Walter Andrews had indeed been revitalized by the news, and he invited Moore and me to celebrate his imminent retirement with a small party. I did my best to appear equally as overjoyed as he, but there was, on that occasion and several afterward, too much talk of the dead killer and the murders he'd supposedly committed for me to relax fully. I was stiff and reserved with Juliana, and although she seemed not to mind, I knew she must be hurt by my behavior. I blamed my withdrawal and antisocial behavior on my back injury, claiming it had started hurting again, and of course she was all understanding and warmth, and she applied no pressure on me to visit her until I was completely better.

In truth, that visit to the opium den had reignited my dependence on the drug. Every morning when I woke—each day later and later—I told myself I would not go again, but every evening, when the darkness of my thoughts and fears overwhelmed me, I would once again find myself back in the sewers of the city, seeking temporary oblivion. My work was suffering as distraction marked my visits to the hospital. The invisible walls of old were creeping up between me and the world as the words of the dead priest haunted my sober waking hours. Each day I took out the package of Harrington's letters and stared at them, caught between the urge to devour their insane contents and my desire to burn them, hoping to obliterate the past.

Now the air reeked of the river everywhere I went, and as my nights were given to the opium, I began to make my days more bearable with laudanum. I wondered anew about the creature I had seen on Harrington's back and despaired of the thin line between madness and sanity.

After two weeks I could tolerate this purgatory no further. The priest was dead, and if I were ever to understand those circumstances or ease the fear that my madness was returning, then I needed to seek out the gentle hairdresser and learn what had happened after our unholy trinity had disbanded on the night of James Harrington's death. I found Kosminski's sister's house easily enough from memory, and although she was clearly displeased to see me, she did unbend enough to tell me that her brother had been in Colney Hatch since 1891 until early 1894, when he had been transferred to Leavesden. When she said sternly that she hoped I would not trouble him there, I nodded and gave my reassurances, although I knew I could promise no such thing. What effect my presence would have on Kosminski, I did not know. His visions had always plagued him—but had our murder of James Harrington turned him completely insane? And was it just coincidence that he had been moved to a new asylum the same year that the priest died?

My questions would soon be answered.

My hansom cab ride to Leavesden was uneventful. I enjoyed the breeze, which shook away the vestiges of my opium hangover, but I confess I did administer myself some laudanum to calm my rising nerves.

By the time we came up the sweeping drive to the imposing modern building, I was ready. I had written to the medical superintendent, telling him I was preparing a paper on patients suffering auditory hallucinations and their links to criminal activity, and I recalled Aaron Kosminski from my time assisting the police on the Jack the Ripper case. It was the superintendent who met me and led me through the institution to the visiting rooms, giving me the guided tour as we walked. I nodded and exclaimed at all the right points, but in truth, I was barely listening.

Finally, he ushered me into the visiting room. "The head attendant can oversee you from there," he said, and he gestured at an office looking down into the room. "You won't be in any danger. Kosminski's not a violent patient—in fact, he shuns contact."

"I would rather be alone with him if possible," I said. "I fear I do not get the most honest answers from patients when they are being watched, especially those suffering from paranoia."

"As you wish," he said. "But I shall leave two attendants outside the door for you to call upon, should you need them."

I gave him my thanks and took a seat. My heart was pounding. In the moments I had alone, I took some more laudanum, and then I waited.

He was thinner than I remembered, if that was possible, and his eyes, ringed with dark shadows in a pale face, darted this way and that as he shuffled in and took the seat opposite me. His restless fingers picked at scabs on his skin.

"Thank you for agreeing to see me," I said, keeping my tone formal until the attendants had closed the door behind them.

"Why are you here?" he asked eventually. His accent was still strong.

"The priest is dead," I said. "He was found dead several years ago, but I only discovered the fact recently."

Kosminski nodded. He did not look surprised. His twitching grew, though, and I felt a pang of sympathy for him. Whatever demons I suffered, I could see they were nothing compared to his.

"I have not seen him since that night. But he left a note for me. One that pertained to our . . . activities." I did not want to speak the details out loud, for fear Kosminski's insanity might create a truth around them that did not exist. If he knew something, I wanted it to come entirely from him. "Had you seen him before he died?"

There was a long pause, and I wondered if he was going to speak at all, and then he sniffed, coughed, and sighed.

"We made a pact," he whispered.

"You and the priest?"

He nodded, his eyes watering. "A terrible pact. I did not think. I did not . . . and they came for him anyway."

"What pact?" I asked, leaning forward.

He was about to speak when he was suddenly wracked with a terrible bout of coughing, his weak body convulsing until his face was red and his eyes were bulging.

"Good heaven, man," I said, getting out of my chair and pulling the laudanum from my pocket, "have you been suffering like this for long?"

He waved his hands at me to ward me away, but his coughing was so acute I ignored him and placed one hand on his bony shoulder so I could tip some of the liquid into his mouth.

Two things happened instantly: his coughing stopped immediately, and his hands, dirty and scabbed, grabbed mine firmly—too firmly.

My own responses were slow, though I frowned at this sudden shift in behavior. His eyes were sharp, and he yanked me so close I could see every pore of his cheeks. The rotten stench of his mouth and filthy skin was nauseously overwhelming.

"I say," I exclaimed startled, although not in any fear, "are you all right?"

"I'm sorry," he whispered. "I'm sorry."

Something shifted in the corner of my eye as I stared at him, confused. There was a darkness—something on his shoulder—and my skin crawled with an overwhelming sense of dread. As I gazed into Kosminksi's bloodshot eyes, I was sure I caught a glimpse of red eyes, and a slick black tongue reached for my throat.

As my mind screamed *insanity* at me, I broke away, gasping. I glanced back at the door, half-expecting to see the attendants rushing in, but it remained closed.

"I'm sorry," Kosminski repeated dully.

I looked at him as I caught my breath, loathing myself both for having gone to the opium den the night before and for having taken oo much laudanum this morning. My brain was drug addled. That's all it was: the proximity of the hairdresser releasing those memories I did not trust to be real.

"I am not hurt," I said, and I retook my seat. "Tell me of this pact you made with the priest." In truth, all I wanted to do was to turn and leave and never look back, but I could not. I had to be sure that whatever they had done could have no impact on my current life. If they had left a record somewhere of my involvement in Harrington's death, then I would not be able to explain that away so easily.

The hairdresser had slumped in his seat. Although he looked terribly sad, his agitations had ceased, and his coughing had stopped. He looked almost as if a weight had been lifted from his shoulders, and that fanciful thought made me shiver in dread. I took two deep breaths. It was the laudanum, that was all. Nothing more.

"He came to see me." His voice was soft, and he stared at a point in space rather than meeting my eyes. "When I had moved here. He was not the same man—I knew it before he came. I had *seen* it. He had killed. He told me what did not need saying: the *Upir* had not gone into the river that night. It was upon him."

The world darkened slightly. "Go on."

"He had believed that he could control it—he thought his weakened arm would stop him from killing, but the beast was stronger." Finally he looked at me. "His hand he cut off, to try and stop it, but it did not work. He heard they were sending others of his order to find him—to kill him, maybe. This did not scare him, but he was afraid it would trick them as it had tricked him. He came to me."

He broke down and started sobbing, lost in the memory, and my stomach in turn twisted sickeningly as he talked of madness I had thought so long ago left behind. But the priest had died in mysterious circumstances. Could his strange order have been responsible? Could such madness be spread among many?

"I thought it would be better than the visions," Kosminski whispered. "I was wrong."

"I don't understand," I said. "What did he want from you?"

He looked at me as if I was fool for not already knowing what he was going to say. "We thought I could starve it," he whispered. "I am touched so little. So I took it from him."

"The *Upir*?"

He nodded. "I have tried so hard. I did not want to see you. But my mind has not always been my own."

"Nonsense," I said. "We have been friends."

"No," he whispered, "no, we are not friends. I have done a terrible thing."

"What?" I asked. "What terrible thing could you do in here?"

His face was desolation itself. "I have given you the *Upir*."

It was madness, I told myself all the way home. The heat no longer bothered me for my skin was clammy with cold dread. Aaron Kosminski was mad—and so was I, for thinking that seeing him might bring me any sort of relief, or that I would find anything more than insanity—an insanity I had been part of.

The next morning, I woke with a fever.

24

LONDON. SEPTEMBER, 1897
EDWARD KANE

He was happier than he had been since he arrived in England. The revelations about the murdering priest, combined with Dr. Bond's eminently sensible comment that if James Harrington had been up to no good at the wharves, there would have been some evidence left had finally banished his doubts about his friend. He had even begun to feel faintly ridiculous for having thought such things in the first place.

As he watched Juliana tend to her dead husband's grave, brushing away the fallen leaves and laying fresh flowers, he made a silent apology to the man's memory. Now they could all finally move on. He hoped that Jim, gentle man that he had been, would have no objections to his pursuit of his widow. If only she could let go of her sense of obligation to Dr. Bond. It was Edward she loved, he knew that, and they had shared several kisses since that first glorious touch, but when the doctor had fallen ill, she had become overwhelmed with guilt, and she had backed away from him physically, leaving him nearly driven insane with desire and love for her. He had tried to persuade her that her loyalty was misplaced, that the heart could be loyal only to itself—that there was no reason why she could not be as good a friend to Thomas Bond as she had been in the past without feeling obliged to marry him. In fact, he sincerely hoped that they could both be good friends, for, putting the matter of Juliana aside, he too had great respect and admiration for the doctor.

At last Charles Hebbert, who had been attending to Dr. Bond during this past month of illness, announced that the good doctor was finally on the mend. Juliana had not visited him, for both her father and Bond had insisted she stay away, in case she should catch his fever. And he himself had thought it best to wait until Thomas was up and about again before revealing that he was back in Juliana's favor after the boating incident.

"We should go," he said, checking his pocket watch. "We shall be late for your visitor." Juliana smiled, and he was glad to see her face free from the grief that had darkened it so often in the past. Little James, who was happily making daisy chains on the grass at his dead father's feet, got up. She took one hand and he took the other, and they left the dead to rest in peace.

William Chard Williams was much closer in height to little James than to either Edward or Juliana, but his freckled face was cheery, and his eyes twinkled as he shook the boy's hand.

"So, you want to be prepared to go to school with all the other boys, do you?" he asked.

"Yes, sir," James said very soberly.

"Then between us we shall get you ready, won't we?"

The boy nodded again, and Chard Williams grinned at him, teasing out a nervous smile in return.

Juliana poured some more tea and told James to go and play with his toys, leaving them to talk in quiet. Edward sat back in his chair and let Juliana make the arrangements. He knew at his own cost how protective she was; he would not make the same mistake again. While he took some credit for this change in her attitude, he had played no part in finding the private tutor for her.

"And you used to be a schoolteacher?" she asked.

"Yes, ma'am, I did." Chard Williams nodded at the envelope on the table between them. "You'll find my references in there, together with several from those I have privately tutored since. I would very much like to be teaching in a school still, but unfortunately I have problems with my back, and long hours of standing are not good for my health." He smiled again. "But at least I can still educate the young in this capacity."

"You are very good with children," Juliana said, smiling, and Edward knew then that she would hire this one.

"Unlike most schoolmasters of my acquaintance"—the tutor leaned in conspiratorially—"I'm rather fond of them."

"Do you and your wife have any of your own?"

"Sadly, not yet—but I do confess that my wife is somewhat younger than I am, and so I hope we shall, in due course. She loves babies herself; in fact, she often fosters and cares for other people's little ones. If young James does come to our home for his lessons, then he will certainly learn what it's like to be around other children. The lessons themselves will of course take place in a private room, and he will need to concentrate and work very hard, but I am a believer in allowing breaks for the learning to be absorbed before moving on."

"I quite agree," said Juliana. Finally, she looked Edward's way, and he gave a slight nod. She smiled. "Then I think all we need do is settle on times and your fees. I will be happy to leave my son in your educational care."

It was as if something had been freed in Juliana that night. Charles Hebbert called in to say that Dr. Bond was in far better spirits—still weak, but dressed and up, and he was well enough for Hebbert to reduce his visits to every other day.

It had been a long way to come simply to impart that news, but Juliana was always pleased to see her father. Edward too was happy to see him, but he was equally happy when he accepted a glass of wine but would not stay for dinner, saying he planned on dining at his club. While Juliana was in such good spirits, Edward wanted her to himself. Hebbert tipped him a wink on the way out—sharp-eyed as he was, he could obviously see that too.

"So now that James's tutor is taken care of, you can start your journey as a businesswoman," Edward said as they finished dinner.

"I feel as if life is starting again for me," she said. "And I do think it would make James happy to think I was looking after his business for his son."

"He would be very proud of you, of that I am sure. Although I cannot imagine he wasn't already as proud as a man could be, just to have you as his wife."

There was silence after that as Juliana looked down into her glass, her expression unreadable. He had never met a woman so warm and yet so contained. What did he have to do to win her over? Why could she not just love him as he did her?

"It's late," he said at last, "and it has been a long day. I should return to my hotel."

She looked up, her dark eyes studying him. "Perhaps you should stay," she said softly.

His heart raced suddenly. He didn't speak, not wanting to break the moment.

"It would not be a promise of anything," she continued, as if they were discussing a business contract. "It would not mean that I am not still considering my obligation to Thomas."

Obligation. She had used the word herself.

"I just wish to feel alive again." Her fear and loneliness shone from her eyes. She had been without a man for a long time. He got to his feet without saying a word and followed her upstairs to her bedroom. They peeled each other's clothes off with increased urgency and fell on the bed, barely able to stop kissing long enough to gasp in a breath. Edward Kane thought he would explode at the feel of Juliana's silk-soft skin on his. He held her full breasts and took a nipple in his mouth, teasing her expertly with his tongue. Her hands ran through the curly dark hair on his chest, no doubt very different from James Harrington's smooth, boyish skin, and as her back arched under his touch any initial shyness she might have been feeling vanished. This was truly a woman in his arms, not a girl. He slid his head down further, relishing the taste of her, and despite his own desperate need to be inside her he held back, instead concentrating on pleasuring her, until she was hot and moist and panting with desire. She pulled him back up the bed and opened herself fully to him, grasping his buttocks to pull him in deeper. He groaned as they grappled with each other, trying to hold back, until with a cry, he forced himself to withdraw, dragging himself out of her just at the last moment and spilling his seed across her smooth belly.

It had been pure animalistic sex, all grunting, urgent *need* and *want*, but as they lay there in each other's arms, the summer night's heat caressing their cooling skin, Edward Kane knew that they had also been making love, perhaps for the first time in his life.

He was content. He was more than content. He was ecstatically happy, and he made a silent vow that he would always protect Juliana Harrington and keep her safe, no matter the paths their lives might take.

25

LEAVESDEN. AUGUST, 1897
AARON KOSMINSKI

Assessment

The patient appears to be making progress. He is calmer, and his visible tics have lessened. He allowed himself to be washed, although this heightened his anxiety levels. His sense of distraction has decreased although his fear of water is not diminished. He is still mainly wary of touch.

He has requested that Dr. Bond not be allowed to visit him again.

26

LONDON. SEPTEMBER, 1897
DR. BOND

It was a relief to be finally feeling myself again, even though my energy was drained and simply moving around my house exhausted me. Charles Hebbert had done me a great service, caring for me throughout the worst of my fever, but now that I was on my way to recovery, I enjoyed having some time to myself.

My head was finally—thankfully—clear. A month confined to my house and under the close supervision of my friend and Mrs. Parks had cured me of my growing opium addiction, and I was determined to avoid even the laudanum when possible, although I had to accept it when the racking pains in my chest were at their worst. I was determined that I would not be dragged into that place again. The priest was dead, and Kosminski was in the asylum, and now that I was rational once more, it was clear to me how the poor Polish hairdresser could have been so deluded. I did not doubt that the priest had visited him, but after much contemplation, I had concluded that the priest was suffering from his own delusions—he clearly was a member of an order whose role it was to fight supposed demons—and he must have convinced Kosminski that he had transferred the *Upir* to him. It would not have been a difficult task, not given the state of paranoid delusion that gripped that unhappy young man so firmly.

Now that I was free of the opium haze I had been locked in, I could see the ridiculousness of the fear that had overwhelmed me on my return home. When I had awakened in a fever and feeling so ill, it was not caused by any mythical *Upir*—I did not doubt that I had caught some sickness from the asylum. Kosminksi was far from a healthy man, and he had pulled me close to him. It pleased me to find that I could think of such madness with a calm head; I could even feel amused by my own involvement in it.

Mrs. Parks had brought me soup for lunch, and she had left cold meat and salads prepared for me in the pantry, her regular routine. My appetite had shrunk considerably during the weeks of my illness, and rather than worry her by not eating her repasts, I had started taking much of it to the back door and feeding the cats that wandered the streets. I had collected several regular visitors in the ten days or so since I had started leaving my bed, and they allowed me to stroke them, wrapping themselves around my legs and purring as I fed them morsels of pork and beef.

This warm evening was no different. When I opened the door, three or four appeared out of nowhere, vocally expressing their eagerness as I tore bits of chicken from the breast that was supposed to be my supper. I murmured at them, finding an easy joy in their presence, even if their affection was based entirely on the food in my hands. A cheeky-looking black and white chap leapt over the back of one of his fellows and sat at my feet expectantly, and I could almost see his eyebrow raised in an expression of *Oh do hurry up, I haven't got all day*. I normally tried to ensure that each got an equal amount, but I do confess I gave him a little more than the others, simply for his attitude.

The air was sticky and humid, but it was a pleasant change from being inside, so I took a kitchen chair and sat there for a while enjoying the heat and the hum of the city, not caring that I looked like a strange eccentric to anyone who passed me by. I must eventually have dozed off, for when I came to with a start, night was falling and the air was a little chill, making my skin tingle. My feline companions had vanished, no doubt back to the comforts of their owners' beds, and I, in turn, sought out my own bed, where I fell into a sound and dreamless sleep.

Juliana visited me the next afternoon, and she was the final tonic required in my recovery. She told me she had been wanting to visit all month and scolded me for refusing her entry, but her reprimand was given with a smile, and I could see she was happy to find me well. Mrs. Parks fussed around her as she told me about little James's new tutor and how that would allow her to spend much more time at the wharves, learning the business. She spoke with great joy, but she seemed slightly shy with me, which I put down to our having spent a month apart. I decided it would be best to leave some time before discussing our engagement further. I hated that I had been so ill—I hoped she would not see that as a sign of my age, just a simple bout of something unpleasant, which truly was all it was. I was older, certainly, but not yet an old man, and I fully intended to ensure that I remained fit and healthy in order to be a good husband to her when we did finally wed.

"I am very fond of you, Thomas," she said as she left. "You do know that, don't you?" She touched my cheek softly and then kissed it. Her lips were like butterfly wings, and they made my heart race.

"I am very glad to hear that," I said, "for you know what you mean to me."

Her lips lifted in something that was almost a smile, but her eyes dropped from mine. "I shall see you soon, Thomas. Now, make sure you get well."

I had almost forgotten how beautiful she was, and now that my mind was clear of drugs and delusion, I could not wait to make her my own. My spirits were truly lifted, and when I fed the cats I added an extra two slices of thick ham to their feast from the larder.

I had hoped Juliana might call on me again the following day, but she did not. Disappointed though I was, I realized that with her new interest in Harrington's business and having to prepare little James for the tutor, she was increasingly busy, and it was not a short trip from Barnes to Westminster. But now that I was recovering, I was stuck in that purgatory between being too weak to do very much but better enough to feel restless and bored. I read for a while and wrote letters—one to Charles, thanking him for taking such good care of me, and another to Andrews, telling him he was welcome to visit whenever it suited him.

By late afternoon I was once again in my new spot at the back door, sipping tea and waiting for my feline companions to arrive. It had become so much a habit that I was beginning to contemplate getting a cat myself—I smiled to myself as I imagined Mrs. Parks's face. But then I was sure that if she saw me sitting in the doorway, a blanket over my knees, feeding morsels of her lovingly prepared dishes to strays and wandering pets, she would probably call for the men from the asylum herself.

I relaxed back into my chair and shrugged my shoulders, trying to ease my back, which still ached from whatever had plagued my chest. I was happy to see the first of my fellows trotting toward me, the others soon following, but sadly there was no sign of the cheeky little black and white tom. *He must have found a better offer somewhere else*, I thought to myself, which made me smile.

Within a few days I was feeling well enough to leave the house, and although I did not wish to walk too far, I took a hansom cab down to the wharves to visit Juliana, which served a twofold purpose. I was curious to see how she was doing—and I missed her company, of course—but I knew this was the last of the ghosts of the past I had to expel. If Juliana was determined to become a businesswoman and I was determined to make her my wife, I was going to have to make my peace with that place, though it held so many bad memories. Even so, as resolved as I was, my heart was beating fast as I made my way to the offices I had not seen for so many years. Thankfully there was no dockers' strike today, and instead of the eerily empty space I saw on my last visit, this time the place was abuzz with men loading and unloading crates and ferrying them to and from the various warehouses and out to the dock, filling the gantries and workspaces with noise and life.

"I hope you don't mind my dropping by," I said, smiling, as I opened the office door. "I thought I would like to see the magnate at work."

Juliana was behind the desk, with Mr. Barker leaning over her shoulder, obviously discussing a document with her. She leapt up as she saw me, crying, "Thomas! What a wonderful surprise!"

She looked beautiful, less formally dressed than normal, and in more severe colors than the bright clothes she usually favored, but nothing could dull her own natural shine.

"I shan't stay long," I said. "I know you have much to do."

"Stay as long as you like. It is so good to see you looking so well."

She swept out from behind the desk and came to kiss me on the cheek, and it was only when I closed the door after her embrace that I saw Edward Kane standing behind it, leaning over an open filing cabinet drawer. My heart dropped. I had known that Juliana would forgive the young man, of course, but I certainly had not expected to find him here.

"Dr. Bond." He smiled at me, and I struggled to return the gesture. Was there something a little false in his own too, I wondered?

"Mr. Kane." I nodded at him, and from the corner of my eye I could see Juliana looking nervously from one of us to the other. My heart melted slightly. She was obviously worried that I would not be happy that she had forgiven him—and I would not want to cause her any worry. And it was perfectly reasonable that she should want his assistance now, for he could help her far more in the world of business than I. Perhaps this was his way of making amends.

I smiled again, more naturally this time. "I am glad to see that along with Mr. Barker here, Juliana has another expert adviser on hand."

"I feel I owe you an apology, sir," the American started. "You were right in what you said, and I should never have—"

"It is forgotten." I waved the rest of the sentence away. "And I was perhaps a little sharp myself."

Beside us, I could almost feel Juliana relaxing, and I was glad. Her happiness was more important to me than my petty jealousies of the younger man, surely just paranoia on my part, for after all, it was me she had all but agreed to marry, and surely she would not have done that if she did not love me.

With harmony restored, Juliana took me on a tour of her new empire. I was pleased to see that the workers already treated her with the correct deference, no sly looks as she walked away, and for her part, she was gracious and courteous to all. I felt immensely proud to have her arm linked in mine as we walked through the noisy heat. My back ached, but the pleasure of her company far outweighed my discomfort. I was also immensely relieved when we bypassed the warehouse where James Harrington had committed his terrible deeds, and where I had put an end to his tragic life.

By the time we returned to her office, I could not have been more pleased with how the visit had gone.

"I shall come down with you," Edward Kane said, as I left to find a hansom cab, and although I was quite capable of finding one myself, I did not wish to appear rude, especially in light of Juliana's forgiveness.

We strolled out from the hubbub, and then he said, "I fear I have another favor to ask of you, Thomas. I have to return to New York for two months or so—I'm leaving next week."

My heart leapt with this news, and my shoulders straightened. My jealousy might have been misplaced and foolish, but that did not stop its existing, and the idea that the younger, richer, and more handsome man would no longer be around Juliana for a while filled me with joy.

"I hope to be back in time for Christmas," he continued, "but in the meantime, I hope you might keep an eye on Charles Hebbert? I might be talking out of turn here—in fact, I probably am—but he seems not entirely himself. His moods are erratic, and he has been visiting Juliana and James less, perhaps drinking at his club a little too often."

"Well, Charles does enjoy company," I said.

"I know," Kane said, "but the past two weeks or so he's been—well, different. Juliana hasn't said anything, but I think she's worried about him too."

My hackles rose slightly with his mention of Juliana, and once again I cursed my ill health for keeping me from her for so long.

"Would you look out for him?" he asked again, and there was such earnest good intention in his expression that once again I felt guilt for my bad feeling toward him. Edward Kane was a good man, and he cared about the friends he had made in London—myself included, I had no doubt.

I shook his hand firmly. "Thank you for telling me, and have no fear, I shall make sure I get to the bottom of whatever is troubling my old friend."

"Thank you," he said. "I have to say, I'm sad to be going home, but let us hope we can all celebrate a good Christmas together."

"I'm sure we shall," I said, climbing into the waiting cab. "I'm sure we shall."

I waved my farewell and then sank, contented, back into my seat. I did not think much about his concerns over Charles, for I was too busy being overjoyed at the thought of a few months without Edward Kane's presence making me feel old and foolish for loving Juliana.

"I've been through the kitchen, and I cannot find what's causing it," Mrs. Parks said, two days later. We had thrown open the windows to ventilate the house, but still the vaguely sweet-rotten smell permeated the rooms. Mrs. Parks, with her sharp eye for cleanliness, was being driven to distraction by it.

"You go home," I told her. "These past few days have been exceptionally warm and humid—no doubt whatever the stench is, it will fade as the temperature cools down."

She did not look convinced. I had spent most of the day in bed reading, exhausted after overdoing it because of my keenness to be back on my feet, and although I too could smell the tang of something odd in the air, it was not plaguing me as it did her. "I can take care of my own supper—I think you have earned an afternoon off after your care of me this past month."

On days like this I could see how much Mrs. Parks had aged. She had been in service with me for many years, and where she had once been matronly, now she was becoming an old woman, and, though I hated to admit it, she had started to fuss like one too. Not that I would ever say such a thing to her. She would be appalled.

"Nothing's quite right," she said, her brow furrowing. "Are you sure you haven't had any visitors in the evenings? I'm sure things have been moved—and that awful smell . . ."

I sighed, suddenly feeling like a frustrated boy in conversation with my own grandmother, many, many years before.

"No, Mrs. Parks—perhaps it is just the heat affecting you. Or maybe you have a touch of my fever coming? Although I sincerely hope not."

She sniffed at that and straightened her back, clearly not pleased with my tone. "Well, there is plenty of food in the pantry, and some of that chicken broth on the stove." She peered at me over her spectacles. "Are you sure you'll manage? Is Dr. Hebbert calling on you later?"

"I shall manage perfectly well, for I am feeling much better," I said, with a smile. "I have no visitors coming so when I have finished my book, I promise I will eat, and then I shall retire early. So please"—and I tried hard to keep the exasperation from my voice—"go, enjoy your afternoon. I shall see you tomorrow."

She bustled out, and I was sure I could hear disapproval in the rustle of her dress, but a few minutes later I heard the front door firmly closing, and I settled back against my pillows, happy to have some peace and be alone with my book.

An hour or so later my stomach rumbled, and I realized that I was suddenly famished. I ventured downstairs in search of food, and as I reached the ground floor, I suddenly understood why Mrs. Parks had been so disturbed by the smell. In my bedroom it had been a vaguely unpleasant tang in the air, but by the time I reached the hallway, it was so thick I could almost taste it.

My appetite temporarily suppressed, I wandered from room to room trying to find the source, and eventually I stopped outside the door to the small cellar under the stairs, and I pressed my nose against the gap around the hinges. I pulled back quickly as the scent overwhelmed me. I frowned, looking down at the small mahogany occasional table that partially covered the doorway. I was sure it had been further along the wall than here. Had I moved it? Or perhaps Mrs. Parks had done so in order to polish the floor . . . ?

The lightweight piece slid easily along the floorboards, and I stared at the door. The cellar was a forgotten place. I did not collect clutter, nor did I keep a selection of fine wines in the house, so it had long been unused. Perhaps some rats had found their way in and died?

I sighed. I wanted something to eat, for I was, for the first time in many months, truly starving, and I wanted to sit outside my back door and eat, away from the smell, but I knew that I would not be able to relax until the cause had been investigated and dealt with. It was not fair to Mrs. Parks to make her work in such an environment, and I would certainly be no gentleman if I expected her to take care of it for me.

It took me a while to find the key—in truth, I could not remember the last time this door had been opened. Then I fetched a candle from the kitchen, and once it was lit, I unlocked the sliding latch from the wooden door and pulled it open.

I immediately started gagging at the stench that erupted from the blackness. I swiftly pulled a handkerchief from my dressing gown pocket and pressed it against my face, but it did little to keep out the noisome smell.

As I began my cautious descent, I could not help but remember the vault at New Scotland Yard, where a poor carpenter had discovered a rotting torso wrapped in newspaper all those years ago. This darkness had the same sense of oppression, and the smell was far too similar. I felt as if time was folding in on itself—except this time I had to go into the bowels of the earth and make that awful discovery alone.

I had expected the air to cool as I edged my way down the stone steps, but the heat from the nearby kitchen combined with the summer outside instead made it humid, almost stagnant. I tried not to think of how it reminded me of the river; I forced my imagination to still and concentrated instead on reaching the bottom without tumbling. I put one hand on the rough cool wall to steady myself, and I was not sure if the damp I felt came from my sweating palm or from the bricks themselves.

Finally, my feet found solid ground, and I turned to look into the main part of the room, wishing I had thought to bring a shovel and sack with me so I would not have to come down again. The stench here was overwhelming, and I was gripped by a sense of dread the like of which I had not felt in years. I wanted badly to turn and flee, to lock the cellar door forever and let whatever was there remain unknown—but this was a child's response, and I would not allow myself to succumb to it.

Upstairs was daylight, I reminded myself. The city was alive with noise only feet away from the silence I was wrapped in. As I fought the awful scent, taking shallow breaths while trying to calm down, I cursed myself for the lack of a gas lamp, for the light from the candle illuminated little, barely more than a few inches from where I held it.

I forced myself forward, moving slowly and carefully, with the rough sound of my breath in my ears and my slippers shuffling on the uneven floor my only company. Suddenly something caught the candlelight and glinted in the darkness: a glassy eye that stared accusingly at me. My heart almost stopped and I yelped, a high-pitched sound more worthy of a young girl than a man approaching his sixtieth year.

With a trembling hand I raised the candle higher, for the dead eye that stared into mine was not at my feet, nor was it small enough to be that of a rat. It was a long moment before I could even begin to comprehend the horror laid out before me. The candle shook as I moved it closer, and I could only imagine the mask of terror that must be my face.

The cat—what was left of it—lay on a wooden bench. Its head was quite separate from its body, which had been cut open and the skin pulled back, clearly in order to facilitate the removal of the internal organs. Two of its legs were missing. I saw the color of the fur in the patches that were not matted with blood—black and white. It was the cheeky little chap I had fed the most meat to only a few night before—and once again I found myself gagging into my handkerchief.

But he was not alone on the bench; there were others around him, all in similar states of dismemberment, and all of whom I recognized from my relaxing evenings by the kitchen door. I staggered backward, desperate to return upstairs, to the daylight. My mind was reeling, and as I clambered up the steps, I was shaking so much I nearly dropped the candle. And now, finally, flashes of what could only be memory started to come to me: my hands, picking up the black and white tom and feeling the *thrum* of his purr against my hands as I stroked his soft fur; me, turning away from the back door and murmuring to him as his paws kneaded my chest—and the sudden, overwhelming *hunger*.

I gasped and stumbled into the gloriously bright hallway with such relief. The dark cellar felt like an ocean in which I was drowning. I leaned against the wall, sucking in deep breaths of air that was no doubt still rancid, but I no longer cared. My head swam, and I sobbed and shook uncontrollably, willing the unwelcome images away: a knife in my hands. Blood. A cat's desperate hiss and squeal as hands—*my* hands—wrung its neck. *What had I done?* And *why?* Was I truly going insane?

When I could trust my legs to move safely, I fetched a glass of water and sipped it slowly, trying to calm myself, but when I looked into the liquid, all I could see was the river. I could hide from the truth no longer. That strange weight on my back that I had dismissed as strained muscles from my coughing, or part of my fever, now felt like lead between my shoulders, and from the corner of my eye I was sure I could see something dark, a shadowy shape, just out of my sight. I sobbed some more at that and then climbed the stairs to my bedroom where I lay, curled up on my side, like a frightened child.

I have given you the Upir.

That was what Kosminski had said to me, and despite everything that we had been through together all those years before, I had arrogantly dismissed it as madness. There had been madness at work, I now knew: my own madness of reason and science, my arrant refusal to believe in everything that had been right before my eyes. I had dismissed the priest as a lunatic, and I had blamed all memory of the *Upir* on drug-addled imagination. What a fool I had been—and now it was I who was cursed, just as James Harrington had been. The evidence sat in the bowels of my own home and in the dark corners of my memory. Why had I gone to see Kosminski? Why had I not just left all alone, let it lie? What good could the truth ever have served?

The skin on my back crawled, and I knew that if I could have flayed myself to be rid of what clung there, invisible and insidious, I would have. I shivered at the thought of it, and once or twice I lifted a hand and almost reached round to touch my skin, but I could not quite bring myself to do that. I would not feel it, that I knew, but all the same, it would be there.

The afternoon darkened into evening and eventually into night as I lay on my bed and stared into space, all hope lost. I was not sure what I was most afraid of—the *thing* on my back, or the fact that I had done such deeds without *knowing*. My skin cooled until my trembling was overtaken by shivers.

Eventually I got up.

I was afraid, but abject terror could be sustained for only so long before exhaustion calmed the body. I needed to think; to consider how I was to manage my new condition. This time I would not hide from the truth. Harrington and the priest had both been tricked by the *Upir*, but I had the advantage of understanding something of the beast; perhaps this would allow me some control. It was attached to me, but that did not mean I had to hand myself over to it—indeed, I had no intention of doing so. I had a good life, and I was not about to give that up.

I had to make plans. I determined to start by reading Harrington's letters properly—but first, I had to clean out the cellar, scrub away the smell of my guilt. Then I would release Mrs. Parks from my service with a generous parting gift.

Now I was on my feet and moving, and I had a sense of purpose, and I felt stronger already. This thing would not beat me; I would not become a monster. I would find a way to live like a decent man.

Some hours later, sweaty and exhausted from my exertions, I threw the sack of remains into the river. There was nowhere else for them to go. I stared at the inky water. I was going to have to make the river my friend.

27

The *Times*
Thursday, June 11, 1896

EXECUTION AT NEWGATE

Yesterday morning at 9 o'clock the woman Dyer, who was convicted at the Central Criminal Court of the murder of a child which she had adopted, was executed at Newgate. It will be recollected that Dyer had carried on the business of baby farming at Reading.

28

Extract from letter from James Harrington
to Edward Kane, dated 1889

. . . I should dread the vagueness that heralds the approach of the fever that leads to my dark deeds. I used to. I used to fight it, drag it out as long as possible before I was overwhelmed. Now, I find I am simply weary and welcome it. I let the other, this terrible demon behind me, take control. I think that perhaps fighting it for so long has weakened me. More than that, I fear that my weakness has allowed some part of its wickedness to seep into my soul, for I have begun to enjoy the darkness, the long nights where secrets can breathe and respectability slumbers.

Sometimes I watch Juliana as she lies in our bed sleeping. She is sweet and beautiful, and I still love her. I'm sure I must do beneath my numbness. Love does not die so easily. The fact that she still loves me despite my illnesses and erratic behavior are proof of that. She does not know how dangerous I am, how as I watch her breathe, her soft skin rising and falling with the action, I want to tear into her skin with my bare hands and see her flesh from the inside. I want to see her eyes widen in fear. I want to feel the powerful surge of the creature that clings to my back—the one they all see in the end. The very thought of it can make my mouth water. These thoughts are terrible in themselves, but she is carrying our child. Her pregnancy is making her ill, and I should be more sympathetic but all my warm emotions are deadened. They are things I have a memory of but can no longer touch. I watch my sleeping pregnant wife and fantasize about slicing her breasts off and feeling those pleasurable shivers as the monster feeds, as I did with Elizabeth when from somewhere deep inside I watched myself pull our unborn bastard from her womb. I am a killer. I can no longer blame it on the visitor I carry. The Upir and I are no longer distinguishable.

I am remembering more and more as time passes. It is as if the creature and I truly are becoming one—symbiotic. I feel old so much of the time, and cynical, as if somewhere just out of reach I have thousands of years of life and knowledge that I can't quite grasp but weighs me down all the same. I know I have had blood on my hands. I know I have squeezed the life out of strangers. I know that I am cursed and doomed, and yet I can't open my mouth to speak.

I do believe that this demon is a kind of drug. Perhaps we provide the pleasure for each other. For when I relax—when I enjoy my madness for want of a better word—then I feel free and powerful and unstoppable.

This is my greatest fear: I have become unstoppable. No, perhaps my greatest fear is that I no longer wish to be stopped.

I have lost any belief that you are receiving these letters, and much of the time I no longer care. I no longer truly understand why I write them except maybe to retain one last thread of my unraveling humanity. I believe that this will be my last. There is very little more that I can say. However, if you do find yourself with this sheet of sorry paper in your hands, take only this from it.

Do not come to London, Edward. Do not try and find me. No good could ever come of it. There is only wickedness here.

Your friend,
James Harrington.

29

LONDON. OCTOBER, 1897
DR. BOND

"I think he may be overworking," Henry Moore said. "What do you reckon?" He hadn't taken his coat off, and for that I was glad. I did not want him staying long.

"I'm afraid I haven't seen him very much since I was ill," I said. It was the truth. I had been to the wharves to see Juliana on several occasions, eager to reestablish our relationship now that Edward Kane was temporarily absent, but I had not been to the house yet, or seen her father, for all his care of me during my sickness. "I have dined with him only once this month—I fear I have had far too much work to catch up on for much socializing."

Moore nodded and glanced up at the bookshelves of my sitting room, where volumes of mainly unread poetry sat alongside novels and plays. Most of my medical journals were kept in my study. "I should read more," he said, pulling a slim blue book free and turning it over in his hands. "But then I suppose the same is true of most men." He reshelved it and turned back to me. "You didn't think he was slightly erratic, then? When you saw him?"

"Not that I recollect," I said, but if I were honest, I would have to admit that I could barely remember our dinner at all. I had still been reeling from my personal discoveries. "I am presuming, however," I continued, "that you have been finding his behavior odd."

"He seems distracted," Moore said. "I'd like your opinion though."

"Of course. I shall arrange to see him in the next week or so, and I'll let you know what I think."

Edward Kane's words at our last meeting came back to me. He had been worried about Charles's drinking and had asked for my help, but I had been so absorbed I had barely listened, and I had promptly forgotten my promise. Now it appeared Kane was not alone in his worry.

"Thank you. And you're well, Thomas?"

"Certainly better than I was last month." I smiled. "But I fear my recovery is slower than it was when I was a young man. In fact, I was about to lie down for an hour or so when you arrived."

"Then I shan't keep you any longer." He squeezed my arm in a surprising and unusual gesture of affection. "But I'm glad you're better. You had us all worried for a while there."

He glanced back briefly at the slim volume that had grabbed his attention, and I took the book down and pressed it into his hand. "You were right. We should all read more. It can be very good for the soul. And also, I think you will enjoy this one."

He took the book and left, declaring that he would start reading it that very night, and I smiled as I closed the door. I was glad he had taken it. Mr. Stevenson's *Strange Case of Dr. Jekyll and Mr. Hyde* was a little too close for my comfort these days, and I was happy the text was no longer in my house.

I let ten minutes pass to make sure Moore was not going to return for any reason before I started to make my way to the cellar, whence I had been headed before my friend's unexpected visit. I took one of the new lamps from the kitchen, and I went down the stairs to where my work awaited me.

After my initial terror on finding the poor cats had eased, my first thought had been to return to Leavesden, to force the thing back onto Kosminski, but my request for a visit had been politely declined, and there was no way I could force myself into that institution without causing the medical staff to think me as insane as their guests.

After several long dark nights of fear and laudanum, I decided that I must approach my new situation in a scientific manner. I would not think in terms of demons and creatures—I vowed I would never even *think* the word *Upir* when considering the thing that I could almost see, the weight I could feel on my back—but instead, I would treat my condition as one of parasitical infection, which if handled carefully, could at least be managed. I had studied Harrington's letters thoroughly, and it was clear to me that he had lost control by fighting the urge for blood for too long; it had made him too weak to fight the thing's desire for wickedness. I would not make that mistake. I intended to feed it little and often—not too much, but enough to keep me healthy and free from fever.

The one thing I was certain of was that I would not take human life. I was a doctor. Although I had spent much time analyzing the dead, my vocation was the preservation of life. I would not become a monster like James Harrington. I would learn from his mistakes. I would live with this condition, and I would remain the master of it.

At the bottom of the stairs I lit the two gas lamps I had left there, and yellow light illuminated the small underground room. In the corner a mop and bucket stood ready with carbolic soap and jar of bleach I had mixed. I had spread old newspapers across the floor under the wooden table, that I would burn in the brazier in the garden when I was done.

The dog lay on the table where I had left it in the early hours of this morning. Its bared teeth had frozen into a rictus grin, and I shuddered slightly looking at it, just as I had when I had pulled the knife across its throat. But I knew that the parasite that clung to me had enjoyed the fear and pain in the animal's last moments; that was what it fed on, and so it could not be avoided. I took some comfort in the knowledge that the dog would have died anyway.

I picked up my scalpel and started to cut through its stomach. I had work to do. The monster needed feeding, and it liked its meat fresh.

The dog had not been difficult to source. My addiction to the smoke of the poppy, both recently and in those dark times past, had led me into many of the poorest parts of London, and it was to these I returned when I worked out what needed be done. In the steamy pubs of the East End, it did not take me long to find out where I could go to gamble a few pennies on fighting dogs, and it was there I met the burly, gruff man introduced only as George who would facilitate my needs. He was a swarthy, well-built fellow missing most of his teeth, but his eyes had a granite sharpness I recognized in the intelligent among the criminal classes. He might not be well educated as my class would recognize it, but the back alleys of the East End were his place of business, and he ruled it like a prince.

Once a week, in a grimy cellar that stank of beer and stale sweat, I joined the crowd that would squeeze in to bet on an illegal dog fight.

"'e won't fight again," he had said to me when I expressed an interest in buying the badly injured bull terrier. "'is leg's fucked."

"I don't want to use him to fight," I had replied. We had left the den and were out in the cooler air of the night, which felt almost as fresh as the countryside compared with the reeking atmosphere inside. "I would like one dog every ten days, and I would rather not have to come here to fetch it. We could arrange a place to meet—somewhere discreet. And I would rather you came yourself than sent a lackey."

He had sniffed and lit a pipe as he watched me thoughtfully. "You rich or something? Government?"

"Neither," I had replied. "I am just a private man." I took out several coins from my pocket. "And I pay well for my privacy."

"And I'm a businessman," he said gruffly after a moment. "If I weren't, then I'd probably wonder what a gent like you would want with a useless cunt dog every week or so." He took another long draw on his pipe and then smiled as he blew out the smoke. "But I find wondering can be bad for business."

"Then we shall get along well."

After brokering the deal with the owner, who was more than happy to be paid for a beast he would no doubt be dumping in the river anyway, George muzzled the dog and I found a cabbie who for the right money would take us somewhere near where I lived. The dog would have to walk the last of the way home, which it did quite obediently, dragging its torn and broken rear left leg along behind it. When I took it down into the cellar and cut its throat, I was sure there was more than a little relief in its eyes.

At any rate, that was what I chose to believe as I sliced through the dead creature and pulled out its slick, cold entrails and held them up for the parasite to admire. It had been a long month of slow acceptances on my fate, but I did not wish to cause any living creature to suffer more than it had to. The fighting dog would have died, whether at my hand or its owner's. Now I just had to ensure that it had suffered enough to satisfy the parasite on me. It would have to.

Still, I felt happier later that night when I had finally deposited the dismembered carcass into the water and the cellar was scrubbed and once again clean and I felt almost my normal self again.

Even though it was past midnight by the time I was done and my back and arms ached, I poured myself a brandy and relaxed in my study for a while. My thoughts turned to Henry Moore's visit and his concerns about Charles Hebbert, and I found myself once again thinking of the lies Charles had told about being at the club and how Jasper Waring had seen him wandering the streets of Whitechapel during the long weeks of Jack's bloody summer.

"Jack" had stopped when Harrington died. The priest had said that the parasite brought a mayhem in its wake that enhanced the wickedness in those around it. Now that I had no choice but to accept that the creature existed—for it was either that or consider myself insane, which could not be true for I had never felt more sane in all my years—then I could see the logic of my suspicions of Hebbert with fresh eyes. When I had first felt those awful bouts of dread and anxiety that had forced me to the opium dens in the beginning, the priest had called it a kind of gift—as if I saw a little of what Kosminski did, but on an emotional level, rather than suffering the visions that so plagued him. What if Hebbert had something similar? What if he was capable of absorbing some of this wickedness that was now attached to me?

It struck me, as I sat there while even the night itself appeared to sleep, that our lives were all webs of lies and deceit. I considered myself a good man, and yet I had killed the husband of the woman I loved. James Harrington had murdered women under our very noses. What secrets did Andrews have? And Moore? It was not such a great leap to consider Hebbert to be Jack the Ripper, that most notorious of all London killers. I thought again of the book I had pressed upon Moore as he left, the tale of a man of two halves, one struggling to control the other. Perhaps it was as true of all of us as it had become for me. I did not know if I found comfort in that or whether it should make me shiver. Perhaps both.

I needed the laudanum to sleep that night.

By the end of the month the weather had turned, and in the bite of the wind and the gloom of the afternoons, I could feel winter once again creeping closer. I did not mind the death of the summer; I preferred the cold air to the stifling heat. It was less claustrophobic, without humidity clinging to me as if trying to bind me further to the parasite on my back.

It was late afternoon, and Juliana had her arm linked in mine as we walked along the road by the river, the breeze making her face flush healthily as she told me all she had been learning, and the new contracts she had secured. She was obviously pleased with herself, and her growing confidence in the world made her walk tall and proud, which in turn made her even more beautiful. But I was distracted from her gay chatter, not just because the world of business was not one I understood well, never having been involved in it, but because of a disturbing discovery the previous night. The visit to Juliana had been meant to raise my spirits, but I confess I was finding it difficult to shake off my fear. The iron taint in my mouth and the nausea in the pit of my stomach suggested that I understood perfectly well what had happened the previous night, even if I could not remember it.

I had taken possession of another wounded dog from my unsavory associate George two nights previously, and I had killed that poor beast in order to keep my own tamed. But when I returned to the cellar last night to parcel up the piecemeal corpse and take it to the river, I could not find the liver. For a long moment I had stared at the bench, thinking my tired eyes were playing tricks on me, but it was not there. I have always been methodical in my work, and I had dissected the animal as I would a human body—after so many years in medicine it was second nature to do so. The dog's liver was definitely missing.

Worse than that, I had awakened that morning with a strange metallic tang in my mouth, as if I had bitten my cheek hard in the night and blood had pooled there while I slept. When the meaning of the missing organ dawned on me, I had run back upstairs and tried to force myself to vomit, but my stomach would not oblige, leaving me with a raw throat and trembling with horror as I clung to the cool ceramic of the kitchen sink, for there was only one rational explanation, however unwilling I was to contemplate it.

I took more laudanum to calm myself and vowed to be more vigilant. I would no longer take laudanum or even brandy before killing the dogs, no matter how much it eased the awfulness of what I was doing. The creature—my *infection*—was always lurking, just waiting to take control where it could, and I had been overconfident in my complacency. I could not allow it to happen again.

"What have you got there?" I asked, looking down at James, who was fiddling with a piece of rope as he wandered along beside us. I ruffled his hair slightly in an attempt at affection. Now that I carried what his father had, I thought I might love the boy more, but if anything, my resentment had grown, for his father brought this curse into our lives, and he was still my living memory of that.

"I'm doing a fisherman's knot," he said, and held it up for me to examine. "Mrs. Chard Williams showed me how."

"That looks quite tricky," I said. "Although I hope you are learning more than just knots."

"Yes, I am," he said proudly, swinging the knotted rope at his side. "Mr. Chard Williams says I will be ready to go to school in no time at all. He says I am a very fast learner."

"I am not surprised, for you are a very clever young man." I smiled at him. I could at least enjoy the pleasure our interaction gave Juliana. "And do you like going to your lessons?"

James nodded and said seriously, "It can be noisy sometimes. Mrs. Chard Williams likes looking after babies." He shrugged. "But we close the door, and then we don't hear them very much."

"Perhaps one day you shall have a baby brother or sister of your own. Would you like that?" I did not look at Juliana, but I was sure she would understand the subtext of my question. I was well now—aside from my ongoing new condition—and she appeared recovered from her grief and the ailments that had plagued her since her pregnancy. It was the perfect time for us to push our marriage plans forward.

James crinkled his nose and then smiled. "A brother. The girl babies cry louder."

Juliana laughed at this and leaned closer in on my arm, and my heart swelled. Why should I deny myself love when I had lived without for so long, simply because of this parasite? I would never hurt Juliana—I would die first. I knew that if she were my wife, if we were living together as a family, then there would be no lapses like that which had just occurred, for I would not allow myself to relax. I would keep them safe.

"Then we shall see what we can do about that," I said, proud of my forwardness.

James ran ahead to look at a barge passing on the river, and I seized my moment. I stopped and turned to look at Juliana. "Perhaps now is the time for us to make our engagement more formal," I suggested. "A spring wedding maybe?"

Her eyes darted downward. "I'm so very busy with the business," she started, and then she drew a deep breath. "I am not sure I would make you a very good wife, Thomas—"

"Nonsense," I said firmly. "I am very proud of you and all you are doing. I have no issue with your securing James's future." I laughed and assured her, "I am no old man who thinks women have nothing to contribute." I squeezed her arm. "Indeed, underneath this professional exterior I am quite forward-thinking."

"I know, Thomas," she said, and she started walking again, "and I am truly sorry for making you wait. I just want to be certain before I marry again."

My heart folded in on itself in a way I did not know was possible. If there was one thing in this world of which I was certain, it was my love for her, and I had hoped she felt the same. I suddenly felt every single one of the years between us.

"I understand," I said. The pain I was trying to hide must have been evident in my tone because she stopped walking and looked at me.

"Never doubt that I love you, Thomas. You have been the kindest, most wonderful friend to me. There is no man in my life like you, and there could never be. But everything is changing at the moment, and I feel like I need to take things one step at a time. Can you understand that?"

Her dark eyes were so full of worry that I just wanted to pull her close to me and keep her there forever. I was being selfish. I was forgetting how cautious she had become since Harrington's death.

"Of course I understand," I said. "And I will wait patiently. You know that."

She smiled and took my arm again and steered us back toward the house. The wind was getting sharper as the afternoon faded. It was time to get into the warm. I did not wish to be walking alongside when it became the night river, the slick black creature I fed from my secret deeds. Juliana did not belong with that river but with the daylight one, the benign Thames, the city's lifeblood. I had managed to separate the two, and I wanted to keep it that way.

"Are you seeing my father soon?" Juliana asked. "He hasn't visited us for a while—I had hoped he would come with you today."

Fortuitously, I had already arranged a dinner date with Charles Hebbert, and I assured her now, "I am looking forward to seeing him tomorrow. I am dining with him and Walter Andrews." I added, "I hear he has been working very hard." I kept the last sentence light, knowing that whatever her own concerns might be, Juliana would hate to think that we had all been discussing Charles's behavior and his heavy drinking behind his back.

"It's not like him, not to want to spend time with James and me," she murmured, her voice low, almost as if she was embarrassed to voice her fears. "I hope he does not disapprove of the amount of time I am spending at the business. Since you recovered, I feel as if I have hardly seen him. Perhaps that's my fault for being preoccupied."

"Nonsense. Your father is very proud of you." I squeezed her arm. "I shall find out if there is anything troubling him. Can you trust me with that?"

She smiled, and the worry lifted from her beautiful face. "I trust you with everything, Thomas. You should know that by now."

The wind no longer touched me. She loved me. I was sure of it. She *had* to love me.

30

The *Colonist*
October 14, 1897

ANOTHER "JACK THE RIPPER"

Paris, October 12

A man named Vacher has been arrested in Lyons in connections with a number of mysterious crimes. He has confessed that he murdered eight women under circumstances similar to the murders committed a few years back in Whitechapel, England, and attributed to "Jack the Ripper."

31

LONDON. NOVEMBER, 1897
DR. BOND

We dined at Charles Hebbert's. Perhaps it was my imagination, but as we sat at the table, even with the lights glowing brightly, it seemed as if the darkness that had filled the house before—when James Harrington had been living here—had once again returned. Shadows crept up the walls, bleeding darkness into the patterns, and although it was cold outside, the air felt stifled, as if no windows had been opened all summer. Even the fire barely crackled in the grate, as if it too felt the weight that hung over the room. Was this my fault? Had some part of what had infected Harrington and now had me in its grip touched Hebbert so badly that it lingered in his house?

He had not redecorated since Mary had died, and there was an emptiness in the building that no amount of forced laughter could fill. I had not realized the depth of his grief over the loss of his wife, instead trusting in his stoicism and his apparent return to good humor, but the house was haunted with echoes of her. They were far more visible now that this "other" bleakness was back.

I let the other two make most of the conversation as the housekeeper brought in various dishes of roast meats and vegetables, interjecting occasionally, but mainly watching Charles's behavior.

His hands were twitching in what had become almost a nervous tic, and he had refilled his wine glass twice before I had finished my first. His speech was too loud and too fast, almost manic, and I had to concede that if he was behaving like this around Henry Moore, the policeman had every right to be worried.

I sipped some more wine, and then at last we fell into a comfortable near silence as we ate. The food was delicious, and for once I found that I was ravenously hungry. It was only when Andrews put down his fork and knife and looked with surprise at both Charles and me that I paused.

"Have you two been out with the hunt today?" he asked quizzically. "I've never seen men eat so much so quickly." He laughed, clearly finding it entertaining, but only then did I realize that I had refilled my plate once already and was about to help myself to more. I had been eating in a daze, but my hunger felt bottomless. I thought of the dead dog and the missing liver and my stomach turned.

I laid down my own knife and fork and looked up at Charles, trying to ignore the gravy dripping down his chin. "It would appear the change in the weather has made us hungry," I said, trying to laugh it off. "And I must confess that I have not eaten yet today—perhaps that was not wise."

"Well, you're obviously completely recovered," Andrews said with a smile. "There's nothing wrong with a healthy appetite—but I foresee two rather portly gentlemen at this table in the future if you carry on in this manner!"

Both Hebbert and I laughed at that, and I resumed eating, more slowly this time, and I resisted the urge to consume much more, instead just finishing what was left on my plate and then declaring myself finally full. When Andrews excused himself for a moment, Charles took the opportunity to break the last chicken wing free and eat it with his hands.

I watched him in silence for a minute, then asked, "Are you well, Charles? I have not seen you much of late, and that saddens me. I owe you a great debt of gratitude for the care you showed me during my illness."

His eyes met mine—and then something shifted in his gaze and his expression became slightly vague and confused as he glanced toward my shoulder, as if he could almost see something there, but not quite. His mouth slackened and hung open, and for a moment I could see the half-chewed chicken on his tongue. He frowned slightly and then snapped his mouth shut around the bone and sucked the remaining meat from it hungrily.

For my part I was suddenly aware of a weight on my back that seeped in through my clothes like a dense chill and wrapped itself around my spine. When Charles's mouth had slackened, so mine tightened as I felt a surge of energy run through me. My back stiffened, and I was filled with a sense of malevolence that threatened to overwhelm me.

Had Harrington felt like this? He must have done—but at least I knew what was causing it, and that meant I had more chance of controlling the *infection*—for control it I must.

Andrews came back into the room, and the moment was suddenly over. The weight lifted, and Charles's eyes cleared of their haze. One thing had been proven, however. My old friend had some sort of gift for seeing things that others could not, and the creature on my back knew it. I had felt the delight in the cold wickedness that had gripped me, and I knew that the parasite reveled in Hebbert's partial awareness. The priest had been right: it took pleasure in taunting those around it.

We drank our brandies, and I longed for Andrews to leave, for he was outside of our bubble of bleakness. At last he did, and as we said our good nights, I envied him his pleasant retirement and peaceful mind.

"Shall we have a nightcap?" I asked when there was just Charles and I left. The stairs loomed dark and cavernous in the hall, and I was sure I saw a flicker of fear in his eyes, although he smiled and said that was a jolly idea. Was he even aware of this reaction he now had to me? Were there some moments more than others when he sensed the presence? I imagined that nights were worse than days; that was certainly the case for me. It was in the darkness that I would feel the first shivers of fever and know that I must feed the river again.

We went upstairs to his study, and I could feel the temperature drop as we climbed. Hebbert paused to turn up the lamps, though they spluttered and did little to shift the atmosphere of gloomy unease. The fire was set, and I lit it while he poured us both drinks and we took our usual seats on either side of the fireplace. Of all the rooms in the house, this felt the most lived-in. Books and papers were scattered across the desk, and a further pile sat on the table next to the cabinet of medical equipment.

"No need to drink it all at once," I said, with a smile, as Hebbert drained his glass. "I cannot keep up."

He sighed and stared down into his glass. "It is this or the laudanum. Sometimes both." With his humor gone, I could see how the years had settled into his face. The skin around his eyes hung in dark circles, and beneath his beard his cheeks were veined, and no longer as plump as they had been.

"What plagues you?" I asked. "Is it Juliana? Are you worried about her? She seems very well to me."

He shook his head, and something darted in the corner of my eye, and the weight on my back almost pushed me forward in my chair. I fought the urge to twist around suddenly in the hope of grasping it and tearing it from me; I knew that would not work. Instead, I gritted my teeth and reminded myself it was simply an infection, nothing more—certainly nothing that would drive me insane with its presence. But sitting here in the gloom with Charles Hebbert, that was somehow harder to believe, and it was my turn to take a long drink of my brandy.

"No, it is not Juliana," he said, wearily. "She is blooming after her loss at last. I think we can thank Mr. Kane for that."

His words were not meant as darts, but they stung all the same, for it was I who had looked after and loved Juliana for all these years, not the handsome American.

"Do you remember," he said, the reflected light of the fire dancing in the dullness of his eyes, "when I suffered those terrible dreams?"

His voice was low, the natural energy normally present vanished. "So unlike me. So vivid."

I nodded; we had sat in this very room when he had spoken of them before. I had been gripped by my insomnia and sense of dread, and he had appeared to me to be everything stable in the world. I had tried to reassure him they were nothing then; now, I had begun to suspect differently. Now, the cause of those dreadful dreams sat opposite him, just out of sight, clinging to my back.

"I have not felt right since your illness," he said. "The dreams have returned." He stared into the fire. "There is such wickedness in them, Thomas, such terrible deeds. I do not understand—they are so strong, so powerful, that the fear they cause in me lingers throughout the days. It is like it was back then again. Sometimes I feel as if I exist in a cloud of claustrophobic darkness. I am not even sure of my own mind some of the time—I find myself thinking things that cannot possibly be. Only the laudanum calms me."

"I have taken that path to ease my own anxiety at times," I admitted. "There is nothing wrong in it—"

"I just wish I were not afraid," he said. "Or that I knew what it was that terrifies me so."

A wave of sympathy for my friend rushed through me, and once again I wished that Harrington had died in Poland, for then we would all have been freed of this terrible curse. I did not blame myself for Charles's predicament—I did not even blame Harrington because he too was a victim, after all—but I still felt some strange guilt at Charles's suffering. For an overwhelming moment I wanted to tell him everything, to pour out the secret life I had lived in that dark year that followed the summer of Jack, to tell him my tales of river demons and possession, of death and darkness . . .

I did not of course. How could I? He would not have believed me. I had not believed the priest, after all, even though I had been suffering in the wake of the beast. I could never tell my story, not without appearing insane or admitting to what others would see as murder.

"Would you like another brandy?" I asked instead. I was the concerned friend, the steady influence. I was as I always appeared to the world.

"Yes," he answered. "Yes, please." I left him staring at the fire as I took his glass and went to his desk to refill it. The room was gloomy, and in an effort to raise my friend's spirits slightly—and in all honesty, my own—I turned the gas lamp above the glass cabinet up—and it was then that my eyes fell on the contents of the cabinet. On the top shelf, tucked behind various bottles, was an old mortar—a large, heavy vessel. After glancing at Hebbert to check that he was still preoccupied, I ducked slightly to peer behind it. A rack of old pestles rested against the wooden back, with numbers painted on them to denote their size. I looked at the middle. The number six was missing.

The weight on my back was suddenly forgotten as my head started swimming. Elizabeth Camp had been brutally beaten to death with a pestle marked with a six or a nine. It had been thrown onto the track after the terrible deed had been committed.

As I fought to keep my breath steady, I took a sip of my brandy. I recalled my own joke to the police at the time, that I used that railway line to visit Hebbert's daughter but that the pestle was not mine. It had not even occurred to me, not for one moment, that Charles Hebbert also had frequent cause to travel that way.

"I dread sleeping," Charles said softly, and with my heart racing in my chest, I turned to look his way, every nerve in my face straining to hold back any expression of horror so that I could feign calm normality. He was still staring into the fire, his face utter desolation. "I wish Mary were still alive."

"It will pass," I said, and my tone was steady. I had become so adept in disguising my own terrors that now it came almost naturally. "It did before, did it not?"

"That is true." He looked up at me. "You are a good friend, Thomas. I know I sound like a madman, that this is so out of my usual nature. I pride myself on my affability."

It was a strange phrase for him to use, I thought afterward when I had cajoled him into going to bed and I finally left the house. To pride oneself on something made it sound forced. Had he dark fantasies in his mind that he controlled in his daily life? Surely all men had secrets, lustful or otherwise, that they hid from the rest of the world. But what were Charles Hebbert's? And what could have driven him to beat poor Miss Camp to death on that train all those months before?

Trails of damp mist wrapped themselves around my ankles, deadening the sound of my boots on the pavement as I walked. In the chill air, my face burned. The sympathy I had felt for my friend still lingered, but the realization that my suspicions might be correct were making me nauseous. If Charles had killed Elizabeth Camp, then he was surely capable of other horrors. I moved from pool to pool of streetlight, but I barely noticed, for my thoughts were darker than the night around me, and no yellow gas glow could lighten them.

Whether he realized it or not, I now truly believed that Charles Hebbert had been Jack the Ripper. I wanted to believe that it was the presence of the *Upir*—the *infection*—that had brought the wickedness out in him, that he had not been entirely responsible for his actions. After all, the Ripper killings had stopped when Harrington had died, and it was only since I had become infected myself that Charles was reporting the return of his bad dreams. But the murder of Elizabeth Camp did not fit: she had been killed while the creature was locked up with Kosminski, miles away in Leavesden—so the question was, why? And why had it been such a vicious attack?

I would watch Charles Hebbert carefully—although what I would do if I discovered he was a murderer, I did not yet know. But I had a moral responsibility to follow my suspicions. I was no monster, and I would not condone such action in others, even in the wake of the mayhem created by the thing on my back.

It would also, I thought as I finally let myself into my own dark and empty home, provide a distraction from my own predicament.

Over the next two weeks I forced myself into Charles's company wherever possible, arranging days when I could be out with Juliana and little James and turn up unannounced at his house. Under the guise of returning the concern he had shown me while I was ill, I asked about his melancholy and dreams; in truth, I was trying to force his hand. If the priest's theory was right and the *Upir* drew out the wickedness in the city, then increased proximity to me should have the same effect on Hebbert that Harrington's presence had had. Because I was well again, I had been called into the police mortuaries on several occasions to undertake postmortems on men and women killed in apparently irrational fights, and I was now certain that these incidences were in part caused by the mayhem that spread out from the thing on my back. I distanced myself from responsibility, however: I could not bear any blame for I too was a victim, much the same as those who were unwitting carriers of typhus but did not themselves suffer: they could not be blamed for an outbreak should the disease be brought onto a battlefield.

My pursuit of Charles gave me emotional balance. I could do nothing about the effect the *Upir* might have on the city unless I left London, and that would have meant leaving Juliana, which I could not have borne. But if I could uncover Hebbert as a killer and prevent more deaths, then I would be at least doing some good from this purgatory in which I found myself.

I started following Hebbert whenever my own schedule allowed, and just as Kane had thought, he had been going to his club often and leaving late at night and much the worse for drink. Then one night I watched him come out of his club and take a hansom cab to Whitechapel. With me not far behind him, he weaved his way drunkenly through the louder streets, though with no apparent purpose. This happened again and again. Although I made sure to keep my distance as I trailed behind him through those vice-ridden streets, I began to realize that I could probably have come face-to-face with him and he would not have seen me. Aside from his drunkenness, there was something confused in his manner on these increasingly frequent late-night walks. He would stop at a street corner and look around him as if puzzled to find himself there, then pick a new direction and set off again until eventually some subconscious decision was made to find a hansom cab to take him home.

The nights grew bitter over those few weeks as winter gripped London. The stench of burning coal filled the air, and smoke once again covered London in a gloomy smog where buildings loomed out of nowhere as you walked and footsteps were all you knew of the ghostly passers-by who flitted quickly in and out of sight around you. It became a city of isolation, and when the last streaks of daylight had faded, the East End alleyways, far away from the light and noise of the Commercial Road, exemplified London at her darkest, and it seemed to me that the Thames flowed like the Styx, dark and deadly, through the heart of hell.

With every visit to Whitechapel, Charles Hebbert stayed a little longer, and his feet strayed toward the run-down taverns and the crowded doorways where gin-soaked women, far from the bloom of their youth, leered at the passing men, cat-calling the offer of their delights. They might have fondly hoped their manner was flirtatious, but to me it sounded like nothing more than weary desperation. Each time Hebbert paused and glanced their way, my heart would race and I would forget the bite of cold in my lungs. He would eventually turn and leave, and in those moments, despite the death of Elizabeth Camp, I felt overwhelming sympathy for my friend and colleague. Was he fighting an urge as I did each time I cut into another poor dead dog? Did his mouth water slightly? He had no cellar in which to contain the horrors that consumed him; I did not know if he was even aware of them. At least I had knowledge to fight my demon, to fight to retain my humanity.

By now I was beginning once again to doubt my suspicions of Hebbert, even with the evidence of Elizabeth Camp's murder—surely many medical men used the same set of pestles and mortars, after all?—and in truth, I was wearying of my nightly vigils. This night, when Hebbert had neither attended his club nor left his house, I was ready to leave the freezing shadows from where I had been watching and go home. I was not quite myself, having abstained from killing any more dogs for the last few days in the hope that the more I starved the parasite, the more Hebbert would feel its effects and be drawn out by them. Then I would be able to capture him— before he committed a terrible deed, but after I had seen enough to convince myself once and for all of his guilt.

My skin burned slightly with the start of a fever, my lungs felt full of liquid, and I had developed a racking cough. I needed my own warm bed. I was about to turn away when the front door opened and Hebbert emerged, wrapped in a dark coat. Even though his face was mostly hidden by his top hat, as he passed under the streetlamp, I caught a glimpse of his expression, and I could clearly see something had changed. On his previous outings he had looked almost confused; now he was focused. His eyes glared darkly ahead, and he moved with dread purpose. As my heart raced, my tiredness vanished. After letting him get a little way ahead, I fell into step and followed him as he strode to the main road to flag down a hansom cab.

He did not go to his club but got the driver to drop him on the Whitechapel Road. Then he strolled along the street, turning this way and that, until he had made his way into the maze of narrow backstreets. The light and noise that spilled from the pubs on most corners only emphasized the threatening darkness that surrounded them. I stayed behind Hebbert, doing my best to keep my tread soft, for I had to stay close to keep him in sight through the rank fog that sank between the buildings and consumed even the cobbles beneath my feet.

After ten minutes or so he went into a public house from which music and raucous laughter spilled out onto the pavement, together with several of its clientele. I hung back for a few moments, watching through the window until I saw him order a drink and take a place toward the far side of the room, and then I went in myself. It was hot inside, a damp heat caused as much by the bodies that crowded the place as by the roaring fire, but I kept my cheap coat collar up and the battered bowler hat I had invested in tugged down almost over my eyebrows. I hunched my shoulders and changed my gait and made my way to the other side of the worn bar from where Hebbert stood. The barman brought me a small glass of beer, and after I had paid him, I settled back against the wall and watched.

I needn't have worried about Charles spotting me. All his attention was focused on the drunken men and women who filled the room. Several of the women, sweaty and much the worse for wear, were attempting to ply their trade, trying to lure men into the alley outside in exchange for a few pennies; some were doing better than others. One woman, however, was rejected at every table with such disdain that I wondered if she was at the point in her career where she would have to give away her services to find a customer who would take her.

She was not young—even if time had been less cruel to her I would have placed her at thirty-five or more—but with the jaundiced yellow of her sagging skin and several teeth missing, she could as well have been fifty or more. Her attempts to make up her face were now smears down her cheeks, rendering her eerily clown-like as she weaved unsteadily between the men who so cruelly brushed her off.

"Go 'ome, Annie," the barman called out. "You're putting the customers off their beer!"

There was a round of laughter, and though the woman shouted something back, it was lost in the noise. She pulled her shawl around her, covering up her drooping breasts that had been threatening to escape the loose ties of her bodice, and she stumbled toward the door. Hebbert watched her like a hawk. After a moment or two he put down his glass and slipped through the side door.

Not wishing to draw too much attention to myself, I exited the way I had come in and moved quickly round the corner, where I hoped to see Hebbert not far ahead. My heart sank as I was presented with a crossroads. I ran forward and peered both left and right, but with the noise of the pub so close by, their footsteps were lost to my straining ears. My heart raced. I *had* to find them. I was now sure that Hebbert meant the woman harm, and I had to catch him in the act but in time to still save her. What I would do after that I did not know, but at least this wretched Annie was so drunk no one would listen to her story. I doubted she would remember any details clearly enough, even if someone did.

I took a deep breath and turned to the right on instinct, my feet carrying me quickly into the darkness. The road narrowed, the slum houses on either side almost leaning in to touch each other, and here and there a black mouth of an alleyway loomed up out of the fog. Where had she gone? And where was Hebbert? I paused and looked around me, feeling lost in an awful maze, and then I heard something: a drunken giggle, a few slurred words, coming from somewhere down a tiny road on my left.

I followed the noise, barely able to see a foot in front of me. The fog deadened the darkness and made it a solid entity. I could hear them ahead now, the shuffle of shoes and the rustle of clothing, and a gruff voice that sounded so unlike the urbane Charles Hebbert I had spent so many convivial evenings with. As I moved more quickly, certain I should have been upon them by now, I could not help but wonder if it was the parasite that was aiding my hearing, if I was somehow attuned to its supernatural powers now that I was so close to a potential murder.

She laughed again, and then I saw, only a few feet ahead of me, a glint of steel in the night and the cream of exposed flesh.

"Charles!" I called out, grabbing at the shroud of his coat. "Charles, no!"

But I was too late. Her laugh caught in a gasp, and then there was a short shriek that was over before it started. As Charles Hebbert stared at me, bewildered, she slid down the wall behind him, her eyes open wide in shock, one hand flailing toward the cut on her neck.

"Thomas?" Hebbert said. "What are you doing here?" He dropped the knife as if he had forgotten he was holding it, and the intensity of his expression faded away, leaving only the face I knew—I thought I knew—so well: open, friendly, generous Charles Hebbert.

"Get her shawl," I growled, crouching beside the poor woman whose head lolled sideways. The cut was bad, and blood pumped from the slash, but she was still alive. I doubted we could save her, but still I had to try. As Charles shakily handed me the tatty material, I wrapped it as tightly around her neck as I could without strangling her. She murmured and muttered as I carefully pulled her up.

"Take the other side," I snapped. Hebbert stood before me like a chastened child who had been caught stealing apples, awkward and ashamed.

"Thomas, I—"

"We can talk later. First we must find a hansom cab—we'll take her to my house, but we need to hurry."

The three of us stumbled forward, the woman still mumbling as she drifted toward unconsciousness, and I could imagine her warm blood seeping into my dark jacket, invisible in the night. Hebbert ran ahead and hailed a cab, and we pushed the woman inside, seating her between us. I forced Hebbert into a jovial and lewd conversation, as much as the very thought disgusted me, so we looked like nothing more than two gents who were taking away a drunken unfortunate for a night of depraved pleasure. I kept my glove gripped firmly over the wound as I continued our charade. On the other side of her, Charles Hebbert looked as if he might cry as he forced himself to laugh along with me. My skin itched, and I thought of red eyes and a slick black tongue winding round my neck to try and reach this dying woman's blood. I fought back a fit of coughing, barely breathing through my nose, all the while willing the horse to trot faster before our façade fell apart and the cab seats were slick with blood.

We called the driver to a halt close by my house but not outside it, and as Hebbert distracted the cabbie with payment and small talk, I made a pretense of flirtation with the dead weight of woman I could barely keep upright.

"I wouldn't give 'er any more to drink," the cabbie said to Hebbert, "not if you want your money's worth." He laughed at that, and Hebbert joined in. The sound made me shiver. The jovial laugh I had known for years was now a stranger's laugh.

We maintained our awful pretense at merriment until the front door had closed behind us.

"The kitchen," I said. The woman was still breathing, but her skin was deathly pale. "Then go upstairs and get my medical bag." Charles looked at me for a moment, still dazed. "Go!"

"Thomas," he started, and then thought better of whatever he was going to say and ran to the stairs. I was glad. We had plenty to talk about, but it had to wait.

I heaved her onto the table and then pulled off my sweaty, blood-soaked coat and threw it to the floor before carefully unwrapping the crimson shawl and peeling it away from the wound. The dirty material clung stickily to the loose skin on her neck at the edges of the gash, and once I had forced it away, I could see the damage clearly. I had known the chances were slim, but I doubted very much that there was anything left we could do to save her. Although he had missed the carotid artery, the cut was three inches wide and deep. Her clothes were soaked in her lost blood.

She gargled, trying to speak, and I leaned over her. "I am a doctor," I said, stroking her hair out of her face. "I am going to take care of you."

It took her a moment to focus on me, and then her eyes widened slightly, her gaze shifting to my shoulder. Claws scrabbled at my back, and I twisted around, instinctively trying to shake whatever it was away. But I could not. The weight of the thing that clung to me could not be shaken off.

On the table the woman tried to scream with the last of her breath, but a wet rattle was all she managed. I was filled with darkness, and tendrils of something thick, wet and rank slid up my neck and wrapped around my head confusing my thoughts and forcing me to look her way again.

Her eyes shone in terror, and as she gasped her last breath, I saw in their reflection the *Upir*, moving jerkily up over my shoulders, its terrible mouth open hungrily, its eyes two tiny pinpricks of soulless red. The air stank of the river and of all the things that had ever rotted in it.

"Thomas."

I jumped and turned, for a moment with no sense of who I was or who the plump, awkward-looking older man in front of me was. He was holding out my medical bag.

"I have your bag," he said. Suddenly the weight shifted and the air cleared of the stench, and I trembled, my face flushing as I panted, desperate to regain my composure. For those few minutes the *Upir*—I could not consider it a simple infection, not in that moment—and I had been one, and I had felt its hunger and wicked delight and the ages of all the years it had existed. I was seeing through my eyes and Harrington's and all who had gone before us. It was overwhelming and terrifying and enticing all at once.

I fought the urge to vomit. My hands were cold and clammy.

"Thomas?" Hebbert said again. He looked afraid of me, and that almost made me laugh out loud. What had become of us? What *would* become of us?

"It's too late." I pulled a chair out and sank down into it, exhausted. I nodded toward another. "There is a bottle of wine in that cupboard. Fetch it and sit."

He did as he was told, a biddable servant. In any ordinary situation, I would have found his behavior disturbing—the switch from violence to such passivity—but this was no ordinary situation. We were both locked in something beyond our obvious control.

"Thomas . . ." His hand shook, the wine threatening to spill over the edge of his glass. "I wish I could explain. I don't know what has happened to me—what happened to me before. I had *hoped*—no, I had *prayed* for it all to be nothing more than dreams . . . nightmares."

"It was you, wasn't it?" I asked. There was no need for elaboration, for the use of the name. He knew whom I meant.

Tears rolled from his eyes and ran down his blotchy cheeks. "I do believe it must have been—but I cannot explain it; truly I cannot." His eyes met mine, desperate for some kind of understanding. I said nothing but sipped my wine, and I let my blood settle back down while my mind freed itself from the image of the thing I had seen in the dead woman's eyes. There was no need for me to ask a question of him, for he had started speaking, and it was my experience that when a man began to bare his soul, he rarely stopped until he was free of his burdens.

"When I was young—very young—I sometimes . . . I had thoughts. *Urges.*" Shame hung heavy in his stilted words. "Ones that I would never act on, Thomas, I promise you that: they *disgusted* me. But they were violent and angry. It was a lust, that is really the only way I can describe it: a terrible lust to hurt—no, not just to hurt, but to *terrify* women. To have power over them. I knew I could never give in to those lusts—I *would not*. I would not be that man. I met Mary, and we married, and I swear by all I believe to be good and holy that I never raised so much as a finger against her, nor against Juliana. I loved them both very much—Juliana is the world to me, you know that. That *other* part of me, well, I locked it so far down inside me that I had almost forgotten it existed. And then somehow, back in that terrible summer, the box opened."

He leaned across the table, his voice suddenly urgent. "I was not myself. There was no intent in my actions—you must believe me. Even as the—the *events* were occurring, it was as if I were in a dream—a nightmare. There were spaces in my memory that I could not reach, or that I would not allow myself to reach. I convinced myself the things I saw were simply that, bad dreams, and I tried to drown them with drink. But all the time I was terrified that there was something more to them." He shrugged, helplessly. "And then Harrington died, and I was so worried about Juliana and her pregnancy that the nightmares simply stopped and I was myself again. You cannot understand the relief I felt. Until these past two months or so when they returned."

He paused to drink. "Perhaps I should just throw myself in the Thames and be done with it, Thomas. I cannot bring the shame of a trial on Juliana. She has suffered enough. She could not bear—"

"I am not going to tell Henry," I said, cutting him off. "We will find another way."

He stared at me as if I were crazy. "But . . . I don't—"

"Why did you kill Elizabeth Camp?" I cut him off. "I know it was you, Charles. The pestle that killed her matches the one missing from the set in your study. Did she know something? Did she recognize you?"

He trembled visibly then. "No," he said softly, "she did not know me. But when I saw her one day while I was on the train to see Juliana, I recognized her. It was like being thrown into freezing water. I watched where she alighted and I followed her. I watched her return. Once I knew that this was probably a regular visit to her family, I knew when I could strike. I just needed to wait for her to be alone in a carriage. One day she was. And then it was done." His eyes darkened with the memory of the deed.

"You knew her from one of those times in Whitechapel?" I avoided using the word "killings." Charles's mind was on the edge of broken, and with the wrecked body on the table in front of us, there was no need to say more.

"Yes." He could barely whisper the word.

"And you thought she might implicate you, all these years afterward?"

"No." He shook his head and more tears came. "No, it was not that."

"Then what? What could possibly have made you carry out such an attack?"

He stared at me for a long moment, two mad men locked in a world of insanity. Finally, he sighed, a terrible empty sound, as if releasing the last of his damned soul into the dark.

"She made me remember." He gazed into my eyes. "I could not bear to remember." Neither of us spoke, the clock ticking the minutes of the night away.

"What am I to do, Thomas?" he said, eventually.

I already knew the answer. He could not stay in this city—not while the *Upir* was here. I would have no more deaths on my hands, nor would I be faced every day with my complicity in his evasion of justice.

"You must leave, Charles—go abroad. Australia or America, somewhere far from here." I was tired, and my heart was heavy. We had all been cursed in some way or another, and perhaps this time

I was partially to blame. My curiosity had driven me to Kosminski, and that had been not only my downfall but Charles's too, and tonight it had cost an innocent woman her life. "Have Christmas with your family, but then you must go. You will feel better out of London, I promise you."

"Leave Juliana? And little James?"

I said nothing more, for there was little fight left in him. I could not hate him. He had been my friend for many years, and there were none who could loathe Charles Hebbert more than he must be loathing himself.

"I shall," he said. "I shall start my preparations tomorrow." His eyes finally fell to the corpse he had been so studiously avoiding.

"What will we do about—?"

"I will take care of her. And now you should go home. Sleep tonight, and then start your travel plans. And you must try and maintain a normal façade. Blame your desire to leave on exhaustion, or a wish to travel now that Juliana is settled, before you are too old."

He said, "Thank you, Thomas."

I did not want his thanks. I did not want him in my sight, nor this woman before me.

He washed his hands and face, and then, with his shoulders still bowed, he finally left.

I did the only thing I could do. First I drank some laudanum to steady my nerves, and then I picked up the woman and dragged her down to the cellar. The weight scratched urgently on my back, and once again I felt the cold tightening around my head and a terrible hunger overwhelmed me.

God help me, I gave in to it. I was too tired to do otherwise.

In the morning, when I went back down to the cellar to parcel up the dissected remains, I tried not think about the parts of the woman that were missing—the pieces I had vague recollections of slicing off with a demented glee and cramming, bleeding and fatty, into my eager mouth. I kept the room in virtual darkness as I wrapped each part in paper and sacking cloth, pausing now and then and sobbing aloud at what I had done—at what some part of me had *enjoyed* doing. I would not feed the river with this one, however; the *Upir* would not have that. I would wait until nightfall and bury her in the patch of unused earth at the back of my garden, hidden from sight by an overhanging tree. If her body was found and Hebbert or I were called in to examine her, I feared I would go truly insane.

Despite my awful horror, I could not deny the energy that filled me once I returned upstairs and my house was scrubbed clean of blood. I felt revitalized, and I fell suddenly into a wildly good humor that was entirely at odds with the events of the previous night. I loathed myself for it, for I knew what it meant: I had not killed the woman myself, but I had allowed the *Upir* to feed from her. I had taken one step toward becoming the monster I had vowed not to, one step nearer to allowing the parasite into me, and God help me, enjoying it.

That night, when my labors in the garden were done and my aging body ached in every muscle, I found a hansom cab and wearily made my way to Bluegate Fields and the respite of the poppy. I needed to forget. I needed to find myself again: Dr. Thomas Bond, police surgeon and respected member of society. I would not let the *Upir* win. I would not.

32

LONDON. CHRISTMAS DAY, 1897
EDWARD KANE

Edward Kane had returned in good humor, eager to see not only Juliana and James but the rest of the friends he had made in London, including his erstwhile rival, Thomas Bond. It seemed, however, as he sipped his brandy and observed the room, that the world he had left behind while in New York had slid slightly off-kilter while he had been away. It was clearer than ever on Christmas Day, only a week after his return.

Juliana had yet to tell Dr. Bond that she was no longer interested in his marriage proposal, but that didn't bother Kane—he understood that it would be better when he was here too, rather than looking as if he had run back to America and left her to break the old man's heart alone. Now that the game was won, he felt a little bad about it. Bond was not himself, although he declared he was perfectly well. There was something distant about his manner, and over dinner, as they all feigned merriment, Kane wondered if perhaps Charles Hebbert and Bond, old friends that they were, had had some sort of falling out. They were as polite as ever, but their eyes slid over each other's, and there was none of the easy camaraderie that had been between them before, the result of years of friendship. They spoke to each other through Walter Andrews, rather than directly, and then when the conversation shifted, one or the other would turn his attention to Juliana or James rather than talk to each other.

Little James too seemed despondent. He had been excited to see his American "uncle," but his small brow furrowed when he was left alone, and even the abundance of toys he had been given—Thomas Bond was apparently determined to win Juliana's heart through becoming more affectionate and generous with the boy—only lifted his quiet mood for an hour or so, after which he would return to playing with a piece of rope and tying knots around one of his toy soldiers. Juliana was doing her best to provide a cheery façade, though Edward knew that she wasn't happy about her father's sudden travel plans, and it felt like only he and Andrews had approached the day in a seasonal good mood. Now he was struggling to maintain it in the oppressive atmosphere that hung over the brightly decorated house.

"You'll miss Charles when he leaves, I imagine, Thomas," he said, leaning back in his chair and allowing the big meal to settle in his stomach. "You two have had a lot of adventures together."

"I shall," Bond said, sipping his brandy, "but a man must follow his heart, and there is a lot of world beyond London. As time ticks on, we all have unfulfilled dreams to chase." He glanced at Hebbert. "When does your ship leave? It must be soon, surely?"

"Two weeks, Thomas." Charles Hebbert smiled, but it wasn't the open jovial expression Edward had come to know. "And then I shall be gone."

"If it's an unfulfilled dream, then you never mentioned it to Mother or me," Juliana said. "It sounds more like an old man's folly to me." She had drunk more wine than was usual, and her words had a bite in them—bite caused by hurt, but a bite all the same.

"Oh, your father has mentioned a wish to travel many times over the years. To me at least," Bond cut in, patting her hand. "You should be happy for his new start. After all, you have the business and James and me—" His eyes darted in Edward's direction, and there was more than a touch of wariness in them, but he covered it with a gentle smile. "We will always be here for you. Isn't that right, James?" He ruffled the boy's hair and the child nodded.

"You can go and play, James," Juliana said softly. "And then we shall sing some carols."

"Our new world has become smaller, my dear," Hebbert said. "I can send you telegrams and letters, and perhaps you can all come visit me when I am settled. It's not an unfeasible idea. I have become tired of London, and I fear it is becoming no good for my health."

She smiled at that, never liking an argument, but her lip trembled slightly, and Kane could see she was fighting back tears.

Walter Andrews looked awkward, and Kane leaned in toward him. "I think a smoke in the fresh air might help my digestion. What do you say to joining me?"

"I most certainly shall." His relief was almost visible, and he followed Kane to the garden, where they stood in the freezing cold of the dark afternoon, the blaze of their matches and the escaping light from the house highlighting the frost that had lingered on the grass since that morning. Kane glanced back through the window. It all looked much more festive from the outside than it felt on the inside. He wondered if Juliana would allow him to stay tonight and take her passionate rage out on his body, or whether she would insist on his return to the hotel and the pretense of respectability.

"May I ask you a personal question?" Andrews said once his pipe was lit.

"Certainly."

"I cannot help but notice the affection between Juliana and yourself. I can also see that you are both trying to hide it—or perhaps fight it, I shan't ask which—but I wondered if your intent was to marry her?"

"You have sharp eyes, Walter," Kane said. "No wonder you did so well as a detective."

"I have an eye for the smaller details, I must admit." He breathed out scented smoke. "As does Thomas Bond. In fact, if I were to be honest, I would say his is better than mine. If I have seen the looks between the two of you, then I imagine he has too."

"I know Thomas loves her," Edward said. "He has been very good to her and James." Was Andrews trying to warn him off? He drew in heavily on his cigarette. "And I have a great deal of respect for him. He is a good man. But yes, I do hope to marry her myself. I believe she loves me."

"I believe she does too," Andrews said. "Will she tell Thomas soon? He is a dear friend, and he has loved her for a very long time. I fear I have encouraged him to do so in the past, and on reflection that was perhaps not wise."

"We were planning to tell him after Charles has left and he's adjusted to that. If you could not mention it to him, I'd be grateful. I'm sure you think less of me now, but . . ."

Andrews waved a hand in the air. "Thomas is my friend, but we are getting old, and you and Juliana are both still young. Your company has brought her back to life; any fool can see that, detective's eyes or not. And you love each other. I can only be happy about that. But it is sad that your happiness will cause hurt to Thomas."

"I hope Juliana doesn't lose his friendship. She does love him, you know."

"He is not that kind of man; she need not worry on that score. But I ask only one thing of you."

"And what is that?"

"Let me know when you are going to tell him. With Charles gone, I think he will need my friendship then. Losing love when you are young and have years ahead of you to find another is one thing. But as we get older, such things are like water through our fingers."

"I will. I promise." Kane's heart thumped with relief, and he slapped Andrews on the shoulder. "Thank you for your understanding."

They turned back toward the house. "I suppose we ought to go back in," Andrews said, with a lack of enthusiasm. "Although I shall be glad when this strange Christmas is done."

"Perhaps the carols and parlor games will bring back our cheer," Edward said with a smile.

"Perhaps," Andrews agreed, but it was clear that neither of them was convinced.

PART TWO

33

The *Woolwich Herald*
August 18, 1899

Young married couple would adopt healthy baby. Very small premium. Write first to Mrs. M. Hewetson, 4, Bradmore Lane, Hammersmith.

34

LEAVESDEN. JANUARY, 1898
AARON KOSMINSKI

Assessment

The patient's condition continues to improve, despite the return of his waking nightmares as reported in his file from Colney Hatch. He is still wary of physical contact and remains unwilling to wash himself or be washed. He has, however, ceased attempts at self-harm, and he is compliant with instructions. He still refuses social activity with the other patients and repeats often that he does not wish Dr. Thomas Bond to be permitted to visit him again. When questioned on this subject, he becomes agitated and distressed. It is my recommendation that in the interest of the patient, further visits from any persons other than immediate family should be denied until he has made further progress.

35

LONDON. FEBRUARY, 1898
HENRY MOORE

"Three serious crimes on London railways in as many days," Henry Moore said. "One damned idiot tried to blow himself up yesterday. Burned the carriage down. And over a woman. I tell you, Thomas, the busier the trains get, the better policing they need. At least this poor bastard's death was just misadventure. But to get drunk and then go and lie on a railway track? Well, I can think of better ways to end my days if I were so inclined."

"Thankfully, I doubt you are that kind of man," Bond said. His eyes darted this way and that, seeking out a hansom cab, which was unusual, for they normally talked for a while on days when work led to their being together.

The inquest had not taken long, and Dr. Bond had given his evidence with his usual professionalism, but now that they were outside and back on the busy streets, Henry Moore could see that the man was distracted. More than that, he looked visibly upset.

"Is all well, Thomas?" Moore asked.

"Yes," Bond murmured. His skin was pale, but there were blotches of red high up on his cheeks that Moore had first thought to be just an effect of the bitter weather. Now that they were standing close together, he realized his friend looked almost feverish. "I just have a slight chill."

Moore studied him. It was bad enough that they had lost the services of Charles Hebbert, but if Bond were to become ill and unreliable, that would be a blow to all the divisions. For a moment, his soul felt heavy. They were none of them getting any younger, and even he was feeling the need for something different. Perhaps a move to the Railway police wouldn't be such a bad idea. It might renew his energy.

"And I received some upsetting personal news this morning," Bond blurted in an unusual rush of words. "I shall be fine once I am at home."

"Is it anything I can help with?" Bond did not, as far as Moore knew, have a vast social circle.

"No, I'm afraid not." He paused and forced a smile. "But it is not a matter of life and death, and I am sure all will be well again soon enough. It was just something of a shock." He sighed. "There is no fool like an old fool."

"And you are no fool," Moore said. Suddenly the cause of Bond's distress was clear to him: a woman, no doubt. Perhaps it was Hebbert's daughter; Bond had always been fond of her. Most of men's follies were caused by women, and he was sure it was the same in reverse. The morgues and police stations were full of men and women who had been drawn to their fates by a love turned sour. Still, it came as a surprise. He had never considered the surgeon to be a romantic man, or if he once had been, he had presumed those days were long done—but perhaps it was true that every man sought a companion against the loneliness. He sniffed hard, his nose running in the cold. Damn these doctors and the misery that seemed to infect them.

"We should meet more often," he said. "I sometimes miss intelligent dining company." He smiled and slapped Bond's shoulder. "You've met some of the men I work with."

"Yes, yes, we should," Bond answered, as a hansom cab came to a halt in front of him. "When I am better, we must."

Moore watched until the hansom cab had disappeared, and he was happy to feel the wave of maudlin thoughts that were so at odds with his pragmatic personality disappear with it. He was left with a more practical consideration, however. Maybe it was time to look for another police surgeon to be his first port of call. In his mind Thomas Bond was by far the best, but he was no longer young, and perhaps having less death around him would help his current decline. He'd speak to Andrews. Maybe he could keep an eye on him.

36

LONDON. FEBRUARY, 1898
DR. BOND

It was a relief to be home and close the front door behind me. I had barely concentrated at the inquest, for Juliana's words were still ringing loudly in my head, and I had been in no mood for idle chatter with Henry Moore.

"I have something to tell you, Thomas—but before I do, please remember that I do care for you, very deeply. But I cannot marry you. I am in love with Edward."

Care for. Those two words had been daggers into my heart. There was pity in them: pity for the old man who had hoped and dreamed of looking after her, of making her happy. I had thought that once Charles had left, she would be more inclined to push our wedding forward, but instead, all this time she had been falling in love with another man and pitying me for still clinging to my hopes.

Though it was early in the day, I went straight to my study and drank both laudanum and brandy because I wished for the awful pain in my stomach to vanish. My whole body was trembling at the memory, which refused to leave my mind. She had arrived early that morning as I was preparing to leave for the inquest, and I had been happy to see her. The first hints of a fresh fever had come on me in the night, filling me with despair, and her goodness and beauty were a rare tonic—they gave me the strength to keep control of the nightmare in which I was living. *She* gave me the strength.

I had known immediately that something was wrong: she could not meet my eyes and paced in the hallway, clutching her bag. I tried to ask her if all was well with James, but she hushed me and said she had something to tell me and that she needed to say it straight away. And then she did. In all honesty, I cannot remember what I said in response. I muttered something about the inquest and that I had to go, and as I hurried her back out into the street, her eyes were so full of concern for me that it made everything worse. Every time I closed my eyes, I could see her expression, and it made my stomach churn. To be rejected was one thing, but to be *pitied*? I could not bear it. I momentarily wished I had left London in place of Charles Hebbert, but even in my grief at her loss, the thought of never seeing her again was too much to bear. In London she was still here, and I knew her well enough to know she would continue to want my friendship. I also knew that like the old fool I was, I would give it to her.

I lit the fire, poured another drink, and stared out through the window. The world sat in a gray mist so damp that I could see water clinging to the leaves of the trees outside. I thought of the poor woman buried in pieces beyond those overhanging branches, and I felt the unnatural heat flood through my veins. Did the *Upir* have a stronger grip when my emotions were unleashed? I certainly felt physically worse than I had when I woke up.

It was all Edward Kane's fault. If he had not arrived, then I was sure that Juliana and I would have been married by now and living happily together, either here or at her house in Barnes. Without Kane, there would have been no reminders of James Harrington and all that I had done in those years, and even with Moore's discovery of the priest's letter to me, I might not have gone to see Kosminski. Hebbert would still be here, and I would be ignorant of his crimes. I ached for ignorance and a return to innocence.

My anger toward the handsome American raged, and with my eyes still focused on that contaminated patch of ground at the far end of the garden, I found myself filled with a sudden and aggressive urge to destroy him, to murder him and chop him up into such small pieces that even if I left them in a pile outside Henry Moore's own house, no one would ever be able to put him back together and identify him.

I trembled with self-loathing and drained the brandy, enjoying the warmth that rushed at once to my stomach and my head. I knew that much of the violence of my thoughts came from the parasite attached to me, but I would not allow it even those moments. It would not want me to kill Edward Kane to feed its hunger—the *Upir* just wanted women, the creators of life, for its sustenance— but it would take delight from it, from my downfall. It wanted to break me, I could feel it. In my dreams, when I had not passed out from the laudanum or drink, I wrestled with it, just as the priest had when he pulled it from Harrington's back. Its red eyes, so full of ancient horrors, were always shining in glee. These were not just dreams, I knew that. I was in a battle for my very soul.

I thought again of Edward Kane, and this time I just felt tired and old. My bitterness at his success with the woman I loved was as much because on some level I had expected it but had chosen not to see. Of course Juliana would prefer him to me: he was the right age for her, he was wealthy and charming, and more than anything he had no links to the tragedies of her past. Edward Kane was a good man. To kill him out of jealousy would both make me monstrous and destroy Juliana's happiness. I wished for neither to occur.

My eyes itched, and I went down to the kitchen and made a small meal I had no desire to eat. If I was to keep the fever at bay, I needed to keep up my strength. Once that was done, I wandered the house restlessly, the twisting knots of heartache in my guts not allowing me to settle with a book. I paused as I caught sight of myself in the hall mirror. I was aging fast. My mustache, although still thick, was filling with white, and the skin was beginning to hang loose at my neck. I twisted my shoulders around this way and that, but I could see no sign of the demon on my back, and its very invisibility paired with my knowledge that it was there made me shudder. I wanted to sob. I was alone with my madness, no longer having even the hope of Juliana at my side in my retirement to buoy my flagging spirits. Unless I could find a way to force the *Upir* to leave me, this was to be my life for the rest of my years: an unholy marriage until death do we part.

I laughed out loud at that, and the sound, ringing around my empty house, unnerved me. I needed oblivion. I needed to let my mind separate from the horror attached to my body for a few hours. I needed to go to Bluegate Fields. I did not care that it was not yet night. The dens were open at all hours, and where once my craving for opium to see me through my sleepless nights had been my most shameful secret, I was now far past that.

I did not even bother to change my clothes but instead, just grabbed my hat and coat and left. What did it matter if anyone saw me? What was the worst that could happen? I would lose the respect of my peers? In some ways I wished for it.

Of course I encountered no one I knew as I alighted in the East End and made my way down the alleyways to find a suitable establishment for a few hours of oblivion. No heads turned as I took my place in a corner of the stinking room and waited for the ancient Oriental to bring my pipe and a hope at peace. In the dens we were all equals, and even those who might murder you for a sideways glance when outside were safe company here, in the grim environment of the overcrowded tenements. Each man was lost in his own reverie, the transient sailors, the lascars, and the lost souls like me. Chi-Chi scurried over to me on his soft-soled slippers, making barely a sound as he moved, and he did not meet my eyes as he prepared the bowl of the pipe. I remembered the man from years before; he had sold me the stranger opium in order for me to see the *Upir* as the priest directed. I wondered if perhaps these men from such faraway lands could *see* more than we did. One day I might pluck up the courage to take that drug again and get a full sight of what was attached to me, but I feared it would drive me truly insane. It was enough to constantly feel its weight and catch the slippery darkness in the corner of my eye.

Juliana's words had weakened me, and all I wished for was a hazy oblivion. I would think not of her or the *Upir* but of happier times gone by. My dreams would be of the joys of my youth and my first love. I took off my hat and greedily sucked in the heady, sweet smoke, and then lay down on the thin mattress and let the stained and chipped ceiling become a doorway to better things.

It was several hours later when I emerged, and the city was in the grip of night, if not of sleep. Although the immediate and debilitating effects of the drug had faded, my head felt thick, and I moved through the streets as if the smog were truly an ocean I had to wade through, and the lights and noises around me were strange creatures that lived in its depths. I staggered toward the main streets in order to find a hansom cab to take me to the sanctuary of my home, away from the too vivid life that surrounded me. I kept my head down, and occasionally I held a hand out on the damp brick wall to steady myself. I no longer felt the elation of my opium dreams; they were now just vague tastes of memory. But at least I felt numb, Juliana and the *Upir* simply abstract problems to be faced again the next day.

"All right, sir?" She came out of the gloom, a mess of tumbling hair and a gait as unsteady as my own. "A gent like you shouldn't be out here alone at night. Not unless you're lookin' for some company? Are ya?"

She leered at me, her mouth widening unnaturally with my altered vision. Every reeking inch of her seemed to consume me as she slipped her arms inside my open overcoat and wrapped them round me.

"I'd keep you warm, I would. Wouldn't cost much neither, not for a gent like you." Her breath was rancid, and my senses were too heightened to cope. Filled with horror at her touch, I pushed her away, gasping for breath and falling into the wall that was all that prevented me from tumbling to the filthy ground, such was my urge to keep this monstrosity away from me. Her red hair was dried out, streaked with gray in the matted curls that hung to her shoulders.

Her skin was doughy and blotchy from the cold. Somewhere deep inside I felt my own fever rising.

"Stay away from me." I spat the words out, and she pulled away, almost laughing.

"All right, all right. Whatsa matter with you?"

She turned and began to walk away, and I noticed, as I got my breath against the wall, that she no longer appeared as intoxicated as she had moments before. Instinctively, even though my hands felt almost separated from my body, I checked my pockets. My watch was gone.

I stared after her, suddenly filled with indignation. She had taken me for a fool. I might have been a fool for Juliana, but I would not be a fool for this creature. It was my watch and I would have it returned.

"Wait!" I called after her. My voice slurred and it did not sound like my own. "Wait."

Her footsteps stopped and she turned.

37

LEAVESDEN. FEBRUARY, 1898
AARON KOSMINSKI

Under the starched sheet and rough blanket, Aaron twitched in his sleep. His mouth fell open in a gasp, but no one paid any attention. Further down the large room lined with beds on either side, others were tossing and muttering, releasing their demons as they slept, or lying awake in the night staring at the ceiling, lost in their own worlds. Since moving to the dormitory, Aaron had begun to find the presence of others comforting, even though he did not interact with them or get close enough that they might touch him. He had kept a wary eye on those who had visitors, waiting for the monster to return to seek him out again—Dr. Bond would try, of that he was certain. Though he cried when he thought of Dr. Bond, and of his own weakness, he had been so relieved to be released. He could not have it back. He *would not* have it back.

At last he slept, and the visions came. The *Upir* was not in Leavesden, he knew that, for the horror gripped him and he *saw*. It was in London, and it was hungry. He whimpered again, dribbling onto his thin pillow, lost in the moments unfolding behind his closed eyes, and somewhere deep in the part of him that was conscious and aware, he cursed his grandmother for her gift and he cursed his own mother for ever bringing him into this world.

She came back because she was greedy and she thought the man a fool. It was there in the shine of her eyes and the smile that stretched across her face. He did not know she had his watch. She'd get some money from him for her services, and then she'd have both. She wasn't old—despite the cheap powder and skin puffy from the drink and cold, she was still in her twenties, and her body was firm under her tired clothes. She walked with more purpose, swinging her hips, looking at the old man as if he were prey. The closer she drew, the more the scent of blood traveled with her: the last dregs of her monthly loss had escaped her, not so much that a customer would notice, but enough to carry in the stagnant air like honey.

"Not in the streets," he said. He was not aware that he was speaking; his mind was still in an opium fog, but watching from his place both there and yet not there, Aaron knew this was not the Upir *alone. She had angered the doctor, and the* Upir *was using his rage, feeding it, to achieve its own ends. They were becoming one. "Come to my house. I will pay you well."*

In his bed, Aaron sobbed loudly, his eyes squeezed shut tight. There was no release from the vision, however. This was not like before. This was immediate, not simply sensory or a terrible dread. It was as if the *Upir* now carried a part of him with it, and that link would never be broken. He had been tainted, and that taint would remain forever.

The woman was excited, that was clear by the racing of her heart and the rise in her body temperature. A night in a gentleman's house? She'd take that happily. She took his arm and held him steady, quite unaware of the unnatural strength that filled him. They found a hansom cab, and he directed the driver to Westminster as she climbed aboard, flashing her legs at him and laughing raucously. She was East End born and bred, and even with his watch tucked into her bodice she felt no fear. Maybe, if he paid properly, she'd drop it on the floor in his bedroom, make it look like it came from his clothes. He was old and drunk, and she doubted she'd be working hard for her money tonight—if she was lucky he'd fall asleep and she'd get to spend the night in a big soft bed in a warm room.

She leaned in toward him and whispered all the things she would do for him. He didn't speak much, but he stared at her and his eyes were filled with lust. She was right, she thought. This wouldn't take long.

Somewhere in his dream, Aaron tried to scream a warning at her. She was not a good woman, this prostitute. Her heart had been hard long before she had ever lifted her skirts for a living. She had abandoned her own newborn babes—two of them—without as much as a backward glance. She preyed on the weak, stealing where she could, even from her own—but still Aaron cried for her, and for what he knew he was going to see.

They walked a bit after the hansom cab had dropped them, but that didn't surprise her. Gents did not like to be seen with women like her, even though they liked to be touched by them well enough, and she was so glad when they reached his big, warm house. She was so impressed by the height of the ceilings, the richness of the gilt on the hall mirrors, that she didn't even notice him locking the door securely behind them.

"Would you like some wine?" he asked. The beast was beating on his back, hungry and filled with anticipation of the moment, and Bond's mouth watered with it—and in turn so did Kosminski's. It was black in the doctor's head, like the depths of every riverbed in Europe, and the Upir's grip was like fronds of weeds gripping him, holding him down until he had drowned. Aaron willed the doctor to fight it, but the opium held him still; there would be no battle tonight.

The woman giggled, a crude sound that lacked anything of innocence. She made a mock curtsey before following him into the kitchen. He watched her as she drank, before coming to stand inches from her face. He stared hard into her eyes, as if looking for something in their reflection. He lifted his hands to her face, softly stroking her cheeks. Perhaps it was the intensity of his stare, or the way she found herself backed up against a wall, but Kosminski felt her stiffen and her mood shift. Suddenly she was wary.

"You took my watch," he said, softly, his hands caressing her neck. "You are wicked."

She tensed at that, the discovery of her theft, but still she thought she could control the situation—she had been in worse than this and got herself out. She laughed a little, denying it, and pressed her body against his. There were ways to control men, and she was schooled in all of them.

"But you don't know what wickedness is," he muttered. He slurred his words as his hands tightened around her throat. "You have no idea. But it wants you, and I must give it what it wants."

"What are you—?" Suddenly the danger was real, and she was no longer in control. The gloved hands around her throat were growing tighter—so much strength for a drunk old man.

"Can you see it yet?" he hissed. "Can you see it?"

And then she did, and so did Aaron, and they both screamed in terror, she silently as the last wheeze of life left her; Aaron loudly enough to wake the attendants, who shook him from the moment even as he continued sobbing and scrabbling at his throat and shouting of river demons.

He did not sleep the rest of the night.

38

LONDON. FEBRUARY, 1898
EDWARD KANE

It was still dark outside, and the winter dawn was hours away, but they were both awake. He liked the nights best, when they were free of the constraints of polite company and business and could enjoy each other as he was sure they had been born to do. Harrington, God rest his soul, had never been the man for her—how could he have been? She was too powerful a woman for someone that gentle. She needed a man who was her match, and Edward was that man.

He loved the feeling of her naked body curled up across his in the aftermath of sex almost as much as he loved the sex itself. She was tall and elegant, but in bed she was like a cat, full of stretches and contented purrs that made his heart both race and tighten. What had his life been like before her? Sometimes he could barely remember. When he had told his friends back home in New York that he had fallen in love with an English widow, they had laughed to his face, so well known was his reputation as a womanizer. He had taken their mocking in good humor, pointing out that it was only because he had had so much experience with the fairer sex that he knew this to be something entirely different—indeed, he intended to marry her and never disappoint her. He had promised that when they met his Juliana, as they would one day soon, they would understand his change of lifestyle.

Now he looked down at her as she stretched an arm across his chest and played with the hair there that was still damp from their exertions. Her own red curls hung loose, and she pushed one out of her face and sighed.

"Are you happy?" he asked.

"I am." He watched her perfect mouth curl into a smile. "I feel so much better than I did."

"You're welcome. Give me ten minutes and I'll do it again."

"Not that." She slapped his chest playfully. "Although I cannot deny you do have certain skills . . ." She looked up at him and winked, her skin glowing. In all her naked glory, she looked about nineteen. Gone was the fraught, uptight woman he had first met, still struggling with her grief and about to resign herself to marriage with a man as old as her father. She was almost a girl again, bright and vibrant and full of life, but with all the good sense and experience of a grown woman.

Charles Hebbert's leaving had been difficult for her, but they had the selfishness of love on their side, and over the past few weeks they had been so wrapped up in each other that had he still been here, he would have been ignored for the most part, however unintentionally. Edward took consolation from the fact that Charles was happy that it was he who would marry his beloved daughter, as he had intimated on several occasions. He was leaving his girl in safe hands, and perhaps he too would find a new love on a different continent.

"I am glad Thomas knows," Juliana said now, changing the subject to one less welcome, "but I do worry for him. He said barely a word to me but just ushered me out of the house—I had expected something more, I confess. I would not have been surprised if he had been angry with me. I half-expected him to be." Her brown eyes darkened with worry. "I fear I was unkind to him by not being honest with him sooner. But I was not being honest with myself either. He has been such a good friend to me, and for such a long time."

"But no regrets now?"

"No," she admitted. "I am sad for him, but I can't deny I feel like a weight has been lifted from me."

Edward took her arms and pulled her up toward him so that her long hair hung around both their faces, as if curtaining them off from the world outside.

"I cannot wait for you to be my wife," he said. "And I promise you now that I will never do anything to hurt you, or James. I will protect you from everything. And I will love you until the day I die."

She smiled again and kissed him, her tongue touching his as their lips met. Even though they had barely finished, he felt a shiver of pleasure run through him again.

"I know," she said, "because I feel the same way about you." She rolled away and lay on one side, propping her head up on one hand. "And that is why I had to break poor Thomas's heart. Perhaps if I had never met you, if I had never known how much more I could feel, then I might have made him a good wife. But not now. Even if I had kept my word and married him, he would have grown to hate me, and I him—and that I could not bear."

"You did the right thing. You did the only thing you could do. He had no claim on you, and you have nothing to feel guilty about. You cannot control your heart." He loved her goodness and her concern for others. New York was full of people who claimed to love each other but who were concerned only with their own gain. It was a thrilling city and he adored it, but it was selfish and hungry, unable to combine ambition and decency. His father, the coldest and most practically ruthless man he had ever met, was venerated in the city, even after his death. Juliana was a million miles away from that mentality. He wanted to take her home—of course he did—and the business would not allow him to stay away forever, but he had yet to broach the subject of where they would eventually settle. Once they were married, it would be his decision to make, but he could never force Juliana into something that would make her unhappy. He felt no less of a man for that; Juliana was his equal, and only a fool would think otherwise.

"Will he be all right?" she asked.

Back to Thomas Bond. He wished she would forget the old man now that she had told him she was no longer his. "Doctor Bond is a good man," he said, and he meant it, for after all, if it hadn't been for his care and ministrations during her pregnancy and in the aftermath of James's murder, then he had no idea how damaged Juliana might have been. She might even have died. "And neither is he stupid. I imagine that he understood why you were delaying better than you did yourself," he said firmly. "I am sure in his heart he knows that this is better for you. Give him time. He loves you, and he will always be your friend. We will just have to make sure he knows he is always welcome in our home, that's all."

"I hope you're right. For James's sake as much as anything." Her right shoulder had risen slightly to her ear, an endearing habit he had noticed she had, something she did without realizing it when she was thinking hard. "I have you—and James is starting to love you, I can see that. You bring out the boy in him. But Thomas has been there all his life, and James needs him, especially now that Father has left."

The mention of James dissipated the rising lust Edward had been feeling. Since he had gotten back from New York, he had realized the boy was not the same. Even at Christmas, when his grandfather had still been here, he had been quiet and unresponsive. He had had moments of good humor, sure, but he had withdrawn into himself a lot more, and his smooth brow was too often furrowed with thought for a boy that young.

"How is James getting on with his lessons?" he asked. It was a genuine concern, but he wanted to distract her from her preoccupation with Bond. The changing light told him he would need to creep back to the spare bedroom soon if they were to get any sleep—and they must if they were to be able to function at all the next day—and he didn't wish her ex-suitor to be the last thing they talked about before separating. It was natural that she was concerned—she had told him only that morning—but Dr. Bond was a grown man. He could cope with this news. They had spent enough time worrying about him.

The distraction worked. Juliana glowed with pride as she said, "Mr. Chard Williams is very pleased with his progress. He says he's very clever. He should be ready to go to school soon."

"Good," Edward said, and leaned in to kiss her again. "He must get all that cleverness from his mother."

He didn't raise James's strange behavior with her, but instead reached for her warm body and pulled it on top of him. There had been enough worry for today, and soon the night would be over. He wanted to enjoy it as long as it lasted.

39

LONDON. FEBRUARY, 1898
DR. BOND

It was dark on the water, broken only occasionally by a dapple of moonlight on the inky surface when a break came in the clouds above. This being our second night out, there was no real conversation beyond the occasional mutter and the grunt of the rivermen rowing us out to where the water was deepest. That suited me. There was little I wished to discuss with these men beyond what was necessary, and they in turn appeared to prefer ignorance as long as I paid well.

"Nearly done." Beside me, George sniffed as he threw the last package over the side, his nose no doubt running from both the cold and the terrible stench of rot and human filth that still rose from the river, even in these modern times.

I could not make out the hour on my pocket watch in the dark, but I knew it was past three in the morning. I huddled in my cheap coat and scarf and enjoyed the splash as the last of her slid into the dark depths, where hopefully the stones wrapped into the package would drag her to the bottom, preventing her from being washed up on the banks.

"Take us back, Jimmy," George grunted, and the other man turned the small boat around. London loomed large on either side of us, but even on the busy water thoroughfare, I felt as if we were in a world apart. I had drawn George into my madness. Not that he knew what was in the packages—he might suspect, but he had not asked. I had told him I was a surgeon and hoped that was enough. I had sown the seeds and could but hope they had grown into his suspicion that I was one of those fellows who paid for corpses of the dead in order to study them and now was simply disposing of my used materials. I pulled a small purse of coins from my pocket— I had bought several such purses from a shop far from anywhere I usually frequented—and handed it over to him.

"Pleasure doing business with you, sir," he said. I could see the whites of his eyes in the dark, and he was studying me. Something had shifted in our relationship over the past few days. I felt there was a new respect there, and more than a little wariness. In our first dealings, with the unfortunate dogs, he had been the confident villain, but though he maintained that attitude with the wheezing, bronchial wherrymen who rode us out, he no longer used it on me. Perhaps he had a native sense of danger; maybe he could feel the unnatural energy that came over me when we were on the water. I could not deny it myself; it was exactly what had forced us all here in the first place.

I had awakened that morning with a terrible sense of dread, and when I had seen my pocket watch on the table beside my bed, I knew that what I had hoped were merely the echoes of the nightmare haunting me were nothing of the kind. When I forced myself to face whatever awaited me in the cellar, I found a terrible mess. The *Upir*—I—had cut the unfortunate woman to pieces; had torn her soft flesh apart and consumed it. The taste was still in my mouth.

I drank a lot of wine and brandy that morning, but I could not get drunk. I was filled with such overwhelming remorse at my actions that for a while I could not think clearly at all. It was only after several hours of railing at myself for being so weak that I had allowed such a terrible murder of an innocent to be committed by my hands that the truth began to dawn on me and I calmed slightly. She had not been an innocent, this woman who was now lying dead in my cellar: she was a thief, and doubtless worse. Who knew what other wickednesses she had been responsible for in her past? For all I knew, she had intended to murder me in my bed and make off with more of my possessions. She had been a criminal, rather than a hard-working member of society.

I drank more brandy as I muttered to myself, trying to justify my actions: if she had not pressed herself upon me—if she had not stolen my watch—this fate would not have overtaken her. I did not seek her out as Hebbert or Harrington had their victims; no, she had forced this situation upon me. And so I was not yet a murderer, in my own mind at least, not truly. I had no doubt this woman had committed a crime in her past that was worthy of the hangman's noose.

By the afternoon I had decided that this was no different in many ways from when I had dispatched James Harrington. Society was safer without her. But it had been a sobering lesson. The parasite had forced my hand last night, and now I knew for certain that the dogs were no longer enough to satisfy it, which was something I had suspected for a while. I could no longer deny that the hunger had become as much a part of me as of it, and that had made me let the *Upir* take over. I might have no choice but to be part of this devil's pact, but I was going to have to approach things differently from now on. I could see that I would have to kill again, and again, but I would *choose* my victims. I would select those who were damned souls already, the criminal and depraved.

I would not kill innocents. I was not a monster.

At first I had considered burying the woman in the garden. It was the most convenient option by far—but it would not be holding up my end of this terrible partnership. The *Upir* needed the river fed, and I would happily do so if it meant there was the possibility one day that the creature would take sanctuary in the Thames and leave me to live my life in peace. Only her head would go in that soft earth— I could not risk any chance of identification—and the rest would take to the water. But I would learn from Harrington's mistakes. I felt no urge to taunt the police by leaving part of her where it could be easily discovered (and on reflection, now that I suffered his condition, I wondered if the torso left in the Scotland Yard vault was more Harrington's doing than the *Upir*'s, a result of his unconscious desire to get caught making itself manifest perhaps). I trusted my medical ability to ensure that the woman was unidentifiable, but I had no desire for her body to wash up on the riverbank. I wanted her to simply disappear, so I could forget my unwelcome *needs*, at least until the next fever struck me and I would have to act again. My plan would require accomplices, but I knew just the man to go to.

And so here I was.

When the small boat finally came ashore on the shingle of a quiet bank, Jimmy—although I was not convinced that was his real name—secured it among the other small craft.

I expected my cold joints and bad back to scream at me as I stood upright after an hour or more in the freezing cold, but instead I rose easily, and I could not deny the pleasure that my renewed energy gave me, even though I knew that I should find it abhorrent.

"You won't be needing any more dogs, then?" George asked quietly as we moved like hollow ghosts toward the steps and the streets to take us back to our lives.

"No," I answered. "No more dogs."

40

LONDON. APRIL, 1898
DR. BOND

The weather cleared for the wedding, and warm sunshine bathed the small church in Barnes that Juliana had chosen. I had to admit, as much as it hurt my heart, she looked radiantly happy as they said their vows. The sight of Edward Kane still made my stomach knot with a fury I didn't entirely understand, but I could not deny they made a fine couple. Standing beside Walter Andrews, I felt suddenly old and tired. The rage I felt toward Kane was, I was certain, driven in part by the *Upir*, but the exhaustion and sadness were all my own.

Juliana had written to me and begged me to remain her friend, even though she would understand if I felt I could not. Once I had dealt with my more pressing situation in the cellar, I had realized that without Juliana, in whatever capacity she would allow, my life was empty of real goodness, true decency. Still, it had not been easy for me to adjust to my new role in her life, not least because I could not shake the feeling that I had behaved like a fool, an old fool, and that was worse than if I had simply loved her and never declared myself.

Little James took my hand as we followed the couple out with our paper cones of rice, and I smiled and clapped with him and the rest of the guests as we showered his mother. We were a small gathering: Walter Andrews, James Barker and his wife, James's tutor William Chard Williams and his wife, and one or two others I did not know but I presumed were business connections of either Juliana's or Edward's. James Barker had walked Juliana down the aisle in her father's absence. I was sure that in her heart she wished me to have done that but thought it inappropriate to ask, and that made me feel even older. To admit to myself that on some level she had always seen me as a surrogate father figure, that her very real affection for me was nothing more than that, crushed me. I would not love again, of that I was certain, but I could not cure myself of the love I had for her.

We went back to the house in Barnes, where an informal wedding breakfast had been set up so that we could enjoy the sunshine. Watching their ease with one another, I realized that Juliana and Kane had probably been man and wife in all senses of the words for some time now, and I could not stop my teeth from gritting as I looked at the rich, handsome young American.

Andrews handed me a fresh glass of champagne from a passing tray as a jovial-looking man said, "You must be Dr. Bond. It is a great pleasure to meet you. James mentions you often in our lessons—allow me to introduce myself: William Chard Williams, James's tutor. I hear you will be looking after the young man while the happy couple are in France?"

"Yes, I shall," I replied. The man's open expression made me think he knew nothing of Juliana's rejection of me, and for the first time that day I relaxed slightly. I looked over to where the boy was playing with a ball and hoop in the far corner of the lawn, and he glanced back but did not smile. "Although I fear that at my age this might prove more exhausting than anything I have done before."

"Hear, hear," Andrews cut in. "Quite a challenge for you." He was being overly pleasant to me, and I could not help but think it pity.

"He's a well-behaved boy," Chard Williams continued. "A credit to his mother."

"Do you have children of your own?" I asked, and the man shook his head.

"I married late in life, I'm afraid. But my wife is young, and she does love looking after babies for others, so perhaps one day . . ." He gestured toward a tall, thin woman, still in her twenties, who was talking to Juliana. She did not have Juliana's beauty, but the difference in the Chard Williamses' ages was not dissimilar to that between Juliana's and mine, and once again I felt a failure and wished for this interminable day to end. I was tired of being sensible, ever-reliable Dr. Thomas Bond. I was a man too, and I felt as deeply as any other.

As soon as Chard Williams had left us to rejoin his wife, little James came back over and lingered at my side.

"He's very fond of you, isn't he?" Andrews said, looking down at the boy. "I think two weeks in his charge might be good for both of you. Will you come here, or take him to Westminster?"

"I'll bring my things over tomorrow," I said. "He has his classes, and Juliana has arranged a nanny to look after him until I return home if I have to work late." James hadn't reacted to my words; he was watching his mother talking to his tutors. I still could not warm to the boy, but I did feel an empathy with him. He had been Juliana's entire world for such a long time—she wouldn't leave him for an hour, let alone two weeks—but now he, like I, had been abandoned, at least partially. His love was no longer enough for her. She wanted instead to bask in the bright sun of Edward Kane. Young James and I, we were inextricably linked to the past, to Harrington and to all the darkness and grief of that time. Perhaps he felt some of the loss that I suffered, although the affection Juliana felt for him would never recede into simple fondness, as it had for me. She would always love him, for he was a constant reminder of the good man she had once loved. To me, however, he was a constant reminder of a monster I had killed.

"Go and play, James," I said, suddenly wishing him away from my side. "Enjoy the sunshine while it lasts." He did as he was told without a word, leaving me alone with Andrews. He appeared to be as reluctant to mingle as I was, and the reason, after another glass of champagne and a little small talk about his retirement, soon became clear.

"Thomas, I've been meaning to talk to you for a while. I called on you two evenings in a row, after Kane told me of his engagement, but you were not home."

So Edward Kane had told Andrews rather than speak to me himself—had the American wormed his way into Andrews's close circle of friends too? Was I to have nothing left?

"I just wanted to say—well, how truly sorry I am."

"Sorry?" I asked. On some level I wanted him to feel uncomfortable; after all, he had encouraged me to press my suit with Juliana. If it had not been for him, my pain would be private.

"For—well, I know how you feel about her. This cannot be easy for you."

"Oh, come, come, Walter. She is a beautiful young woman—anyone can see that Edward Kane is a better suitor for her than I could ever have been. In part at least, my proposal was because she was still fragile, prone to illness, and I was very worried about her. However, she is clearly flourishing, and I could not be happier for her." I was overdoing it, I knew that, but I could not stop myself. "I can now enjoy my impending retirement without worrying about domestic duties."

"I know that you are a true gentleman," Andrews started, studying me, "but there is no shame in admitting hurt feelings. I too feel bad, for I know I was eager for you to propose to her, and I know she was not clear in her responses."

My hand tightened slightly around the delicate glass stem of my glass. It appeared that Kane and Andrews had had quite the heart-to-heart about me. Heat burned my cheeks. Was I to be left with no dignity?

"I did feel hurt, I will admit that," I conceded. Andrews had a sharp eye, and I did not want him to be worrying about me or paying me undue attention, not in my current situation. "But I have had time to adjust to the idea." I looked over to where Kane stood, strong and handsome and laughing in the bright sunshine, not a care in the world. "And you and I, Walter, we are no longer young men. I think perhaps love is best suited for the young, don't you?"

Finally he smiled, his face filled with relief. "I am glad you see it that way too, Thomas. I do think he will be very good for her. She has certainly changed since she has known him, wouldn't you say?"

"Yes," I said, forcing a smile. "Yes, I do believe she has." So even my old friend was relieved that Juliana had escaped a future with me. I drank my champagne too quickly, the fizz of bubbles racing to my head. I knew I was being unreasonable; of course Andrews was right—indeed, more than he could ever possibly know. I would not have been the best match for Juliana, even before my terrible affliction, but she had been my one hope of a happy future. But I realized I had hoped that Walter Andrews might at least have seen some positives in my steady, if unexciting, love. Apparently not. And now all I saw in my future was a ceaseless struggle against an evil that should never even have been part of my life.

"We should have dinner soon," Andrews said, relaxed now that our awkward moment was over. "We used to do so regularly, and of late we have not—we must rectify that."

"We shall," I said, "once my temporary parenting duties are over." In that moment, I could happily have never laid eyes on Walter Andrews again, for all he had been an old and true friend to me for so many years.

It was strange to be alone with James without his mother there, but we quickly settled into a quiet, comfortable routine. For the most part we did not see each other that often. I would spend the day in the city and then return in the evening, and we would eat a quiet supper together. I would ask him about his studies, and then it would be time for him to go to bed. Our relationship was stilted—I had never been quite sure how one was supposed to engage with children—but I did my best. When I asked him if he missed his mother, he shrugged and said a little, but he would not be drawn out on the subject. One night, when I had a very early inquest to attend, he stayed at the Chard Williamses' house—for which I paid them a generous fee—and although he did not complain, he was quieter after that. I found myself feeling bad that I had been so happy to spend a night in my own home with no company. The boy had, after all, lost his father, and now his beloved mother had remarried; the world must have seemed a very different place for him. Many boys of his age were more independent, but it was not his fault he was not like them. His mother had kept him tied to her apron strings. I made a promise to myself that I would try to engage with him more, and after that I attempted to play games of his choosing rather than merely dryly discussing the events of the day. The weather was still warm so we took to the garden, and I was pleased to discover the fresh air did as much to raise my spirits as his. I had had no new fever, and I could almost imagine that my life was normal again, especially away from the presence of my cellar and the knowledge of the deeds committed there.

His screams woke me first at the start of the second week. I sat up in bed, my heart pounding, staring wildly around me, disoriented by the unfamiliar surroundings. I pushed back the covers and ran in only my nightshirt along the corridor and burst into James's room.

"What? What is it? What has happened?"

I looked around in the gloom for a sign of some intruder, but there was nothing, just the boy, sitting bolt upright in his bed, his eyes wide and staring at some remnant of his disappearing dream. I sat on his bed, and in the dawn light I could see that his face was covered in sweat, darkening his blond hair at the hairline. For a moment it made me think of blood.

"It was just a bad dream," I said, as slowly his focus came back to me. "Everything is fine—there is nothing to worry about." I eased him back down and tucked his sheet around him. "Now, go back to sleep." He didn't speak a word, and I wondered if he had really woken at all. His eyes closed, and after a moment his breathing steadied, and I went back to my own bed where I lay awake until breakfast, my imagination forcing images of Juliana and Edward Kane into my head that I had no desire to see.

The nightmares came the next night, and the night after, and on the third, by which time I was exhausted as much by my broken sleep as by the expectation of being woken. This time I lit the lamp in his room and shook him gently until he was fully awake. Once again his skin was clammy and his nightshirt damp.

"What is it, James?" I asked. "What is bothering you? What do you dream?" My own skin had started to burn slightly in the night, and I knew that soon I would feel the first touch of the fever that came with my peculiar infection. I needed my strength, and for that I needed a decent night's sleep. "Your mother will be home in a few days. There is nothing to worry about."

He stared at me for a moment. "I was in the river," he said, eventually. "All tied up."

My heart froze, and I pulled my hand away from his. Suddenly I saw every echo of his father in his young face. "It was just a dream," I repeated. "You are safe in bed, James, in your own home."

"I . . . I . . ." he started to say, his bottom lip trembling, "I *saw* something."

"Don't be silly." My mouth had dried. What was this? What could he possibly have seen? "It was just a dream." I stood up, no longer wanting to be near him, as if he were the *Upir* itself detached from me and taken human form.

"But I—"

I tried to calm myself. I was being ridiculous. There could be nothing sinister in young James's dreams; this was simply a memory playing out in a dream.

"You fell into the river, not so long ago," I said. "Do you remember? When you tumbled from the rowboat? I imagine that is what this nightmare is about." My heart rate was returning to normal; of course that was what this was about. I had to stop seeing suspicion everywhere. What could young James know about my deeds, after all? Nothing. I might not be able to bring myself to love him as I should, but that did not mean he somehow knew of my secret life. And yet still I trembled. It was the words he had used: *I saw something.* It had made me think of Kosminski and his strange visions.

He shook his head, as if trying to clear it. "I *saw* something," he repeated plaintively, almost as if he knew how much the phrase disturbed me, although of course he could not possibly know that.

"Go to sleep," I said, firmly, turning the light out. "You are too old for this kind of childish fear." Cowed by the sharp tone in my voice, he curled back up under the covers, but his face was still full of woe.

"Dead girls in the river."

He spoke so quietly that I almost missed his words, but they drifted across the room and snared my attention. *Dead girls?* Was that some kind of threat? Had he seen me in his dream? I stared at him from the dark doorway. "Go to sleep," I snapped, barely able to draw breath.

I closed the door and then almost fell against the wall. I clutched the doorjamb and let out a juddering sigh before summoning the strength to get back to my room. The house felt claustrophobic, and I craved the sanctuary of my own home, even with all its dark secrets.

I stared into the mirror, my reflection shades of blue and black in the gloom. Patches had appeared on my cheeks, and my skin was hot. Fear made the *Upir* hungry, and if I was to make some attempt to save my soul, I could not leave it much longer before I found a villainess for the part.

The next night when he screamed himself awake, I pretended not to hear. I remained in my room and stared at the ceiling until the sobbing finally stopped.

It was a relief when Juliana and Kane returned two days later. They were flushed with happiness and health and breezed into the house full of energy and vitality and clearly entirely in love with each other. It was a sharp contrast to the depressing atmosphere that had hung over the house since James's nightmares had started, but they appeared not to notice. James ran to his mother, then Kane swung him up onto his shoulders, and for the first time in two weeks the boy laughed aloud.

"Has all been well?" Juliana asked as she kissed me chastely on the cheek and thanked me for all I had done. Her eyes were kind, but I saw pity in them, I was certain. How could she even respect me after the apparent ease with which I had accepted her marriage to another?

"Yes, of course," I said. "We have gotten along fine, haven't we, young man? But now I really must get back to my own home and leave you to unpack and settle back in."

"Stay for dinner!" Kane exclaimed. "There's no need to rush off." He grinned, the easy smile of the victor, and I gritted my teeth as I returned it but shook my head. "Sadly I cannot," I said. "I really do have work waiting for me."

"Then you must come for dinner soon," Juliana said. "You really are the kindest friend I have, Thomas. There is no one else I would have trusted with James." She looked at her son. "James, come say thank you and good-bye to Uncle Thomas. He has to go home."

The boy dutifully came over, and I crouched and let him hug me. He squeezed me tightly—almost too tightly. Was there menace in it? What did he know? What had he seen?

"Good-bye, James," I said, breaking free and forcing myself to ruffle his blond hair. "I shall see you again soon."

"Good-bye, Uncle Thomas." His voice was soft, and he half-smiled at me, as if we shared a secret. Suddenly those blue eyes no longer looked so innocent, and even though the house was warm, I shivered. Harrington had been infected when James was conceived; it was not unreasonable to think that perhaps something of the *Upir* had transferred to his unborn child. Had James been threatening me, or was it that he could somehow see in his dreams the dark deeds I had been forced to do? Did he even understand what he was seeing? Or—a dreadful thought!—was there another *Upir*, an awful procreation of the one attached to me, growing inside him? Would he become a monster too?

Whichever was the truth, I could not stand to be around him.

And now I could really feel my fever growing.

41

LONDON. MAY, 1898
DR. BOND

It was nearly midnight when the heavy knock at the front door disturbed my preparations. The packages had been wrapped and were now in the kitchen, packed into the two small valises I had bought especially to carry them. Even though it was well into the night, the heat of the day lingered in the house, and I was sweating from my exertions, carrying the parcels up from the cellar. I was not tired—I could still feel the immediate invigoration that came after feeding the *Upir*—but I was looking forward to getting the last of it—of *her*—dispatched into the river. Once George's man had taken me out onto the river for the second night, all traces of her would be gone from the house, and until the next time, I could padlock the cellar door and pretend nothing had ever happened.

My heart raced as the knocker went again, loud and insistent. I hesitated in the hallway, not knowing what to do. Whoever it was, he was keen to see me—but I needed to leave shortly if I were to make my rendezvous with George on the riverbank. But if I were to leave while whoever was knocking so insistently was still waiting outside, that would look highly suspicious—how ever would I explain the valises, let alone my sudden need to leave my house so late at night. I had no choice. I had to let whoever it was in.

"Thomas," Walter Andrews said as he stepped in to the hall. "You are still up. I thought you must be asleep."

"I am not long in from a dinner engagement." I did not move too far back, keeping him close to the door, not wanting to encourage him to linger. I itched to be rid of him—of all people, I did not want a retired detective in my house. I knew only too well how keen an observer of people and detail Walter Andrews was. "But what brings you here so late?"

"We have all sent messages to you." He was agitated, almost irritated, and that in turn irritated me.

I glanced at the table by the door and saw three envelopes on the plate there, which came as a surprise to me. When had they arrived? Now that I no longer had Mrs. Parks in my service, I must have put them there. I must have picked them up from the floor when I got home and placed them on the salver—but I had no recollection of it.

"I'm sorry," I said, "I have been busy—what on earth is the matter?"

"It's young James—he has a terrible fever. The local physician has seen him, but Juliana is insisting on your care." His brow furrowed. "We are all being very positive, but I must be honest with you, my friend, he does not look at all well."

A fever. My stomach churned. A fever like mine, perhaps? "Has the physician seen him this evening?"

"Yes, and he has given him something to help the lad sleep, but he is almost continually coughing, and his skin is burning very badly. Juliana is beside herself."

"I shall go first thing in the morning," I said. From the corner of my eye, I could see a thumbprint of red on one of the envelopes that I had chosen to ignore either while in the grip of the parasite or in the midst of the awful task in the cellar or in the laudanum and brandy haze afterward. I moved slightly and leaned against the table, blocking it from view. "There is little point in going now: the boy should be sleeping and so should Juliana. But I will be there by breakfast time."

Andrews nodded, and I could see his disappointment—but what exactly did he expect me to do? Drop everything and run to the side of the woman who had chosen another over me? Juliana was Edward Kane's responsibility now.

My bitterness surprised me. I had thought myself a better man than that. What the *Upir* made me do was one thing—I did not consider that any part of who I was. I was a good man, one who had always held reason and dignity over emotion. But it would appear that over the years I had forgotten the power that love had to twist into something dark inside.

"I am sure she will be grateful to see you whenever you can get there," Andrews said, a snip of reproach in his voice. "You are the only one she trusts, Thomas."

I felt a pang of something close to guilt at that. I should leave immediately and go to the boy, but I could not, for I had dark deeds to finish. There were men waiting for me, and they would not be happy if I missed our meeting.

"First thing," I said. "I promise, the boy will be fine until then, Walter. Waking him at this hour will likely do more harm than good."

We said our awkward farewells, and then I ushered him out of the house. I turned the lights down to create the impression I was going straight to bed, in case he was studying my house from the street, and then I waited. After a while I went to my study window and looked down at the pavement outside. Even though I could see no sign of him, I still waited as long as possible before I dragged my laden valises out into the night and headed once more for the river, trying to think of anything except the butchered contents.

She had been a wicked woman, of that I had no doubt. I had studied her for nights, watching her steal and lie and beat another unfortunate woman until she had handed over her meager earnings. I was no monster. I did not consider the life of an unfortunate, someone who had fallen into despair, to be in itself a crime, and I did not believe that any woman would choose that life for herself if it were not out of dire necessity. And I would not feed the *Upir* from those whom life had forced into such lowness—I would not become like Harrington or Hebbert. I did what I must to protect the innocent from the creature on my back that drove the bloodlust, and I considered the easy prey of prostitutes to be as innocent as any other. I had vowed to kill only the criminal, and I would be firm on that front. Still, I did not like to think how the aftertaste of my activities, that metallic tang on my tongue that no longer made me retch, or that perhaps I crammed the soft parts into my mouth with occasional relish. That was not me. That was *it*. I refused to believe otherwise.

I thought of James and his fever. I thought of his father and what he had done. The idea that the *Upir* might have left its seed with Harrington's inside Juliana plagued me. Her pregnancy had been terrible, and the labor had almost killed her. Could that have been because of the unnatural monstrosity growing inside her?

The river had never felt more filled with secrets than it did that night.

42

LONDON. MAY, 1898
EDWARD KANE

He hated seeing Juliana like this. Neither of them had slept properly for days, and when at last she did drift off from exhaustion, he would hear her crying in her sleep, calling out for James. Sometimes the James she shouted for was her dead husband, and sometimes it was her terribly sick child. No doubt memories of the former were haunting her because of her fear of death of the latter. Edward was not jealous; he knew that whatever love she had had for her first husband was nothing compared to what she felt for him—but he felt so damned helpless. There was nothing he could do to ease her suffering. He would not insult her with platitudes, not when it was so clear the boy was gravely ill. Although it hurt him to see it—he had grown genuinely fond of the child—he knew the worry he felt was nothing compared with what his wife was suffering.

Despite the beautiful spring weather outside, a pall hung over the house in Barnes. Although he had never considered himself a superstitious man, Edward Kane could not stop thinking of it as a visitation of death, as if the Grim Reaper himself had come to call but was not yet sure if he was staying. Even with the windows open wide to allow a healthy warm breeze, the air was greasy with the foreboding of death.

Dr. Bond had been a godsend. Over the past week he had barely left the boy's side, and Edward knew that although it did nothing to ease Juliana's terror at the thought she might lose her child, at least she knew he was in the safest of hands. Bond had promised her he would not leave until the boy was well again. Edward had nothing but the utmost respect for the doctor; for his own part, he wasn't sure he would have been so generous of spirit in defeat.

"It is very kind of you to call on us." Juliana looked strained, but Edward was glad that they had visitors. It was good for her to see that others cared, and the Chard Williamses had clearly become fond of James during his lessons there, for this was not their first visit since he had taken ill. "I am sure that when James is well enough, he will enjoy your cakes a great deal."

"I know he likes them," Ada Chard Williams said. Her face was almost as tight with worry as Juliana's. "It was the least I could do. Is there any improvement?"

"It's hard to tell," Juliana said, carefully sipping her tea, "but Dr. Bond seems confident he will recover." Her voice was hollow, and Edward knew she wasn't convinced. He couldn't blame her for that. Neither was he.

"Let's hope the fever breaks soon," he said.

"I'm sure he will soon be running around and tiring you both out as boys do," Chard Williams said.

"It's his dreams I cannot stand," Juliana admitted. She glanced up at Edward, who stood behind her with one hand on her slim shoulder. At least she had not shut him out in her grief; they were still able to take comfort in each other. "He talks of such horrible things—'dead girls in the river,' he keeps saying, though why, I cannot begin to understand."

Ada Chard Williams's eyes widened, and she visibly shuddered. "Children do have such imaginations, don't they? Maybe I could speak to him? I'm very good with the young 'uns."

"That is kind of you," said Juliana, "but I could not bear for anyone else to catch his sickness. And he is barely conscious most of the time."

"Dr. Bond says it is most likely his memory playing tricks on him from his fall in the water," Edward cut in. "For that, I will never forgive myself."

"He keeps saying he doesn't want us to throw him in the river," Juliana was speaking as much to herself as to their awkward guests. "Why does he think I would do that?"

The Chard Williamses exchanged a glance, and Edward gave them a small, sympathetic smile. Even Walter Andrews was uncomfortable when he visited now. Edward knew that he felt like he was intruding on someone else's pain, however well meaning his intent.

"We should probably get back," Ada Chard Williams said. "We have taken up too much of your time already. Mrs. Kane, you really should get out in the fresh air for a walk while he's sleeping—you must take care of yourself, you know. You will need to stay healthy for when he gets better."

Juliana smiled gratefully. "Yes, yes, of course you're right. Perhaps I shall."

Edward knew she wouldn't; she had no intention of leaving the house, not while her child's life hung in the balance.

When the Chard Williamses had left, Edward made fresh coffee and took the pot and one of the small cakes the tutor's wife had brought up to Thomas Bond. The doctor was half-asleep in a chair beside the bed where the boy was lying, sweating and shivering. James had always been small for his age, but he seemed to have shrunk over the past few days. His arms were stick thin, and the dark hollows around his eyes amplified the pale, waxy sheen on his skin. Edward's heart sank yet again. If Dr. Bond was on one side of the bed trying to save the boy, then Death was surely on the other, trying to drag him down to the depths.

"How is he?" Edward asked as Bond took the coffee and cake and placed them on the table. He didn't touch either.

"Not good," Bond said. He was obviously exhausted. "I am trying everything I know, but the fever refuses to let him go; indeed, I fear it is getting worse." He rubbed his unshaven chin, but he appeared oblivious to the two days' growth of stubble. "His pain is increasing.

He can keep down neither food nor water, and that has made him very dehydrated. He is still delirious, but he no longer vocalizes his dreams."

"I'm glad about that at least," Edward said. "I fear his ramblings remind Juliana of Harrington's death. They're strange dreams for a child, don't you think? I haven't said anything to his mother, but I wondered if perhaps his grandfather told him stories of some of the cases you two worked on? The Whitehall case, and those like it? Or maybe he overhead Charles talking—children always listen when they shouldn't, after all."

"It's entirely possible," Bond said, looking down at the floor, "but if he did so, it was not in my company."

"I hope you don't think I was suggesting—" Edward started, but Bond immediately started shaking his head and held up a hand to stop him.

"I know you meant no accusation. I'm sorry—I think we are all feeling the strain. Perhaps we should get James to a hospital? I truly don't think there is much more I can do here . . ."

Edward leaned over the child and stroked his damp head tenderly. "Juliana trusts you, Thomas, and so do I. No one has been more of a father to him over the years than you." His throat tightened with emotion. How could James have come to this state? And gone downhill so fast in the past week? None of it felt real—but real it was. The wheezing, uneven breaths counted out the seconds as James struggled to hold onto his life. His eyes moved behind his closed lids as his dreams continued silently.

"Should I prepare her for the worst?" he said quietly.

For a long moment, Bond said nothing. He looked old and tired, as if he carried all the worries of the world on his back. Whatever the outcome, Edward and Juliana owed many debts of gratitude to this fine man.

"I shall try one more medicine," Bond said softly, "but if there is no improvement after that, then, yes, I think we should all expect the worst."

* * *

Little James died at just before noon the next day. It was not a peaceful death. From the hours just before dawn until he took his final breath, he was racked with stomach pain, his frail body doubled over and his limbs tensed so tight that Edward could not believe they did not snap. His weak screams were worse than if his cries had torn through the house. Though he was lost in his delirium, nevertheless he called out for his mother to make it stop, and every time she squeezed his hand and told him through her tears that she was with him, he called for her again, for he was so confused in his terror and pain that he didn't know she was there. Juliana could not comfort her baby in his last moments, and the tragedy of that, for both the boy and his mother, broke Edward's heart.

The hours seemed endless. Walter Andrews arrived at some point. Kane could not remember when, or who let him in, but he joined the gathering around the soaking bed where James lay writhing, and Edward watched the horror that they were all feeling settle onto the ex-policeman's face. The boy's agony and suffering were so unbearable to see that when the moment finally came, Edward could not fight the wave of relief that came over him. It was done. It was over.

Then Juliana filled the house with her grief. She screamed her pain: every animal that had ever lost its young, every mother who had ever lost her child. She was broken, and there was nothing Edward Kane could do but hold her.

43

LONDON. JUNE, 1898
DR. BOND

Rain fell as we stood around the small grave, the drops pattering steadily against the leaves of the overhanging trees. The humid air was still, and overhead the sky was an endless gray. The priest committed James to the ground, and Kane steadied Juliana, who let out a small sob of anguish that rippled out across the graveyard and almost made the trees shiver. I could not see her eyes behind her heavy veil, but I knew they would be red and sore, as they had been ever since James had fallen ill. I tried to feel something—there should have been myriad emotions raging inside me—but I could not. There was nothing but a pleasant emptiness. I had taken too much laudanum and smoked too much of the poppy over the past few days, trying to free myself of the boy's agonized shouts for his mother, but I heard them still, over and over in my head as I lay in bed, so often that I had almost convinced myself that his spirit had returned home with me, that he was haunting me. Perhaps he was.

"She is selling the business," Walter Andrews said softly as we watched Juliana take a handful of earth and throw it onto the coffin. "Kane tells me they are going to go to America."

"Perhaps that is wise," I said. I searched my heart for some pain at the news. I had fought so hard to have her, to keep her in my life, and now, after everything, I would be losing her anyway. She would be gone. There was only numbness. "She has had too much tragedy in London. Kane has a good life there, I imagine. It will be easier for her to heal."

"Hebbert is going to join them there rather than stay in Australia. That will be some comfort to her."

"So, they will all be together again. That will be nice." I felt a prick of bitterness at that. Perhaps the drugs were finally wearing off. So I was to be quite alone. Hebbert, whom I had saved from justice, would be with his family, and I, who had gone to such great lengths to protect us all, would be left alone to face my fate. I watched as Juliana held onto Edward Kane's arm and leaned against him. It was not just for physical support, I could see that. James's death had not diminished her love for the American—if anything, it appeared to have made their bond stronger. My stomach, already queasy from the laudanum, twisted into a knot as they approached.

"Thomas," she said, "I wanted to thank you for everything you did. Before . . . and after."

I took her hand and squeezed it. "I am so sorry. I wish I could have saved him."

She managed a wan smile. "No one could have tried harder. And you made everything, well, a little easier."

After the boy had died, I had taken over all the arrangements. Juliana had seen this as a sign of my love for them both, but the truth was that I could not risk another doctor's examining the boy's dead body. Not that such a thing had been suggested. My reputation was without tarnish, and the boy was known to have been sickly— there were none who would suspect anything other than a fever had carried him off. There was no call for a second opinion. It was exactly as I had hoped it would be—but even so, it was a relief that the boy was finally in the ground.

"When are you leaving?" I asked, directing the question at Edward Kane. I could not look at Juliana, and I was not sure why she suddenly filled me with unease. It was as if perhaps she would somehow *know*.

"Soon. The house can be packed up when we're gone. We can trust Barker to run things sufficiently until the sale is completed."

Barker was on the other side of the grave talking to the Chard Williamses. We all looked so awkward, standing around the grave: this dispirited group mourning a child.

"Are you coming back to the house?" Kane asked.

"Yes, of course," Andrews said, "but we will not stay for long. I know this is a very difficult day for you both."

Juliana had drifted off into her own private world of pain, and as Edward Kane led her away, I wondered if she too had embraced the laudanum to dull the echo of those awful last cries. I waved Andrews on and took a moment by the grave. Two men stood a few feet away, sheltering from the rain under a tree. They leaned on their shovels as they chatted, waiting to get to work sealing James into the earth. I looked at the first James Harrington's gravestone. I had killed them both. The thought was still a strange one.

I had administered the poison slowly at first, nervous that my actions would be discovered, but the boy, already weak, was really very ill and may not have survived anyway. But I could not take that risk; if he lived, then so would the part of him that was a monster, and I could not allow that. I was strong, a grown man, and yet I struggled to control the beast that cursed me. What would the boy have become? He was not like me—his *Upir* had clearly been inside him, a part of him: symbiotic, not parasitical. No wonder it fed him with images of what his father and I had done. *Girls in the river.* I shuddered slightly as I remembered the phrase he had repeated, over and over. But they had not been girls—that implied innocence. I would not touch the innocent.

I gestured to the waiting men, and they hurried over and started shoveling. I watched as the damp earth thudded into the hole, scattering against the wood. It was a relief. I had not enjoyed watching the boy in pain, and I did not like thinking about what I had done. But there could not be two of us; that was something I could not allow. And the fever would have killed the boy anyway, I was sure of that. I had just helped it along.

*　*　*

The wake at the house was a somber affair. I could not grieve James as the others did, not burdened with my terrible knowledge, knowing what he truly was, but even I felt the emptiness in the house that his absence brought. I kept expecting to see him playing quietly in the corner of the room, or hovering by his mother as he used to before he had become more confident. Before Kane had arrived.

I made polite conversation with Andrews, but the laudanum was wearing off, and I felt old and weary. We were spokes on a broken wheel. Everything was changing, and even though it was Kane who had ultimately brought all this misery upon me, I found that a part of me was unhappy about the prospect of his departure. The young were leaving England, and there would be only old men left behind: Andrews, Moore, and me. Looking into the future was like staring into a grave. Moore might have the energy and enthusiasm of a much younger man, but Andrews had already retired . . . and what was left for me? I would be sixty years old soon, the woman I loved, the woman I relied on to keep me strong, was leaving to start a new life. My only constant companion in my old age would be the monster on my back.

I would have taken my own life if I had thought the beast would allow it.

44

London. Christmas, 1898
Dr. Bond

I spent the day alone at home. Walter Andrews had gone to some cousins in Cornwall for a full week, and I had met Henry Moore the day before Christmas Eve. He had invited me to join him for dinner, purely out of pity, I was sure, and pity does nothing to encourage a fine appetite or good humor. I had claimed exhaustion and left as soon as we had drunk our first brandy.

I had not gone straight home but wandered London's streets until I found myself outside the wharves that had once been James Harrington's and then were Juliana's and now belonged to someone entirely unconnected, as if Harrington's family had never existed. Everything that Harrington had done in that small warehouse, the fight that Kosminski, the priest, and I had had here—none of that mattered anymore. The past was so easily whitewashed, scrubbed out of the buildings that would outlast us all. People came and people went—perhaps there would be an echo of them here, a trace of them there, but within a year or so, those too would be gone. I wished it were so easy to erase people from one's thoughts.

Juliana's farewell had been something of an anticlimax. Although I still loved her, I loved a past her, when I was a different me. Face to face, watching her cry as she said good-bye, I had been almost unable to bear the sight of her. Although I knew I had done the right thing in hastening James's demise, it still played on my mind. I did occasionally wonder if perhaps I should have left it longer, in the interests of scientific research, and watched the creature develop. At night I still heard the echoes of his agonized cries, and they tore at my heart in a way I could not understand. All this left me unable to look into Juliana's hollow eyes, her grief a constant reminder that I had taken her husband and child from her. If she were ever to find out, she would not understand. I would be the monster, not the savior I knew myself truly to be. That I could not bear.

Once Juliana and Edward Kane had left for their new life in New York, there was little focus to my social life. Andrews and I had met once or twice, and Moore made an effort to get the three of us together too, but it was clear that things were not the same and never would be.

I found that this did not bother me as much as I had expected. In many ways it was something of a relief. I was beginning to find other people's company hard work. I had too much business of my own to take care of.

The mess in the cellar was testament to that.

45

Extract from letter from Edward Kane to
Walter Andrews, dated April, 1898

*You will be happy to hear that we have settled well into New York life.
I think the change is doing Juliana the world of good. She still grieves,
of course; we both do. There is an empty space beside us where James
should be, but over the past week or so she has begun to be able to speak
about him without tears, and we remember him fondly. I am hoping—
although I haven't voiced this to her, of course—that soon we will have a
child of our own, and that will ease her pain.*

*I was very sorry to read of your worries regarding Thomas Bond. He
was very kind to me—especially given his own warm feelings toward
Juliana—and I hope that he comes out of this self-imposed seclusion
you describe. I know that back pain can be a terrible thing, but it strikes
me that he has changed somewhat in the time that I have known him.
His illness and injury aside, I feel as if he has been withdrawing for a
while now. I had thought it was simply my presence and my marriage
to Juliana, but now that I am back home I find myself looking at things
differently.*

*I can't help but wonder (and this could well be nothing more than
paranoia on my part; I feel plenty of guilt where Bond's well-being is
concerned) if maybe I affected his relationship with Charles Hebbert.
Charles visits us often here in New York, and he is generally in relatively
good spirits, but he changes when we mention Bond to him. It is as if he
closes down. Given how well Bond looked after Juliana in the years after
James Harrington's death, I find Charles's reaction to any mention of him*

*strange, and it bothers me that maybe something occurred between
them as a result of my asking Bond for help. Of course, I'm probably
wrong and it was nothing to do with me, but the thought still niggles.*

*You see, when I first came to England, I had some concerns about
my old friend James Harrington. One of the reasons for my initial visit
was to find him and allay my fears. He had written to me—letters I did
not receive at the time; you know about my domineering father, of
course—and they contained tales of dark deeds and murder. Of course,
I soon found out that Harrington was dead, but I realized that Bond was
in a position to understand the contents far more fully than I was. More
importantly, I knew him to be an honest and trustworthy man. I gave the
letters to him and asked his opinion, and after he had examined them at
some length, he assured me that the contents were nothing more than
the result of hallucinations deriving from Harrington's frequent fevers.
I believe him on this because he gave me practical evidence to support
his conclusions. I no longer have the letters so I cannot go back through
them, but I am beginning to wonder—even though Bond assured me that
there was no truth in the main content—whether there was something in
them that I missed, something that affected him in some way or revealed
something about Charles Hebbert that disturbed him . . .*

Extract from letter from Edward Kane to
Walter Andrews, dated June, 1899

*. . . with regards to your questions about the letters I gave to Thomas
Bond, I cannot remember the dates, but it was sometime after I first came
to England and found out about Harrington's death, after I had met
Juliana. He kept the letters, but I am sure he must have destroyed them
by now as he was insistent—and I believe him—that there was nothing
more than madness in them. On reflection, I probably shouldn't have
mentioned them, and you should give them no more thought.*

*I am very sorry to hear that you are still worried about him, that he is
still avoiding society. His back must be causing him a great deal of pain,
and Juliana tells me that he is prone to insomnia, so I imagine the two are*

not a good combination. Juliana has written to him—I told her you were concerned for his well-being—but she has as yet had no reply.

I wonder if perhaps he too is grieving still? He was a father to James for most of the boy's life, and we must not forget that not only has he lost the boy who was to all intents and purposes a son to him, but he has lost Juliana too. And Hebbert as well, of course—their friendship seems to have undergone some shift, but they were obviously close for many, many years.

It is strange how life changes us. You don't see it when you're young, but I suppose neither we nor life can stay the same forever. Friendships come and go as men grow old. And I guess that's not always a bad thing, but I don't like the thought of Thomas Bond being alone. He's a proud man, and I can understand him hiding away if he feels weak, but he hadn't been well before we left. I do hope you manage to get through to him.

Please ignore my worries of previous letters. Whatever is plaguing Thomas, it can't be anything to do with Hebbert. The two have been apart a long time now, and I cannot see how any argument they might have had could still be affecting him now, when they are living in separate countries.

Speaking of separate countries, you really should come visit us in New York. I know you have been here before on police business, but trust me, you won't have seen the best of our city. I swear it changes and grows every month, and I am not sure even London can match the energy and life that fills New York streets. I know Juliana would love to see you and show you our beautiful home. Perhaps when he's feeling better you could persuade Bond to come with you? Hell, everyone needs a vacation every once in a while. So why not come here and be among friends?

46

LONDON. AUGUST, 1899
WALTER ANDREWS

"We do not do this often enough," Henry declared, leaning back in his chair. "Us old dogs should stick together."

"I'm afraid my back pain is not making me very good company," Thomas Bond said, sipping his brandy. "Most days simply walking around my house is quite enough to bear. It keeps me from sleeping well too, and inflicting my bad mood on others is not what I wish for my friends. Although I must admit this has been a pleasant escape from the tedium."

"A fall, was it?" Moore asked.

"Yes. I doubt I'll be back at the hunt anytime soon—if at all."

Andrews watched them both. Henry Moore had grown thicker around the waist over the years, but his eyes were still as sharp as ever, and he exuded the same earthy energy that he had when they had worked together. He would never tire of detecting; it was in his blood. Bond, however, had changed dramatically over the past ten years, and even more so over the past two or three. Andrews wondered if their friendship was nothing more than habit, rather than based on any solid foundation. How had that come to pass? And why was he now sitting here studying the tics and twitches in the older man's face, feeling some sort of vague mistrust that he did not understand?

Bond had laughed and joined in the conversation as much as he ever had done, but Andrews could not shake a feeling of distance coming from the doctor. *What was he hiding?*

Whatever it was, he doubted he would discover Bond's secret anytime soon. He changed the subject, saying, "I have heard from Edward Kane. Apparently they are settling in well, and Juliana is slowly recovering from her loss."

"Good to hear," Moore said. "They're young. The death of a child is a terrible thing, but time will heal her."

"Kane says that Juliana has written to you, Thomas, but has not heard back. I think she is worried about you. I told them that you had been suffering with your health somewhat."

"How strange," Bond said, his eyes slipping down to his glass. "I have not received any correspondence. But this is their new life, and they do not need me in it. However, if a letter does arrive, of course I shall be sure to answer it. I'm glad they're doing well and putting the past behind them."

"Not entirely behind them," Andrews said, lightly. Perhaps it was time to probe a little. "Kane mentioned some letters that Harrington wrote to him before he died—quite worrying letters. He said that you had looked into them for him. That must have been strange."

"He mentioned those, did he? He seems to have forgotten that he asked me to be discreet. I did not expect him to tell anyone else."

"What letters were these?" Moore asked.

"Did he tell you their content?" Bond looked directly at Andrews, who nodded, then continued, "They were disturbing, to be sure. Harrington was ill and delusional. He had convinced himself that he might in some way be connected to several murders of the time—the Whitehall one, for example."

"Ah, the priest's murders?" Moore said.

"Exactly." Bond glanced once again at Andrews. "I fear," he said, "that Hebbert and I had perhaps spoken too frequently on the subject in front of him, and it had somehow confused Harrington's fevered mind."

Andrews was a little taken aback; he would have sworn Bond had looked almost *triumphant*. What was going on?

"A terrible business," Moore said. "I am glad I have never suffered any problems with my sanity."

"I doubt you ever will," Andrews said with a smile. "I don't think I have ever known a more practical man than you, Henry. I imagine you do not even dream."

"If I do, I don't remember them." Moore smiled. "And I like it that way. My mind is busy enough during the day. I like to sleep like the dead at night."

Andrews wasn't sure why, but the words made him shiver slightly. He looked back to Bond. "What did you do with the letters?"

"I burned them. I did not want anyone else reading them—or worse, Juliana finding them. She was fragile enough after Harrington's death, and there was nothing in them that was a real cause for concern. They were just a sad insight into a sick man's mind." He looked at Moore. "Anyway, I have been of little use to you or anyone else lately, but tell us what cases you've been working on? Anything interesting?"

Life came back into Moore's face as he leaned forward; he was always most animated when he was talking about chasing criminals. Andrews only half-listened, and he was sure Bond was only half-listening too. The question had been to change the subject from the letters, Andrews was sure of it. But why? He could not forget what Kane had said: that perhaps something in those letters had prompted the change in the relationship between Hebbert and Bond—what could that have been? On the afternoon that little James fell in the river, Bond had heatedly called Hebbert a liar, a strong accusation to make against a colleague, let alone a friend of many years' standing. And he had said it with such *vehemence*. What suspicions did Bond have of Hebbert? Could it have been something suggested in the letters and then confirmed by that private detective work Andrews had provided for him? Had there been something relevant in the registers of Hebbert's club?

He sipped his brandy and smiled and nodded during the pauses in the conversation, but his mind was elsewhere. In their old friendship,

Andrews would have been able to ask Bond directly, and he would have gotten a direct answer. In fact, in past years Bond would probably have come to Andrews to discuss anything that might concern him.

But sadly, those days were gone.

He watched his two companions as they laughed, and he wondered if maybe he should just let sleeping dogs lie. Whatever Bond had discovered, how terrible could it be? The past was a different country, and perhaps now that he was retired, he should not seek to revisit it. There could be very little good in trying to unpick another's secrets.

But no. Perhaps if it had been just another person's secrets, he would have been able to let it go, but it was not. It could be part of his own unfinished story. Moore might not have nightmares anymore, but Andrews still did. They had discovered the priest, and he was quite sure he was guilty of the Torso murders, but try as he might, Andrews could not convince himself that the priest was also Jack.

He looked at Bond again. What had he said when he had asked for the Members' Ledgers? That the dates were a coincidence?

Andrews did not believe in coincidence. Coincidences were something people with less of an eye for detail saw.

Three nights later and he had his answer, or at least the shocking glimmer of one. It had been easy enough to get the club's records again, and this time it was his turn to study them. It did not take him long to realize what Bond had been checking, and as soon as he had returned the ledgers, he called a hansom cab to take him straight to the doctor's house. There was no answer—even though he was not shy with his use of the door knocker—and he hesitated impatiently on the door step. His heart was racing with what he had found, and he needed to speak to Bond tonight or he would not sleep a moment. He would wait—surely the doctor could not have gone far? Perhaps he was out for dinner. Maybe his back was giving him some respite and he was making the best of it.

It was still faintly light, and the summer night was warm, so he strolled up and down the street while he waited. Slowly the night gathered in, the sky darkening, and his legs started aching. Perhaps he should go home and come back the next day—it wasn't as if Hebbert were in the country and could be confronted. There was nothing that could not wait until the morning to be answered, but that didn't stop his nerves tingling with anticipation and excitement. The Ripper case had destroyed his love of policing, and their inability to catch the killer haunted him still. If there was even a glimmer of hope that an answer could be found, then he would at last be able to relax. His head was still spinning at the thought that Charles Hebbert could have been involved in any way, even though all of their findings had pointed to a medical man, despite the fact that both Bond and Hebbert had denied it, on behalf of their profession. Had the evidence pointed to a policeman, he had no doubt he would have done the same.

A hansom cab pulled up further along the street, and he was about to flag it down when he saw it was depositing Thomas Bond. He almost called out to his friend, but something stopped him, even before he saw the woman climb down after him. That questioning mind that had served him so well as a policeman made him pause. Why had the hansom cab pulled up half a street away from Bond's house? The place was quiet; it made no sense—unless of course he did not want the driver to know where he lived.

Andrews stepped back into the shadows as the woman stumbled and leaned into Bond, laughing. She was clearly drunk, and her cheap, revealing clothing made it clear that she was not the sort of woman he would ever have expected to see in Bond's company. The hansom cab left them behind, passing Andrews, and he watched as the couple weaved their way closer to Bond's house. So there was the reason for the driver's stopping further along: Bond did not wish him to see he was bringing a woman of ill repute back to his home. She was not attractive—her face was hard and her mouth thin with misery and a hint of meanness. What on earth was his old friend doing with a woman like this? Was this his way of forgetting Juliana? There could be no two women more different in appearance although this prostitute—for that must be what she was—did have brassy red hair. Was that what had appealed to him?

Finally they reached Bond's front door and disappeared inside the house. Andrews stared at it, filled with pity for his friend, who had come to this. Why bring the woman to his house? To try and make his actions feel more respectable? He was not a poor man; he could certainly afford a better class of prostitute, and there were up-market bordellos to cater to the needs of gentlemen like Bond. So why drag a woman from the back alleys to his own home for his pleasure? He could not imagine she would be able to provide much in the way of pleasure, not given her obviously drunk condition. Was this perhaps the reason he dismissed his housekeeper? So he could indulge in a new hobby?

Perhaps it should not have surprised him. Men were men, and there were plenty who enjoyed the more carnal pleasures that were often lacking in their marriages. And Thomas Bond had been on his own for a long time. He must be terribly lonely—not to mention having a fair amount of self-loathing—to want to take his pleasure in such a sorry way. He could not knock on the door now—he would not wish to embarrass his friend—but now that he knew he was home, neither did he want to wait until morning. The woman would not be there all night, he was sure. Bond would not want any of his neighbors to see such a woman leaving his house. He doubted she would be longer than an hour, if that. He had his coat and, anyway, the night was not cold, and he was used to such times from his years as a private investigator.

He would wait longer.

But she did not come out, not before dawn and not after, nor when the rest of the houses around him slowly lurched into light and life. His eyes were gritty with tiredness, but his curiosity had now doubled. He waited until after eight, a respectable time, and then went and knocked at the door. There was no answer, and his concern for Bond rose. If he had allowed that woman to sleep in the house, then God only knew what she might have stolen or damaged while Thomas was sleeping. He knocked again, and when there was still no response, he stepped away and continued to wait, even though his limbs were screaming at him to go home to a hot bath and rest.

At half past nine, the door opened. He expected to see the woman scurrying away, but he was wrong: it wasn't her, but Bond himself. He was fully dressed and looked alert, if a little preoccupied. He walked briskly toward the main road, with no sign of any back trouble. Andrews frowned. Now his need to talk to Bond about Charles Hebbert was being overwhelmed by his need to know where the woman had gone. He could not have left her inside, surely? He waited until Bond had gone and stared at the house. He knocked at the door again, but there was only silence. He gritted his teeth. He had come here expecting answers, and now all he had were more questions. *Tonight*, he decided. He'd come back tonight.

Once home, he bathed and then ate before crawling into bed, exhausted, but determined to sleep for only a few hours. But his body betrayed him, and by the time he woke it was already night. He rushed to dress and return to Dr. Bond's, shaking away the vivid dreams of murders from years gone by as he did so. He took a hansom cab to Westminster, and when he turned onto Bond's street, he saw that a cab was already waiting outside the doctor's house. Did he already have a visitor? Or was the woman finally leaving? He made his own driver pull over to the curb a safe distance away, and he watched as the door opened to reveal not the woman but Bond himself, clearly visible in the pool of light from the gas lamp above. He was carrying two valises. He walked quickly down the stairs and loaded them into the carriage. They looked heavy, but he was moving with ease, and there was no sign of the back ache he had been complaining about. Was he leaving London? Why at this time of night? Could this have anything to do with Andrews's mention of the letters Harrington had sent?

He had too many questions, and there was only one way to get the answers. He would follow his old friend and find out just what was going on.

With his own hansom cab keeping a distance, they moved through the city, from the quieter, cleaner streets toward the seething East

End, where life was lived loud in the darkness. Even with no Ripper at large, death came easily and unnoticed here. Andrews waited for Bond to stop, but the wheels kept turning, until they arrived at the river and followed its course out to the quiet banks past the wharves, where no light shone and the Thames was a wide streak of endless black that slithered alongside them like a monstrous slick serpent. He shivered in the warm night, and for a moment he felt such a rush of dread that he wondered whether he should turn back. What was he to learn about his esteemed colleague tonight? Wherever Bond was going, this was not normal behavior. Perhaps he should just go home, sip brandy, forget his suspicions of Hebbert, and leave Bond to whatever seedy madness he chose to fill his time with.

The choice was taken from him as Bond's hansom cab finally stopped a hundred yards or so ahead of them. Andrews quietly climbed down from his own and paid the driver well, telling him quietly to wait a few minutes before leaving, and then he crept along the dark street until he was close to where Bond and his valises had alighted. The summer air was filled with the sweet, stagnant stench of the river, and Andrews breathed shallowly as he paused at the wall and watched Bond disappearing down a flight of stone steps that led to the wet shingle and sand below. He peered cautiously over the edge to see a small light shining, and he heard a gruff voice muttering a greeting.

A second man's words drifted up through the quiet night: "Two cases for two nights. Whomever you're getting your dogs from now, they're getting you bigger bastards than George did."

"No questions, Jimmy, or you'll be going in the river too. He's paying the piper; that's all that matters."

Bond said something, too quietly for Andrews to catch, and then the group fell silent as they pushed a rowboat onto the water, put the heavy valises into it, and climbed on board.

Andrews kept his crouched position, fully aware that even in this poor light he might be visible from the water. He stared in horror as the lamp was dampened and the boat pulled out and was swallowed up by the darkness. Whatever he had been expecting, it was not this. What could be in those cases that Bond needed to go to such lengths to dispose of? Who were these villains? Bond obviously knew them. Why had the man laughed about dogs? Had Bond been experimenting on animals in some awful way? But surely no man would come out here in the middle of night simply to dispose of a dog carcass. He crept back across the street and once immersed back in the shadows, he shakily lit a cigarette and leaned against the wall. His whole body trembled with the knowledge that he was trying to avoid a thousand other questions that led to no helpful conclusion.

The woman: she had gone into Bond's house, but he had not seen her emerge. Bond had left, but she had not—and now he was here, depositing *something* into the river. It was true that she might have left during the hours he had gone home and slept—but would a man like Thomas Bond really leave a woman of that sort unsupervised in his own home? Not if she were still alive, surely . . .

His stomach churned, and he could not help but think back to Elizabeth Jackson and the other poor women whose body parts had been pulled from this very river a decade before. He thought of Charles Hebbert, and the days he had not dined at the club. Perhaps his suspicions of Hebbert had been wrong, and it was Bond who was responsible? His mind blazed in the darkness, a whirling mass of accusations that sat badly with his personal knowledge of these two men. What the hell had happened? What dreadful secrets were they hiding? He thought of the dead priest and the note he had left, addressed to Bond. Could they have been in collusion?

It was all too terrible to contemplate: the thought that his rational and highly respected friend could be in any way involved in such atrocious murders beggared belief—and yet he could not stop the details' forming into a solid suspicion, one that he could not ignore. He felt sick, weak—but he knew he had to confront Bond. He could wait no longer.

The small boat returned eventually, and Andrews stayed hidden in the shadows as he watched Bond hand over a small purse of what had to be coins. Then he waited until his rough companions had disappeared into night.

As Bond picked up both valises and turned to walk away, Andrews stepped out into the street.

"Thomas?" He did not need to shout; his soft word carried easily on the stinking river breeze. Bond froze, and then he turned slowly to face him.

"Walter," he said. "This is a surprise." He spoke casually, as if they were meeting simply in passing on a busy thoroughfare at midday. "Were you following me?"

"I had some questions," Andrews said. His heart was in his throat: fear, but not for his own safety, more for the imminent shattering of his illusions of all he had thought respectable, the expected revelation of terrible secrets. "About Hebbert. About the records you asked me to get for you."

"Ah, those," Bond said. "Yes, I see."

"But now I have some questions for you. The woman who came to your house . . . ?"

Bond raised a hand and sighed.

That was not the reaction Andrews had been expecting, and he paused. He had anticipated anger perhaps, and probably for Bond to run—but this calm resignation? Perhaps he had read this awful situation completely wrong.

"Shall we go to your house?" Bond asked. "We can talk there, and I will explain everything." He looked around him, as if trying to place the location. "I think perhaps it is closer than mine."

Andrews watched him warily for any sign of aggression, but could sense none: this was just his old friend, Thomas Bond, now nearly sixty, standing in front of him . . . in the middle of the night.

"I have something I want you to see, and I think perhaps there is best."

Andrews moved closer to him and asked urgently, "Were you Jack, Thomas?" He desperately needed this answer. "Before we go any further, I must know that."

Bond's eyes widened in surprise. "Walter! How could you think that of me?" Then he paused before saying quietly, "No, I believe Charles Hebbert was Jack. I am no murderer." He sighed again and admitted, "It is somewhat more complicated than that. It will do me good to share it. But I think I need a glass of brandy first."

"You want to come to my home?" Andrews said. "You will tell me there? Everything? Regardless of the consequences?"

"Yes," Bond said, "yes, I shall. I promise you that." He turned and began to stride back into the heart of the city, an empty valise in each hand.

Andrews followed silently.

47

Extract of Florence Jones's testimony
at the Old Bailey, 1899

*I live at 16, Spicer Road, Finch Road, Battersea—in December, 1897, I
was living with my father and mother at Woolwich—I am single, but on
December 17th, 1897, I was confined in a Home at Clapham of a female
child—it was named Selina Ellen Jones—the lady in charge of that house
recommended a Mrs. Muller to me, and the child was put into her charge
till March, 1898, when it was taken from her and put into the charge of Mrs.
Wetherall, of Gee Street, St. Luke's, and I paid her 5 shillings a week from
March to July, 1898, for the care of the child—I went there and visited it,
and, as far as I saw, it had good health and flourished under
Mrs. Wetherall—in July the father ceased to contribute, and I then paid
only half-a-crown a week for it—I saw this advertisement in the Woolwich
Herald on August 18th, 1899: "Adoption.—A young married couple would
adopt healthy baby; every care and comfort; good references given;
very small premium. Write first to Mrs. Hewetson, 4, Bradmore Lane,
Hammersmith"—I wrote to the address, saying that I had a child, and
asking how much she wanted to adopt it—I got an answer, saying that
they wanted it for their own, and wanted £5 down—I answered that,
and said that I could pay £3, and sent this photograph (Produced) of the
child—it was sent back to me in a subsequent letter—it was taken in 1898,
when the child was about nine months old—I asked for an interview, and
an appointment was made to meet at Woolwich Station about Thursday,
August 24th, a week before the child was handed over—I met the female
prisoner at Woolwich, and went with her to my mother's house—mother*

said we wanted her to take care of it for a certain time, and then have it back again—I made arrangements to see the child once a fortnight, and mother said she would come up and see it presently—the prisoner said that her husband was a clerk in Hammersmith, and I understood her to say that she lived at 4, Bradmore Lane; that was the address in the advertisement— no arrangement was made about the money on that occasion—I said that I should always like to provide it with clothes—I told her I would tell Mrs. Wetherall that I was going to take the child away, and I wrote to the prisoner that she could have it on Tuesday—I made an appointment for the next Thursday after the interview at my mother's, to meet at Charing Cross Station—I then got this letter from the female prisoner; it is the only letter I got—(This stated that they had taken a new house in Hammersmith, and all the neighbours would think the child was their own, and inquiring at what part of Charing Cross Station they were to meet.)—Some days before August 31st I bought some child's clothes—I took those clothes to Mrs. Wetherall on Thursday, and she handed me over the child that day, and all the clothes which it had been wearing—I took the child to Charing Cross Station, main line, and the clothes—I saw Mrs. Hewetson, as I knew her, at Charing Cross Southeastern Station, and went with her to Hammersmith by bus—we went to the Grove, and stopped at a house there, and she said that that was the house she had taken—it was not occupied, but there were some workmen in it—I then went with her to 2, Southerton Road, Hammersmith—she said that the house belonged to a friend of hers, and told me to say nothing about the child not being hers, but gave me no reason for that—when we got to Southerton Road I was introduced to the friend, Mrs. Woolmer, as her sister-in-law—I had some tea in the house, and paid the prisoner £3, and gave her the bundle of clothes—I had definitely arranged to pay her £5—after tea the child and I and the prisoner came out, and went to Hammersmith Station—I then went home, leaving the child behind with the prisoner—I was to pay the other £2 on the next Sunday—she said that she would write me a letter, and let me know where—she was going to send her husband with the child to meet me at the station—I got no such letter, and did not know what station to go to— notwithstanding that, I came up to Hammersmith on Sunday . . .

48

London. August 27, 1899
Henry Moore

"I can't believe it," Bond said. He looked up at Moore, his eyes wide, and the policeman saw the doctor's hand trembling as he sipped his brandy. It was still early, but they were both drinking; the situation demanded it. "But why?" Bond continued. "He was younger than I am—there was no sign of any illness."

"He was younger than both of us," Moore said. "He didn't leave a note or letter, not one that's been found anyway." Outside the sky was overcast and heavy with rain, and only a little light crept into Bond's study from the world outside, adding to the oppressive gloom that filled the room. "Who knows? I haven't seen so much of him recently. Maybe he had suspicions of an illness that he didn't share with us. I wondered if perhaps he had mentioned something to you?"

"No, nothing." Bond shook his head. "But lately I have seen him less too. The dinner the three of us shared was the first time I had seen him in weeks. I wish that was not the case now . . ." His voice trailed off.

"As do I," Moore added. Wearily, he took the opposite seat by the unlit fire and leaned back into the creaking leather. "He was a religious man, did you know that? He kept it to himself, but he was a pious one, was Andrews. Saw it a few times when we worked together. Something must have been really plaguing him for him to take his own life."

"We have let him down," Bond said, "and I more than you. We were close friends for a long time."

"You can't see into another man's soul, Thomas. If we could, then my job would be a damned sight easier."

"True," Bond said. There was a long pause. "I have not been much help to you with that of late either. But at least London is full of skilled surgeons. How are things?"

It was good to change the subject from Andrews's death, and normally talking about cases invigorated him, but recently he had begun to tire of the awful mundanity of death in London.

"Another dead baby pulled out of the water, trussed up like a fowl. When men and women want to get drunk and kill each other, I can see a reason, but baby killing . . ." He paused for a moment. He was not a sentimental man, but as he grew older, he found he was questioning more. "Baby killing is the most barbaric thing to me. Maybe even more barbaric than our Jack was."

"Another?"

Bond sounded vague; his mind was no doubt still reeling with shock after the terrible news Moore had brought him. He pitied the man. Bond had suffered really bad luck lately—first Charles Hebbert's leaving, then little James's dying, and then Juliana's marrying and being carried off to New York, and his back injury, and now this. There was a real sense of tragedy hanging over him now. Moore had to admit to himself that it had kept him away: he was a pragmatic, down-to-earth sort of man, and he didn't dwell on the past as others might. Perhaps that was why, despite the obvious signs of age in his physical appearance, for the most part he was still as invigorated by life as he had been when he was a younger man.

He turned his mind back to the subject at hand. "Yes, pulled out of the Thames at Barnes, a month or so ago. She had been dead for a while. Tied in the same complicated fashion." He heaved a sigh.

"No one claimed the first, and I doubt anyone will this one either." He sipped his brandy. "It's hard to investigate something like that. You know what I mean."

"You sound tired, Henry," Bond said. "Not yourself."

"You might be right, Thomas, you might well be right." He met Bond's gaze. "Perhaps it's time for a change for me."

"Retirement?"

"A *change*, Thomas." He smiled. "No life of card games and reminiscing for me! A man needs to work to stay young. But I have started to look around me for opportunities for a man of my experience."

"We all get old," Bond said.

"I don't feel old yet, but you're right: I am tired. I'm becoming too cynical. I want to work somewhere I can sink my teeth into a case rather than being able to do nothing more than *hope* clues turn up."

"I would be happy just to rid myself of this wretched back pain."

Moore studied his old colleague. There were dark rings around his eyes, and his pupils looked large, eating the color in his eyes. Perhaps it was just the lack of light in the room, but maybe laudanum too? He wouldn't blame him for that. He was a doctor, after all, and quite capable of self-medicating with whatever he wished to make himself feel better.

They spoke for a while longer, some small talk, some talk of Andrews and what a good man he had been. After twenty minutes or so, Moore took his leave. It was clear that Bond needed some time alone. Moore knew he wasn't the right man to help with grief; he dealt with anything emotional by applying himself practically to things. Right now, he would deal with his sorrow over Walter Andrews's death by burying himself in work.

He was glad to get back out on the street and into the throng of life. The storm had not yet broken, and it smelled like every foul and great scent of London was hanging in the air. He sucked in a deep lungful, thinking here was life in all its torrid glory. He was not yet ready to give up on it as Andrews had, or fade away from it as it looked like Bond was doing.

He didn't take a cab back to the division but strode through the streets, enjoying the time to think in the midst of the city he loved. It might be time to retire from the police, but not from thrill of the investigation. Ever since the Elizabeth Camp case, he had been drawn to the railways. There were cases to crack there: each month the trains were getting busier, and each month saw more and more crimes. *Me: an inspector on the railways?* he thought as he began to hum to himself. Perhaps that was where his future lay.

49

LEAVESDEN. AUGUST, 1899
AARON KOSMINSKI

Assessment

The patient has become more agitated over the past few days. In his waking hours, he has become obsessed that Dr. Thomas Bond might return to visit him, and he is adamant to the point of near hysteria that we prevent such a visit from happening. His speech often veers back into his native tongue at these times, but he repeats the phrases, "He wants to give it back. He tried to pass it on. He can't give it back."

Records show that the patient gave Dr. Bond nothing by way of a gift on his one visit, but the patient is prone to hallucination. In an attempt to return him to a calm state in which to discuss this current delusion, I recommend no visitors at all for the present.

His aversion to water has also grown stronger again, and he reacts strongly to any physical contact. I would not suggest that anything in his behavior makes him a danger to others, however. His delusions and nightmares clearly terrify him, but his fear does not translate to overt aggression.

50

LONDON. AUGUST, 1899
DR. BOND

The flames were mesmerizing, and I took some small comfort in the steady crackle that came from the fire, and the way each screwed-up ball of paper shriveled first to black and then to gray ash. I watched them as they burned, eliminating each of Harrington's desperate messages one by one, until it was as if they had never existed. I should have done it sooner, rather than simply wishing them away and avoiding that drawer in my desk at the hospital. Now Edward Kane was the only other person who knew of them, and he was far away. Only Andrews would have made the link between my reading the letters and then becoming suspicious of Hebbert. And now Andrews was gone.

My heart was heavy and my throat tightened in grief as I fought to evict memories of the previous night from my mind. My head ached from the fall I had taken, and the large lump that had grown on the back of my skull throbbed continually, despite the laudanum and brandy I had consumed. It had been hard to concentrate when Henry Moore had called with the news I had been expecting, but it had not been hard to feign my shock, as I was still in denial of the whole event. I kept hearing him calling my name on that dark road, seeing him there and realizing that everything was unraveling, no matter how hard I had fought to keep things under control. I should have employed a different private investigator when I first became suspicious of Hebbert—I had been foolish to go to a friend, let alone one as sharp-eyed and intelligent as Walter Andrews. I had grossly underestimated him, of that I was most certainly guilty.

My friend. Walter Andrews had been my friend, I could not deny that: a good friend. And no doubt we would have been firm friends into our old age, if Fate had not worked against me. Why had he followed that night? Why had he let his curiosity get the better of him? Why could he not have left well enough alone?

I screwed up the last of Harrington's letters and tossed it onto the flames, followed by the envelope with his careful writing. These were questions I could just as easily apply to myself as well. Andrews and I had always been similar; neither of us could let something go when our curiosity had been aroused. The *Upir* had taken its toll on us all: first James Harrington, then Charles Hebbert, poor little James, me, and now Walter Andrews. London was awash with the wickedness that had seeped into its streets so silently that none had noticed. We were tainted. *I* was tainted.

I could not stop thinking about the previous night. As I had poured out the whole story to Andrews, I had seen him look at me as if I were quite insane. At first I had wanted only to show him proof—and then, when I felt the weight shift on my back, a thought came to me, a plan that might allow me the freedom to live normally again.

And now I felt ashamed twice over: for having thought to try and pass this cursed existence on to a dear friend, and for the regret I had felt when I had to admit that I had not succeeded. I hated what I had done, but I felt such deep relief that I had not killed him—as much as I loathed the deeds I had committed with the wicked women who fed the river, I was still no murderer. *I was not.*

I stared into the flames, and with no warning, I began to weep.

51

LEAVESDEN. AUGUST, 1899
AARON KOSMINSKI

The sheets were soaked with sweat as the dreams came for him again. This time he saw a man, swinging from the tree, muttering a prayer as he threw the rope over the branch and tied it around his neck.

He saw the long talk, the man's disbelieving face; he waited for the drugged wine to take effect on Bond and saw the sudden feral look in the doctor's eye. He could not look away from the fight that followed, and he saw the Upir scrabbling up Bond's back, its tongue stretching long around his neck, and Bond trying to hold the man close and make the beast leave him as he fought to hold on to his consciousness.

He shuddered and moaned as he felt the creature's pleasure in the man's horror. He hissed in his sleep as the Upir had hissed when the man had thrown Bond off him and stumbled backward on unsteady legs to crash into the dresser. Bond's head had hit the corner of the heavy piece of furniture and he had crumpled to the floor, knocked senseless.

He heard the creaking branch and the desperate prayers, and he heard the hissing of the Upir, over and over, and inhaled the stench of evil. The red eyes were sharp and wicked; the beast was so much stronger than it had been before.

It broke the man and sent him to his death.

He moaned and cried and muttered in the old tongue. He loathed the closeness of the filthy demon, filled with every sin that had visited the earth. He felt it in every pore of his body. It was so much worse than it had been before, and it had almost broken him then. It had been weak on Harrington, just out of the river, but it had gotten stronger as it fed, and it would grow stronger still. He felt Bond's madness growing too, even if the man himself didn't. He wanted to weep for him. He wanted to weep for them all.

52

Extract of David Voice's testimony at
the Old Bailey, December, 1899

*On the morning of September 27th, Stokes called my attention to a brown
paper parcel in the Thames—I looked at it, and saw a baby's foot sticking
out—I took it from the edge of the water to the mortuary at Battersea, where
I took from the outside of it the paper in which the whole thing was wrapped
up—then I came upon a kind of pink-coloured flannelette sewed round the
body from the shoulders down to the haunches, with double white thread, and
between the legs and around the haunches was a white napkin—the head
was covered up with a white cotton bag, tied round the neck with a piece of
cotton stuff, the same as the bag was—it was a piece of selvedge torn off—on
removing the flannelette from the body, I found it was tied up with a kind of
sash cord or blind cord, the heels being drawn up over the chest, on each side
of the head, under the ears; the left arm was thrust under the left leg, between
it and the body; the right arm was squeezed between the body and the leg in a
straight attitude and secured by the cord or line—I sent for Dr. Kempster, who
cut and removed the cord—I cut nothing myself except the outside string and
the paper—I took the pink flannelette off; but left on the head covering and
the string on the body—this (Produced) is the bag which was over the head;
this is the napkin which was round the bottom part of the body, and this is the
flannelette whichwas sewn round the body, from the shoulders down to the
haunches—this string was outside the brown paper; this sash-line was tied
next to the flesh round the arms and neck—I am familiar with knots and the
making of them—I was in Her Majesty's Navy for just over 12 years, and there
we learned to tie all knots which are required in the Navy—in the blind cord*

there are knots which are well known to those familiar with knots—there are three knots here known as the fisherman's bend, and here is another known as the half-hitch—there are 11 of those in the string round the brown paper; there were six half-hitches in the blind cord—a reef knot is well known to me; it is used for reefing sails—I find one in the cord round the body, and only one of that kind—"overhand" knots are known to me—seven of them were to be found in the cord around the brown paper, and one in the cord that tied up the body—I took particular notice of the position of the child's limbs at the time it was found, as well as the position of the strings and cords which bound it up—I have prepared a doll about the size of the child, with just the same presentment as I found the child when I took it to the mortuary—(The model was produced)—this shows exactly the position of the child's limbs and the way in which it was tied after the flannelette had been removed, and also it shows the cord and the position of the knots—I have placed similar knots in the same places as near as I could get them—I was not present when the string was found in the house, but these pieces of cord were afterward shown to me (Produced)—there is a piece of sash-line, a good bit thicker than the other—[described the piece which was about the child's body as blind-cord or sash-line]—in this piece found in the house there is one overhand knot and one half-hitch—in this other piece there are three fisherman's bends, thirteen half-hitches, and eight overhand knots—the sash-line has one half-hitch and one overhand knot—they are broken pieces tied together—this piece is a bit thinner than the piece found round the child's body—it is the same kind of stuff, but not quite as thick—the sash-cord and the blind-cord are all the same kind.

The *Lloyds Weekly Newspaper*
December 10, 1899

LONDON BABY MURDERS
ARREST OF THE HEWETSONS

Late on Friday night Detective Inspector Scott of the V division, Metropolitan Police, succeeded in effecting the arrest of the "Hewetsons" against whom a coroner's jury delivered a verdict of "Willful murder" a fortnight since. The accused, who were apprehended in the neighbourhood of South Hackney, admitted their identity. The woman, who gave her age as 24 years, stated that her name was Ada Hewetson, and her companion gave the name of Chard Williams, and his age as 41. They had quite recently parted with their household effects, and at the time of their arrest were, it is said, on their way to Liverpool.

The *Standard*
December 11, 1899

THE BATTERSEA CHILD MURDER CASE

At the Southwestern Police court on Saturday, William Chard Williams (alias Hewetson), age 41, described as a clerk, living at 26, Gainsborough-road, Hackney Wick, and Ada Chard Williams, age 24, his wife, were brought before Mr. Garrett charged with the willful murder of Selina Ellen Jones, age 21 months, the daughter of Florence Jones, a single woman, living at 73, Gee-street, St. Luke's, whose body was found in the Thames off Church Dock, Battersea, on September 27. It will be remembered that the evidence at the inquest tended to show that the woman Williams, or Hewetson, accepted the care of the child for £5, and took it to a house in Hammersmith. She and her husband suddenly disappeared, and nothing more was heard of the child till its body was found in the river. The medical testimony of Dr. F. C. Kempster, police surgeon for Battersea, was that death was caused by injuries inflicted on the child before the body was thrown into the water, the skull having been battered in, and the head enveloped in a sack. The jury returned a verdict of Willful Murder against the couple, and for some days Detective Inspector Scott, Detective Sergeant Winzan, and Detective Joseph Gough have been searching for them.

The *Morning Post*
Saturday, December 30, 1899

THE BATTERSEA CHILD MURDER

William Chard Williams, aged 41, a clerk and his wife Ada Williams, aged 24, having recovered from their attack of influenza, which prevented them from being brought before the court a week ago, were yesterday placed in the dock at the Southwestern Police court to further answer the charge of being concerned in the murder of Selina Ellen Jones, aged 21 months, the daughter of Florence Jones . . .

. . . the bodies of three children having been found in the Thames, and as in each case they were tied up in a peculiar manner—string similarly knotted having been found in the possession of the prisoners—the Treasury will charge the accused with causing the death in each instance.

In the case of the child Jones, the police evidence is to the effect that it was for some time placed out to nurse and well cared for. Then, in consequence of an advertisement the mother met Ada Williams and arranged for the child's adoption. Ada Williams gave an address at Hammersmith, and there the child was delivered up and £3 of the premium paid. The balance was to be paid later, and an arrangement was made for the mother to see the child during the following week. On her calling at the house she learned that the accused had only engaged the room for a few hours . . .

. . . On September 27th the body of the child was found in the river. Death was due to suffocation, and the head bore marks of violence.

. . . The woman, in a letter addressed to the police, admitted having carried on a system of baby farming, and explained that the children which she had received she caused to be readopted at a less premium. The accused were remanded.

53

LONDON. DECEMBER, 1899
DR. BOND

"This man was James's tutor?" Henry Moore said, as he studied the newspaper articles I had spread over my desk. Despite my aversion for company, I had called on him. I felt I had to. In many ways, this felt like the old days, the two of us poring over information, but in truth, the old days were long gone. Moore had retired from the Metropolitan Police the previous month to move to the railways, and I had retired from my position as surgeon at Westminster a week before. Nothing was like the old days, least of all, me. But I needed to know the truth of it, and Moore was the only man who could find out more for me than the tittle-tattle of reporters.

I had seen the first article only by accident, while I was in the cellar in a laudanum haze and using the paper to wrap a torso, just like the first one in Whitehall had been. I remembered how appalled I had been when it had been discovered, and I could not help but wonder now if my horror at the time was perhaps a subconscious knowledge that I would myself come to be such a monster; was it that which had given me that terrible dread? It was hard to tell. It was all such a long time ago. A lifetime ago.

As my bloodied hands had folded the paper around the meaty flesh in the dim glow of lamplight, the name had snagged my attention. The two words—Chard Williams—hooked in my mind, even through the drug-induced haze, and I had frozen momentarily, then peeled the damp paper carefully away and read it with my heart knocking grotesquely in my chest.

Since then I had devoured the papers for news of the case. It could not be true, I told myself; it must be a mistake. I should ignore it. But as always, my curious mind was ever my downfall, and despite the awfulness of my cellar, I sent a message to Moore, asking him to find out what he could for me.

"Are they guilty?" I asked. My mouth was dry, but I did not try to hide my fear: as far as Moore—or anyone else—knew, I was concerned only for Juliana and her poor dead son.

"Definitely," Moore said. "The strange knots have given them away. They found the same knots in Ada Chard Williams's house as on the bodies. They moved from Barnes in October, not long after the first two babies were pulled out of the river there. Baby farming was her business, but rather than selling the babies on to wealthy couples as she promised, she often just took the money from their natural mothers and then killed them and put them in the river. Like that Reading devil did." He paused, then said quietly, "Damned if I know how many victims she really had."

The world spun beneath me. I needed laudanum. I needed opium. I needed an escape from myself as the true horror sank in.

"Will you write and tell Juliana?" Moore asked, steady as ever.

For a moment I loathed him for his normality.

"I am not sure," I said after a moment. "She would want to know, but I fear it might not be good for her. She would blame herself for anything young James might have witnessed there, and for bringing them into her home—although I doubt very much he was exposed to anything."

Dead girls in the river. That was what James had said to me when the nightmares woke him night after night. *Dead girls in the river.* My hands trembled, and I balled them into fists at my sides to hide the shaking.

"I think she should know," Moore said. "Perhaps you could write to her husband?"

"Perhaps I shall," I said, trying to sound normal. The world shimmered, its edges too hard and bright. I had dragged Moore over to my house, but now I just wanted him gone.

"Thank you for finding out for me," I said, walking over to the study door, "especially when you are so busy with your new line of work occupying you now."

He followed me out, and we headed downstairs. As he gripped my shoulder and told me to enjoy my retirement, I thought of the bloody scene beneath our feet, not yet cleaned out and scoured. I remembered Andrews's face when I turned to see him in that desolate street, and later, once my consciousness had returned after our fight, the lolling of his head and tongue as I staggered out into his garden to find him and fight him once more, instead finding him dead already and hearing the terrible slow creak of the rope tied around the branch . . .

If Moore knew any of that, he would probably strangle me with his bare hands himself, *Upir* or no *Upir*. I doubted the beast would hold any sway over a man like Henry Moore, always steadfast, always grounded in reality. For a moment I was tempted to tell him everything and have done with it once and for all, but my lips and tongue would not comply, and instead I bade him a warm farewell and accepted his invitation to join him for dinner very soon.

It was only when the door had closed behind him that I let the shudder that had been building run through me. I could barely move. My legs felt ready to collapse under me, overwhelmed as I was with the terrible weight of my guilt. What had I done? Oh dear Lord, *what had I done?*

The pieces fell into place in my mind. James had not changed until he started going to Chard Williamses' house for his lessons. Until then, he had simply been a quiet, sickly child with whom I could not bond because of my aversion to his father—no, I must be honest, with myself at least; my *guilt* over his father.

He had grown quieter after that, and he had started playing constantly with knots—I vividly recalled him showing me the fisherman's knot that he must have learned there. And that Christmas Day, he had barely spoken a word, just played with the rope instead. What had his young mind been trying to make sense of? Babies who had been there and then vanished? Or worse yet: had he seen Ada Chard Williams at her "work"?

I remembered their concern when James fell ill and then became sicker at my hand. They had wanted to speak to him—they had been so insistent. What had they wanted? To say something? To see what he knew? Or perhaps they had intended to hasten his end themselves, to prevent him from accusing them of anything should he recover. James had been a quiet, docile boy, the very sort of child who always saw something or heard something he should not. So what had happened in that house to disturb him so?

My legs gave way, and I sank to the ground, my back pressing into the door behind me as if I could somehow grind the *Upir* to extinction. I wanted to die where I sat, sobbing into my hands, a broken fool. I was a monster. A *murderer.*

I had been blinded by my own madness. I had disliked poor little James from the moment he had struggled into this world—but how could this sickly child who had nearly killed his mother during his birth and who looked like his father have brought such insanity into my life? I had wished he had never existed for he was a reminder of a past I longed to forget, and that had colored everything in my relationship with him.

The scales had fallen from my eyes, and I could no longer hide from the horror of the truth. James had loved me in his quiet way, and I had pushed him away. Then when he was afraid, it was me he had turned to—he had been trying to tell me about the Chard Williamses. *I saw something,* he had said when I woke him from his nightmares, but I had shut him up, allowing my own guilt to distort the truth. How could I possibly have thought James could ever be a threat to me? How could I have thought he might have a part of my own monster inside him? Of course he did not; he was just a child. A terrified child, and the son of the woman I loved.

And I had murdered him.

I had given him a slow, painful death that had left him screaming for his mother. This little boy had only wanted my help, for his Uncle Thomas to listen: the uncle he loved, although I did not deserve it.

For the first time since the *Upir* had claimed me, I saw myself for what I really was: a cold killer. Damned. For all my arrogance in casting judgment on those I had murdered, chopped up, and fed to the river, none had deserved to die—and if they had, it should have been by the hangman's noose, not by my hand.

I hauled myself to my feet and stared into the mirror on the wall. I did not recognize the haggard man who looked back at me. I did not know who lived behind the familiar eyes; all I saw was a child murderer. A madman. A monster. The priest had said the *Upir* would drive the host insane, but I had been too full of my own self-importance to pay attention. I should have thrown myself into the river as soon as I left Kosminski at Leavesden, while it was still weak.

Now I was too late; it would allow me no such end. My shoulders ached with the weight of it, and always there was the small black space at the edge of my vision where I could almost see it but not quite.

I needed brandy. I needed laudanum. I needed opium. I needed to forget. For all the women I had killed, it would be James who would haunt my waking hours for the rest of my life. I had murdered him, the child who had been the closest to a son that I would ever have. I had broken Juliana's heart, and I had destroyed myself.

The next morning, my clothes disheveled after a night in the seediest den I could find, I took a train to Leavesden. My feverish opium dreams had been full of the child's pale face and accusatory eyes, and in my head I could still hear his weak screams of agony. When I finally staggered out onto the street I saw him everywhere, on every busy corner, a small blond boy staring at me as I passed. He was *not real*. He was *dead*. I knew that in my heart, for it was I who had killed him, but still I shuddered and gasped at each sighting until I knew I could not go on this way. I had to give it back. I had to go to Leavesden and persuade Kosminski that this was the only way.

They would not let me in.

Even if I had appeared sane, rational, and well dressed rather than overexcited, filthy, and stinking, it was obvious the polite refusal would have been the same. Aaron Kosminski was having no visitors at present, nor for the foreseeable future. Visitors were not good for his emotional state. I wondered as I stood and begged in vain what the attendants made of my emotional state; even through my haze of fear and guilt I could see their pity and concern.

In the end, I had no choice but to return to the grime and stench of London. Worse, I could feel the fever coming upon me, as if the shock of the previous day's revelations was making the *Upir* excitable and hungry.

I would kill a woman that night, and this time I would not study her for her crimes. What did it matter anymore? Behind my eyes, the blood was already endless.

All the way back to London, James sat, silent and still, on the seat opposite me. I did not look at him.

54

The *Morning Post*
Monday, February 19, 1900

At the Central Criminal Court on Saturday, sentence of death was passed on Ada Chard Williams, twenty-four, for the murder of a nurse child, whose body was found in the Thames off Battersea. William Chard Williams, the woman's husband, was acquitted.

The *Times*
Wednesday, March 7, 1900

EXECUTION AT NEWGATE—Ada Chard Williams, 24 years of age, who was convicted at the Central Criminal Court of the willful murder of Selina Ellen Jones, a child which had been placed in her care, was executed at Newgate yesterday morning. There were present at the execution Lieutenant-Colonel Milman, Governor of Newgate and Holloway Prisons, Mr. Under-Sheriff Metcalfe, representing the High Sheriff of the county of London, Dr. Scott, medical officer of Newgate and Holloway, and other officials. Billington was the executioner. An inquest was subsequently held in the Sessions-house, Old Bailey, before Mr. Langham, Coroner for the City. Lieutenant-Colonel Milman gave evidence, stating that the execution was carried out satisfactorily. Death was instantaneous. The prisoner made no confession. The jury returned the usual verdict.

55

LONDON. AUGUST, 1900
DR. BOND

I lived most of the year in the dark, succumbing to that which I could no longer even pretend to fight. The night had become my world; I could no longer bear the daylight and those who carried on their normal lives within it. It was too loud and noisy, and in my rare moments of sober clarity, it was too painful a reminder of everything I had lost.

I employed a woman—no Mrs. Parks, but an earthy creature who needed the money—to fetch whatever shopping I required from that alien world outside. Visitors, mainly ex-colleagues from Westminster Hospital, still attempted to call on me, but I rarely answered the door, and when I did, I pleaded back pain and illness to get rid of them quickly. Even with the hospital so close by, the stream eventually became a trickle as the world moved on without me. Only Henry Moore remained persistent in his attempts to secure my company, and on the rare occasions I agreed to meet him, I could see that he was concerned for me. No matter how hard I tried to achieve the veneer of the honest and respectable man I had once been, it was always just out of my reach. I was a poor imitation of myself, and Henry Moore was too clever a man not to notice it. Our dinners were short, and I escaped them gladly. In some way,

I loathed Moore now, not for what he had done but for who he was: he was everything I so desperately wished to be: sane, clear of conscience, and invigorated by life.

I took too much opium and laudanum, and drank anything else that might drown the last tiny shred of decency inside me that screamed and railed at the horror of my existence and haunted me with visions of James. I was no longer afraid of the dark spot in the corner of my eye. I had accepted that the *Upir* and I had become one being, but every sighting of the dead boy filled me with awful dread. I would find him in the most unusual places, on the landing as I turned the stairs, or his shoes and legs visible in my closet as if he were hiding behind my clothes, and a thousand other places, and always when I least expected it. I did not grow used to the sight, even though I knew the boy could not be real.

I rarely slept, not even when I was exhausted and the drugs had taken their toll on my body. Perhaps by accepting the *Upir,* I had relinquished that small mercy, and hell had come for me early? There were times when I wondered if I were indeed dead, for my craven existence, so flooded with blood, was hell indeed; I could scarcely imagine a worse one. The days and weeks blurred into one, and the only true gauge I had of time was the changing weather and the longer days as I waited for night to fall, when I could hide in the darkness.

I had become depraved. There was no other word for it. I could no longer deny that the *Upir*'s lusts had become my own. Where once my deeds had reviled me, now I was beginning to revel in the moment of the kill and the sweet delights that came after it. I did not limit myself to Whitechapel in my search for my prey; I would not risk the notoriety Hebbert had drawn, working only in those unhallowed streets. The *Upir* most enjoyed the homeless and the wandering immigrants from the east of Europe, relishing in the taste of their soft organs as I squeezed them into my mouth.

Not all my victims went into the river. The woman Hebbert had killed was no longer lonely in her grave at the bottom of my garden. I knew George was becoming suspicious of my activities, having witnessed the feral energy I exuded after such a kill, and with each trip he demanded more money from me. I was beginning to think I would have to deal with George himself before long. Whatever fear I might have had of him was long gone; now it was he who looked at me warily, his survival instincts honed from a life in the alleys of the East End.

Sometimes I wondered if I now killed as much for myself as for the devil on my back. It was so very hard to tell when my hands were tight around a throat and I could feel the surge of excitement running through me. The beast's transferred energy was a drug in itself.

It was perhaps good that I no longer slept, for the cellar always needed scrubbing these days. My fingers were raw from the bleach and carbolic soap.

If only I could clean my soul so easily.

56

LONDON. NOVEMBER, 1900
HENRY MOORE

In many ways, he blamed himself. He had thrown himself into his new job with such vigor that there had been little time for checking up on his old friend, even though he knew Thomas Bond had not been himself for some time.

Tonight the doctor's appearance and behavior had shocked him. His words were slurred, and his clothing and hair were unkempt, to the point that even in the more basic restaurant that Moore preferred, the waiter's displeasure had been obvious. Bond had barely touched his food, but he drank too much wine and brandy before complaining of illness and stumbling outside.

Moore had followed and helped him into a hansom cab, then watched as it disappeared toward Westminster before lighting a cigarette and strolling, still sober, toward his own part of the city. He was not a man predisposed to fanciful thoughts, but there was an air of death around Bond, almost seeping from his very pores. Moore thought he might even go so far as to say there was a sense of both mania and resignation to his coming end—for his end was coming, he had no doubt about that. Thomas had grown almost skeletally thin, and he stooped badly, perhaps to relieve the incessant back pain that had plagued him this last year or so. He had a permanent phlegmy cough that he appeared not even to notice. He was a far cry from the man who had written his report on Jack the Ripper a decade before, the man he had chosen as his police surgeon whenever possible. That man had been serious, sober, and sharp of mind. This "new" Thomas Bond was anything but.

Can it be some form of brain disease causing the changes? he wondered as he enjoyed the cold, crisp night air. Or was Bond overdosing on laudanum?

It was no good, whatever it was, and it left Moore with a bitter taste in his mouth. He was still angry at Andrews's unexpected suicide. He hated that he had left without so much as a letter of explanation, leaving only another unsolved mystery behind him. Andrews was gone, and he knew—because he was a man who could not avoid hard facts when placed in front of him—that Bond would be the next of their little group to fall under the scythe.

For his own part, he did not feel old—he was a man who lived in the moment; he did not dwell on the number of years left to him, as so many men did as they aged. He had seen enough dead bodies to know that a lifespan could not be measured that way. To be alive and healthy on this day, to make it through to the comfort of your bed and the hope of waking the next morning, that was all any man should wish for. And in his new career Moore was feeling more alive than he had for a long time—but his renewed enthusiasm for life had been at painful odds with his old friend's strange shambling toward the end of his. It was clear that Bond no longer wanted his friendship, that he had come to meet him only out of some sense of obligation, but that did not mean that Moore would abandon him. Bond was not himself, and if whatever life he had left to him was to be spent in some kind of comfort, he would need those who cared about him around him.

He had walked briskly, as was his style, but even so, by the time he reached his front door the tips of his fingers were numb and his nose was running, and he was happy to get inside. His mind was still on Thomas Bond, however, and he poured himself a drink and settled down at his desk. Perhaps Andrews's death had been the straw that broke him. Moore was no fool. He had known how the doctor felt about Hebbert's daughter, and if anyone could help him now, it would be Juliana. He also wondered if Bond had ever written to tell them about the Chard Williams case; he had expected her to have returned for the verdict and execution. Once again he cursed his driven mind; he was so focused on his work that he excluded so much else. He had taken Bond at his word that he would write to the Kanes, but he had then forgotten all about it.

He was tired, but he knew that if he went to bed without having taken some action on the matter, he would not sleep. Instead of finding himself back at his desk at some ungodly hour, he would rather get it done now and be able to sink into oblivion with his day's work completed. He would write a letter and send it in the morning.

His mind made up, he pulled a sheet of fine paper from the top drawer and laid it on the blotting pad. This would not take long. He was a plain-speaking man in all forms of communication. He picked up his pen.

Dear Mr. Kane,

I hope you will not consider this letter an imposition as we are not well acquainted, but I feel I should write to you on two matters, that of the recent case of the Chard Williams woman, found guilty of the murder of a child pulled from the river, and of the more personal matter of Dr. Thomas Bond's health, both physical and emotional. I shall lay out the details below, but I wish you to know that I am simply passing the information on and not expecting any action from you other than to impart it to your wife as you best see fit and allow her to decide whether to contact Thomas Bond or not . . .

57

NEW YORK. JANUARY, 1901
EDWARD KANE

Edward had waited until the Christmas festivities were done before sharing the contents of Henry Moore's letter with Juliana. It had been a glorious holiday, filled with feasting, new friends, and laughter, and for the first time in a long time, Juliana had glowed the way she used to in the first flush of their love. She had shared the reason with him on Christmas Eve, as they had placed their gifts for each other under the trimmed tree.

"I have something else for you," she had said, unable to keep her smile from dancing in her eyes, "but it is too well wrapped for you to see at present."

"Too well wrapped?" He had looked around the room, confused, until she had taken his hand and pressed it to her stomach.

He had stared at her quizzically for a moment before her meaning sank in. His heart had leapt.

"You mean, you're—*we're*—?"

"Yes. We're having a baby."

He had whooped with delight, right there on the rug, and she had laughed at his childlike joy, and then they had laughed together and kissed each other and laughed some more. Happiness was returning to their family. They would never forget James, that wasn't possible, but this was a new life, a new child to love and nurture and have as their own. There was a purpose to life again, and he could see Juliana's vitality returning in every passing moment. They made plans and talked of all the toys and books they would fill the nursery with. Christmas was wonderful.

He had thought about just burning the letter and pretending he had never received it. London was a lifetime ago, a place now filled with unhappy memories. New York was their home now. Charles Hebbert had never quite been himself since leaving England, and after a brief visit to New York, he had returned to Australia to make some kind of life there; to all intents and purposes, he was dead to them. What was the point of sharing more bad news from her home country?

But he could not unsee the words, and he could not bring such a secret into their marriage. Some men would, no doubt, but then, some men weren't married to Juliana. Once the world had settled into the new year and winter had gripped the city, he had finally sat her down and gently broken the contents of Moore's letter to her, hating the horror on her face as she learned of Ada Chard Williams's awful crimes—and the realization of the meaning of little James's nightmares and delirious words—and then, once she had taken that in, he told her about Moore's concerns for Thomas Bond.

"He doesn't think he has much time left," he said. "He thought you should know."

For a while she had said nothing, but he had passed the letter over to her, knowing she would want to read it for herself. At last she came and found him in his offices.

"He cannot die alone," she said. Her chin was high and defiant, and her voice was strong. He knew this Juliana well; this was not a woman who could be persuaded from whatever she had decided. "Perhaps, if he has friends around him he will not die at all. We must go to London."

"But in your condition?" Edward said. Her belly had started to show the signs of new life. "Maybe we should wait until after the baby comes?"

"I've thought about that," she said.

"Have you now?" Edward leaned back in his chair and smiled. Of course she had. Juliana hadn't come here to ask his permission for anything. She had come here to tell him their plans. God, he loved this woman. He thanked the good Lord every day just for bringing her into his life, even in such dark circumstances. She was *his* Juliana—she had been, even before they had ever met, no matter how much Harrington might have loved her—and he would stand by her side and do everything he could to make her and their child happy. Even if it meant a trip back to London, and the past.

"I could have the baby there," she said. "I would like that." Her eyes softened and sadness darkened them. "I would like to show James his little brother or sister. I think it would . . ." She struggled for the right words. "I think it would make things better," she said at last.

"Then that is what we shall do," he said, getting up from the desk and wrapping his arms around her. "We'll go to London and look after Thomas Bond, and we'll have our baby there. But you must see a doctor first, and I think we will go nowhere for a month or so. Let's make sure our baby is happy to travel first."

She smiled at that and cried a bit, and then they kissed and the heat between them that had never faded grew urgent, and he locked the door and closed the blinds and they loved each other slowly and gently right there on his desk. Life was good. They would go to London and say farewell to the past. It was time to focus on the future.

58

LONDON. MAY 29, 1901
DR. BOND

Things were changing. I could feel it. The *Upir*, so strong now it gorged regularly on the products of my crimes, was becoming restless. I could feel its impatience, its longing for freshness. I knew why: I was broken, after all. I shuffled through my existence, a puppet to the thing on my back, with no fight left in me. I had begun to realize that the *Upir* gained as much joy from the destruction of its host as it did from the deaths of others. There was no fun left to be had from me. I also knew that when it moved on, it would not end well for me, but I found I cared little for that. I was tired; I wanted it done. I wished for my whole sorry existence to be over. I had started to go out during the day, trying to engage with people, in the hope that the creature would select one and move on, but it did not. Instead, I suffered its increasing rage and frustration as none seemed to fit whatever strange requirements it had.

On those days the killings were more brutal. They barely touched me.

The first human emotion I had felt in a long time came this morning when I received a letter from Juliana: she and Edward Kane were in London, and they wished to call on me, for they had heard I was unwell and this made her unhappy. She wanted to nurse me back to good health and then perhaps persuade me to return to New York with them until I was myself again. I stared at the delicate sheet of paper, my eyes running over her words again and again. *Juliana*. In London. *Here*. I was filled with a sudden terror. She could not come here! She was the only goodness left in my world, even after I had destroyed so much of hers, and although I longed to see her, I knew I could not. As my heart raced and my hands trembled, I felt the cold excitement of the creature on my back, and dread overwhelmed me, for it was clear it had found a new pleasure, a new way to taunt me. My love for Juliana was all I had left of my former self, and I knew without a doubt that if Juliana came here, the *Upir* would force me to take her to the cellar. But I would not do that. I *would not*.

I went to my study and sat, shaking, at my desk. Henry Moore must have told her I was unwell—it was the only explanation. My loathing of him burned bright, and I fought to control it. I needed to master my feelings—so many of which I was sure were not my feelings at all but the wickedness of the *Upir* running through my veins. I needed to call up the last of my energy, the last dregs of the man who had once been Dr. Thomas Bond, respected police surgeon. I needed to focus.

For the first time in a long time I did not reach for the brandy bottle or the laudanum, even though I itched for both. I had to *think*. This was no longer about my survival; this was about Juliana's. I needed clarity—and I also needed to free myself of my secrets, to face the growing list of deadly sins that I hid from in drug and alcohol use.

Juliana was in London, and the *Upir* wanted her. That could not happen. I needed to separate myself from the demon, if only in my own mind, if I was to protect her. I thought of the priest and the way he had wrestled the creature from Harrington's back. I needed to see the beast that clung to me if I was to fight it. Later, I would go to the dens, not to partake, even though my stomach was already clenching in sharp need, but to hunt down that special opium we had used so long ago. I withdrew into a cool corner of my mind, away from the heat and emotions that the *Upir* drew on, and hid within myself.

There were long hours ahead before I could venture east, and I knew how I needed to fill them. I needed to get the wickedness out, whether as a warning or a confession, or maybe both. I had to write it all down so there would be a record when I was gone. And I would leave it for the attention of Henry Moore, the strongest, most rational man I knew, to do with what he would. I knew exactly where to begin: on that grim day in October, 1888, when, plagued by insomnia and anxiety, I was called to Whitehall.

The memories came flooding back, and I could see the events of that day as if it were yesterday. I pulled a blank journal from the shelf, and once I had steadied my hands, and I began to write.

"How much further?" The shafts of bright sunlight filling the building site above were finally petering out and leaving us in a cool, gray darkness that felt clammy against my skin.

"A little way, Dr. Bond," Hawkins said. The detective was grim. *"It's in the vault."* He held his lamp up higher. *"We're lucky it was found at all."*

Huddled over like the rest of the small group of men, I made my way under the dark arches and down stairways from one sub-level to the next. We fell into a silence that was marked only by the clatter of heels moving urgently downward. I'm sure it wasn't just I who found the gloom to be claustrophobic — especially given what we knew to be waiting for us in the bowels of this building — and I'm sure part of our haste was simply so we could face what we must and get back to the fresh air as quickly as possible.

The workmen above had downed their tools, adding to the eerie quiet. We were a long way down, and with the walls damp and rough beside me, I could not shake the feeling that I was in a tomb rather than the unfinished basement of what was to be the new Police Headquarters. But perhaps I was — an unintentional tomb, of course, but a resting place of the dead all the same. I shivered. There had been enough death of late, even for someone like me, who was trained in all its ways. Recently I had begun to think that soon this city would be forever stained in cold, dead blood.

Finally, we made our way down the last few steps and arrived at the vault. It was time to work.

"They moved it over here before they opened it," Hawkins said, standing over a lumpen object nearby, "where there was better light to see it." The foreman and the poor carpenter who had found and unwrapped the parcel were keeping their distance, shuffling their feet as they stayed well clear of what lay at the detective's feet. As I looked down, I found I did not blame them.

"Dear Lord," I muttered. After the slayings of recent weeks I had thought we must all be immune to sudden shock, but this proved that was not the case. My stomach twisted greasy and I fought a slight tremble in my hands. More gruesome murder in London. Had we not seen enough? The parcel the workmen had found was approximately two and a half feet long. It had been wrapped in newspaper and tied with cheap twine, the ends now hanging loose where they had been cut open to reveal the horrific secret inside.

"We've not touched it since," the foreman, a Mr. Brown, said nervously. "Fetched the constable straight away, we did, an' he stayed with it while we fetched the detective. We 'aven't touched it."

He didn't need to repeat himself to convince me. Regardless of the sickly stench of rot that now filled the air, who would choose to touch this? The woman's torso was lacking arms, legs and a head, and across its surface and tumbling from the severed edges was a sea of maggots that writhed and squirmed over each other as they dug into the dead flesh. In the quiet of the vault, we could hear the slick, wet sound made by the seething maggots. Here and there they dropped free to the black ground below.

I fought a shiver of repulsion. Whoever this woman was — and despite the physical trauma it was clear this was the torso of a woman — her death was no recent event.

I crouched lower to examine the damaged body more closely, and held the light close as I bent down to the floor in order to peer into the largest cavity. What was left of her insides was a mess: whoever had done this had not been content with just amputating her limbs. Much of her bowel and her female internal organs had also been removed. This killer had taken his time.

I did not notice the hours passing and the day darkening as I scribbled, my hand struggling to keep up with the terrible story unfolding on the pages. I relived every step of the doomed journey I had taken, flinching from nothing. At points in my tale I wept, loud, racking sobs that blurred my vision and spilled salty drops that made the ink run words into each other, but I did not stop until my shame had been laid bare for anyone who opened the book to see. When I had finished, I leaned back in my chair, my hand and spine cramping from the task I had undertaken, but my heart felt lifted. I had faced my slow downfall, and I felt better for it.

I sealed the journal in an envelope and marked it for the attention of Henry Moore in the event of my death. There would be no more killings. The cellar would remain clean. One way or another, the *Upir* and I were done. Little Kosminski had managed to starve it, and I would do that too. I had to protect Juliana. I had to keep her safe.

When night had enveloped the city, I ventured out. The beast squirmed on my back as if it could sense my rebellion, but I kept myself resolute, even as I passed the women who called at me from doorways, seeking out business and completely unaware that they were toying with their own deaths. I had a large purse of money with me, but it was not for them. The Chi-Chi who had first sold me the strange drug had long since vanished or died, but there would be others, I was sure of it. The Eastern men had different knowledge from ours, and if one Chi-Chi knew of the drug that enhanced men's ability to *see*, then I could not believe that he was alone.

59

LONDON. JUNE 5, 1901
EDWARD KANE

"We have called on him several times for days now," Edward said, pacing around the sitting room of their hotel apartments, "and never an answer. His neighbors say they haven't seen him for weeks, although they hear coming and going at night."

Henry Moore smoked and listened, his brow furrowed into a frown. "He's not a well man. He hasn't answered my notes either."

"But what can we do?" Juliana, hot and flustered and weighed down by the child who was so very nearly grown inside her, fanned herself. "It can't go on. Is there any way you can call on some of your police colleagues to get us into the house?"

"It's not impossible—there are plenty on the force who owe debts of gratitude to him. But to break into a respectable man's house with no real cause . . ." He paused, and then said, "It could do more harm than good. He will not welcome the intrusion."

"I do not care about upsetting him, Mr. Moore," Juliana said. "I care only about his welfare."

"You make a good point." Moore smiled at her. "Leave it with me. I shall go make some inquiries and let you know this evening. We won't be able to do anything until tomorrow at the earliest, though."

"Tomorrow is plenty soon enough," Edward said, relieved. He shook Moore's hand. "And we owe you for this. I know you're a busy man."

"No, you owe me nothing. My problem is that I'm often too busy or distracted by work," he said. "I've neglected my old friend, and I feel bad about that." He got to his feet. "You've come a long way to see Thomas"—he looked at Juliana—"at a time when you should be concentrating on other things. I won't add to your worries. We'll get you in that house."

After Edward had seen the erstwhile policeman to the door, Juliana asked for the hundredth time, "But why won't he let us in? We are his friends."

"You are, my darling." Edward poured a cup of tea from the tray and took it to her. "Me? Perhaps not. I stole you from him, after all. Maybe he doesn't want me to see him weak and old."

"That is not like Thomas. He's a good man—a kind man. He always has been."

"Sickness changes people," Kane said. Although he didn't wish to upset Juliana, he was regretting their trip. Andrews was dead, Bond was sick, and there was something deeply oppressive about the city that he could not quite shake. He wasn't sleeping well, and as he lay awake with his hand on Juliana's stomach, taking comfort from the kicking child, he thought if anything were to happen to her or the baby, he would never forgive himself.

He had no idea where this dread had come from. Juliana had been in perfect health throughout her pregnancy, unlike when she had carried James, and the travel had caused her no sickness at all. They were staying in one of London's finest hotels and wanted for nothing. There was no danger—and yet still his skin prickled with it. Whatever love he had had for London was gone. He ached for the grime of New York.

"Perhaps we should try calling on him again?" Juliana asked. "Today?"

"Let's wait and see what Moore says. I suggest we take a day for ourselves."

"We could visit James's grave," she said softly. "And perhaps Walter Andrews's." She looked out of the window. "While the weather is so pleasant."

The air felt clammy to Edward. He had hoped they might walk in the park and then have an early dinner before a quiet night in, but it looked like that was not to be. The graveyards were where she wanted to go. He shuddered, for no reason. Why was he so overwhelmed by the presence of death? Why wouldn't it leave him?

"If that's what you want," he leaned over and kissed her soft cheek, enjoying the scented warmth of her skin, "then that's what we'll do." He smiled, and she smiled back.

He wished he truly felt like smiling.

60

LONDON. JUNE 6, 1901
DR. BOND

I lay on my back in my stinking sheets, ignoring the pain from the lacerations that covered my skin. I needed the agony to distract me from the terrible hunger. I was weakening, not only in body but in spirit. I knew that. I had allowed the beast to grow so strong that there was little I could do to fight it.

I reached sideways to pick up the pipe, and the welts on my back shrieked in pain as the scabs caught and tore away as I moved. The stink of the pus confirmed my suspicions: the cuts were infected. Trembling, I prepared the bowl and sucked deep. I had not managed to get the same clarity as when I had taken this strange drug before, but it did numb the pain and calm me, and I was certain it helped to distance the true me from the raging *Upir*. Though I might be happy that the cuts were infecting my blood, the creature was far from pleased. I hoped the heat burning through my body was a symptom of a poisoning that might carry me off once and for all. And if no one found me, then the *Upir* would finally die. It could sense that too, and it was taking all my resolve to keep myself pressed to my bed and not throw myself around the room in its anger.

When I had first seen it after returning home with the opium, I had been less affected than I had expected. In fact, it was rather a relief: I was not crazy; I had not invented any of this. I was a victim as much as Harrington, or Hebbert, or all the poor dead women we had left in our wake. The hideous, malignant creature on my back was testament to that. It had grown since I had first seen it on Harrington; the red eyes were more sentient, and they were filled with terrible wickedness. When I turned sideways, I could see the bulbous growths on its misshapen body and the shades of blue that spread out from my own skin where we were connected.

I went back to the East End and paid a woman who specialized in extreme pleasures to score my back with a knife in the hope that I could dislodge the *Upir* slightly, maybe even make it more likely to jump to someone else. But still it clung on, even though it writhed and hissed behind me as I screamed into the rag stuffed in my mouth. My own blood incensed it, and if it hadn't been for the terrible pain of the knife slicing through my skin, I was not sure I wouldn't have turned and strangled the woman there and then before tearing into her body and devouring her soft organs.

I staggered home, and once through the door collapsed to the floor where I lay, semiconscious and bleeding for several hours. When I came to, cold, aching, and with a pounding headache, there was another envelope waiting for me. Juliana had called again. I stared at it and then clutched my head in my hands. I railed against her persistence, and against the love she had for me—if not the kind of love I had craved—that was bringing her closer to her undoing.

I had given in to the *Upir* for too long, and I knew I had left it too late to change. My current resolve would crumble, I knew that—and then what? I could see it all so clearly: I would open the door and tell Kane I had no wish to see him, but I would let Juliana in. She would be shocked by my appearance and rush to my aid, telling her husband in no uncertain terms to go back to their hotel and wait for her, which he would do because he loved her and respected me. Then the door would close, and I would take her to the kitchen to make tea, and there I would kill her. I would kill her and mutilate her and eat those parts of her I had once wished to touch so tenderly, and then I would run until the *Upir* had no more use for me. I knew all this would come to pass should I let her visit because although it disgusted me to my very core, I could not stop my mouth from salivating at the thought of wringing the life out of her and cutting through her tender flesh.

I clenched one fist, shoved it into my mouth and started moaning and rocking backward and forward on my haunches like a lunatic in an asylum. I could not let it happen. *I could not.* I stared at the door for a long time, and finally I pulled myself to my feet and breathed deeply. I knew what I had to do.

As I locked the door from the inside, I filled my head with random thoughts of Juliana, allowing the *Upir* to become excited and distracted at the thought of his ultimate prey. I then went to the kitchen and did the same. I took the keys upstairs with me. I imagined Juliana's eyes wide in terror as I squeezed her throat and the creature behind me squirmed with delight and unfulfilled hunger. I had fed it so well I had made it greedy, and now we both starved.

I opened my bedroom window and suddenly launched the keys out into the summer air, smiling as the silver glittered in the sunlight and tumbled to the pavement so far below. The creature shrieked in anger, but it was too late. The doors were locked and I could not get out—and more importantly, I could not let anyone in, no matter how hard they knocked or begged.

I lay on my bed and smoked more opium, allowing a quiet sense of satisfaction to overwhelm me. My back was bleeding, but I did not care; it would weaken me and that was a good thing.

And weaken me it did. Within three days of entombing myself, what little food was left in the house was gone. When I found the energy, I would drink a little water, but mostly I lay on my bed with the curtains closed, smoking the strange opium and growing weaker. The weakness was a good thing. There were moments when the urge to run down the stairs and beat against the door almost overwhelmed me. I thought of smashing my front room windows and climbing out, but even with the *Upir*'s hunger raging at me, my body lacked the strength. I drifted in my strange fever and opium haze, through memories, good and horrific, from my childhood until now.

A life was very short when it folded in on itself at the end. It all came down to a whisper at midnight, the echo of a laugh. The years just rushed by in a whirlwind. I remembered the boredom of childhood in long hot summers, and then in a snap they were gone and I was on the battlefields, saving lives rather than taking them. It all passed in one breath. I did not dwell on how different things might have been if Harrington had never returned to England. What was the point in that? What had been, had been. I thought of little James, though, and how badly I had misunderstood him, from birth until my murder of him. As my fever grew, I saw him in my bedroom doorway, standing perfectly still and staring at me and the beast that writhed on my back, but I was no longer afraid; instead I drew strength from him. He was there to stop me from leaving, to remind me that if only I could save Juliana, then perhaps I could redeem some part of myself.

All I needed to do was lie here until I died. It was a simple task when put like that, and I intended to go through with it.

I was in a mildly delirious haze, which was why it took a moment for the noise downstairs to wake me. Not noise—*noises*. I sat up and pain shot through my torso. I was slick with sweat and shivering. What was that? I got out of bed, my legs unsteady and went to the hallway. Someone was ramming at the front door—even from upstairs the sound was loud and clear—a heavy thud against the wood that rattled the solid frame. That was not someone knocking. This was more. Someone was trying to break the door down. My heart raced, and the *Upir* squirmed excitedly on my back, giving my weak body a surge of energy. I ran back to my bedroom window and opened it wide so that I could peer out. There were two constables on the street, and there, standing a little way back, was Juliana. She was pacing a little up and down the pavement, her beautiful face tight with worry. Her deep red hair shone in the sunlight. My eyes rested on her, and I realized she was heavily pregnant.

The creature hissed in anticipation behind me, and I was filled with both its mouth-watering excitement and my own overwhelming dread. The house shook with every hit of the battering ram, and I moaned in fear, not for myself but for the woman who waited outside. I was about to run back to the hallway and down the stairs to scream at them to leave me alone, to go away, when I heard the sharp retort of heavy wood cracking. They were getting in. Henry Moore must have arranged it at Juliana's insistence. She would be the first to rush in, I knew that. Even if I did not harm her now, at this moment, as soon as I had recovered enough, I knew I would.

I paused in my bedroom and stood in front of the mirror. The creature was squirming on my back, its tongue running round my neck and up and down my face as it hissed wetly, red eyes shining out from the black mess that was its body. It was Death. It was Madness. It was everything I had become. I looked at myself, a stinking wreck of a man with hollowed-out cheeks in my skeletal face. I was a man teetering on the precipice of a grave.

"Dr. Bond?"

"Oh! What is that stink?"

"Where is he?"

"Dr. Bond—?"

The voices drifted up from downstairs as I faced myself. Feet started to pound on the stairs.

"Thomas?"

Juliana—! They would have told her to wait outside, but Juliana was strong willed. For a moment, time froze. The air was still around me, and I was completely calm. There was only one thing left for me to do. Suddenly I moved. I reached around and clawed at the *Upir*, grasping its slimy, river-soaked body, catching it by surprise. As I did so, I staggered and spun backward in circles, moving away from the door. It shrieked at me, but I was focused on the sounds from downstairs, getting closer. They would get to my bedroom at any second.

If I was going to do it, I had to do it now.

Wheeling and lurching as I fought with the devil on my back, I threw myself out of my open bedroom window.

The sunlight was beautiful. I did not close my eyes as the ground rushed up to meet me.

"Thomas! Oh God, Thomas—!"

Faces bent over me: Juliana. Moore. Kane. I fought for breath despite the agony. The world was a haze. I tried to speak, to tell them to stay away, but though my mouth moved, no words came out, just a terrible wet rattle from my ruined lungs.

"Let's get him to the hospital. Juliana, step back—someone, take my wife!" It was Kane, strong and handsome, looming over me. "It's okay, Thomas. It's going to be all right."

I wanted to smile. I was the doctor—I had been a doctor a long time ago—and I knew this was not going to be all right. Black clouds were forming at the edge of my vision that had nothing to do with the sunny day the rest of them occupied. I could hear Juliana sobbing, but I could no longer see her. She was safe, though. I had saved her.

My body screamed in agony as the men lifted me from the ground and began to carry me across the road to the building I knew so well. The sky juddered overhead. My broken bones scraped against each other, and the pain was terrible and distant and very nearly over. Death was coming for me, but I was happy. I had not killed Juliana. She was safe.

Suddenly I gasped and my hand shot out and grabbed Kane's arm, pulling him toward me with a strength I did not know I had left.

"What? What it is?" Kane leaned forward, his face full of concern.

It was not my strength, I realized as the dark clouds grew larger. I wanted to scream, to sob and cry. Kane's eyes filled what was left of my vision, and in them I saw it reflected, strong and eager and rushing forward with such speed. Kane's eyes widened, surprised and confused, as I felt the terrible weight leave me.

I had been so stupid. I had been blinded by my own love. It had not been Juliana the *Upir* had wanted after all. It had been Edward Kane. And I had delivered him. My damnation was complete.

the subject of melancholia, a form of insanity with depression in which attempts at suicide are not infrequent.

The *Morning Star*

July 13, 1901

TRAGIC DEATH OF A DOCTOR
A FAMOUS LONDON SURGEON COMMITS
SUICIDE AT WESTMINSTER

Dr. Bond, the famous medical coadjutor of the British Criminal Investigation Department, the man whose name has been professionally associated with practically every sensational London murder mystery for the past quarter of a century, has himself become the central figure of a tragedy. He committed suicide on June 6 by throwing himself from the third-floor window of his residence, 7, the Sanctuary, Westminster. He was carried across the road to Westminster Hospital, on whose staff he had been for twenty-six years when he retired in 1899. He had been suffering from melancholy and was confined to his bed.

It was in the De Tourville case in 1875 that Dr. Thomas Bond's name first came prominently before the public as that of a medico-legist. De Tourville was a waiter in a French restaurant who was taken into service by a traveling Englishman, with whom he visited a number of places. The Englishman mysteriously disappeared, and De Tourville came to London, entered the Temple, was called to the Bar, cut a great dash at Scarborough as a French count, married a young woman of fortune, and killed her mother. But no suspicion was aroused at first. The body was buried after a brief inquest, and it was not until both the first and second wives of De Tourville died strange deaths, leaving their large fortunes in his hands, that the body of the first wife's mother was exhumed. De Tourville had declared she had accidentally shot herself while looking down the barrel of a pistol. Dr. Bond's examination of the skull proved that she had been murdered from behind.

Then came the Wainwright case, when Dr. Bond discovered three bullets embedded in the brain of the victim, Harriet Lane—bullets which had been overlooked in the first

61

The *Times* of London
June 7, 1901

OBITUARY
MR. THOMAS BOND

Mr. Thomas Bond, F.R.C.S., surgeon to the Westminster Hospital, who destroyed himself yesterday morning in a fit of insanity by jumping out of a third-floor window at his house, 7, The Sanctuary, Westminster, was educated at King's College and King's College Hospital, and became a member of the Royal College of Surgeons in 1864. In 1865 he graduated as Bachelor of Medicine at the University of London, in 1866 as Bachelor of Surgery and gold medalist, and in the same year he became a Fellow by examination of the Royal College of Surgeons. After a short period of service with the Prussian Army he returned home, and was appointed assistant surgeon, and in due time surgeon to the Westminster Hospital and to the A division of police. By reason of the last-mentioned appointment his attention was early directed to medico-legal questions, in which he soon became an acknowledged expert; and he has been concerned in the inquiries which have been made into almost all the important murder cases for many years past. His experience was also frequently appealed to in cases of real or alleged injuries received by railway passengers, and he was permanently retained as surgeon or consulting surgeon by both the Great Eastern and the Great Western Railway Companies. He contributed the article on "Railway Injuries" to *Heath's Dictionary of Surgery*, and he was an occasional contributor to the medical journals. Mr. Bond's health is understood to have been failing for some time past, and during the last few months he is said to have been postmortem examination. His researches also led to the establishment of identification conclusively.

In after years Dr. Bond's knowledge and skill were employed in the Richmond (Kate Webster) case, the Lefroy and Lamson murders, the Whitechapel series, and the Camp train crime, to detail a few of the many occasions in which Scotland Yard called him as an expert.

62

LONDON. JULY, 1901
HENRY MOORE

He loved Sundays in summer: late breakfast, a long read of the newspaper, and then perhaps a walk. This morning he had done the first two, but now he stared at the journal sitting on the kitchen table amid the empty plates. The door was open, and a warm breeze darted around him. Even knowing to whom the book had belonged, it was hard to dampen his good mood on a day as glorious as this.

They had brought him the envelope, still sealed, after Juliana had begun the task of clearing out Bond's house. He had left them his property—which came as a surprise to Juliana and Kane as much as anyone—and she wished to return it to its former glory before either renting it or closing it up to keep for any future visits to London. They would be staying there at least until the baby arrived, and perhaps longer. Edward Kane, usually so hardy, had been struck down by a fever and had taken to his sickbed, and Juliana had already employed a nurse to help her when the baby arrived. After the loss of James, Moore was not surprised she wanted to stay in England until her new child was of an age to travel safely, and so perhaps Kane's illness, as long as it passed, was a godsend.

He was impressed by Juliana. She had been stoic in Bond's death; she had efficiently gone about organizing the funeral despite her own grief. She was a woman who had become accustomed to loss but had been strengthened by it rather than made fragile. Moore could see that most of that was down to the love between her and Kane. They made a fine—and handsome—pair, and although Juliana obviously loved London, he hoped that they would get back to their New York lives soon. She had clearly thrived there, and there was little left for them here. Bond's house was no place for them—there were too many ghosts to be seen in the corners.

He lit a cigarette and stared again at the journal. That too was full of ghosts: a ghost of himself in a past life lived in those pages, as did all the rest of them. He picked it up, feeling the weight of Bond's words against the paper.

 He hadn't read much. The first few pages he had rather enjoyed, in a strange way—they were a glimpse back into those first days of the Whitehall case, so much of which he had forgotten—but when he had reached Bond's journey to the opium dens of the East End, he had closed it up and made more tea. There were places in a man's soul that another should not see, not even after death. His dilemma was, of course, that Thomas Bond had clearly wanted him to read his account and that was what was giving him pause.

He picked the book up once more and looked again at the first page. The writing was a mockery of Bond's usual neat hand that Moore knew so well from so many reports. Thomas had been sick at the end, not just with the melancholy that he obviously suffered from, but he had blood poisoning, from the cuts that the hospital doctors presumed were some strange treatment he must have tried to ease his back pain. It was also clear from the pipe found beside the bed that Bond had taken to the opium to ease his symptoms. Whatever was between these pages was not an account written by a man in command of his senses.

He poured himself a fresh cup of tea from the pot as he smoked, evaluating the evidence. He had to decide whether to read on in the book or to destroy it. There was no in between. He was a curious man—that had, after all, made him such a good detective—and he knew that if he kept it in a drawer somewhere, the day would come when he would look to the pages again. It was now or never.

He sat there for several minutes. Then, when he had finished smoking, he stood up and took the book to the stove. He opened the metal door, and before he could change his mind, he threw the journal inside. He felt an immediate sense of satisfaction. The Thomas Bond who had written it—who had wanted him to read it—was not the Thomas Bond he had known, the man he had been proud to call friend and colleague. That man was quiet and private, not a person to spill out his life onto the page for another to read.

He looked out at the bright, glorious day. The past was done. He had no time for it. All the world was in the future. As the book disappeared to ashes, he picked up his hat and stepped outside. Tomorrow would bring more investigations on the railway, but for today he would enjoy simply being alive.

63

The *South London Press*
June 14, 1902

GRUESOME DISCOVERY
Alleged Murder and Mutilation in Lambeth

A horrible discovery was made during the early hours of Sunday morning in Lambeth by Charles Whiting, a stoker in the employ of Messer Doulton, who on leaving the works leading to Salamanca Alley, a narrow, ill-lighted thoroughfare, came upon the remains of a young woman scattered on the roadway. A constable was immediately called, and the remains were conveyed to the Lambeth Mortuary, only a short distance away.

The *Times* of London
June 19, 1902

THE DISCOVERY OF HUMAN REMAINS AT LAMBETH

Yesterday Dr. Michael H. Taylor, the acting coroner, resumed his inquiry at Lambeth into the circumstances attending the death of an unknown woman, whose mutilated remains were found . . . in Salamanca Alley.

64

Leavesden. July, 1902
Aaron Kosminski

Assessment

The patient has made sudden and remarkable progress over the past two weeks. He is willing to see his sister again, and his agitations have almost entirely ceased. His nightmares—which have plagued him for more than two years—have calmed.

When questioned on the sudden reduction in his anxieties, all he will say is, "It has gone to America. Too far away to see." He will not be drawn out further, and I recommend that attendants do not try to probe him more as it might affect his current state of balance.

He still has a wariness around water but will now wash and will eat with the other patients. He allows staff to touch him when necessary—without force.

I am not convinced that this patient will ever be well enough to leave Leavesden, but I do believe that if this improvement continues and he does not relapse to his more serious condition, then he may well progress further and live a relatively contented life as a functioning part of the community life here that staff are keen to create.

EPILOGUE

The *Times* of London
March 3, 2001

NEW RIPPER FEAR AS SECOND BODY IS FOUND

SCOTLAND YARD fears that a new serial killer who preys on prostitutes could be on the loose after discovering a second severed torso in the capital's waterways in less than two months. Detectives believe that the latest Ripper may be keeping some of his victim's dismembered limbs as trophies as some body parts are missing from both women.

The *Times* of London
March 7, 2001

RIPPER FEAR AS ANOTHER BODY IS FOUND IN THE THAMES

THE discovery of the third woman's body in one of London's waterways in three months has led to fears of a Ripper-style serial killer, who murders prostitutes before throwing their bodies into the capital's rivers or canals.